D1562121

HER BITTER DEBT

"The house is big. So long as you put up a 'happily married' front to the world, you two can come and go without meeting . . ."

That was the way Major Bill had asked Gabrielle to return to Brian. The proud old gentleman had helped and comforted her in the past. Gay wanted to please him. . . . But could she return to the man who had hurt her? . . . Whom she had once loved so completely?

Could she become a wife in name only?

Books by Emilie Loring

- FOR ALL YOUR LIFE
- WHAT THEN IS LOVE
- I TAKE THIS MAN
- MY DEAREST LOVE
- LOOK TO THE STARS
- BEHIND THE CLOUD
- THE SHADOW OF SUSPICION
- WITH THIS RING
- BEYOND THE SOUND OF GUNS
- HOW CAN THE HEART FORGET
- TO LOVE AND TO HONOR
- LOVE CAME LAUGHING BY
- I HEAR ADVENTURE CALLING
- THROW WIDE THE DOOR
- BECKONING TRAILS
- BRIGHT SKIES
- THERE IS ALWAYS LOVE
- STARS IN YOUR EYES
- KEEPERS OF THE FAITH
- WHERE BEAUTY DWELLS
- FOLLOW YOUR HEART
- RAINBOW AT DUSK
- WHEN HEARTS ARE LIGHT AGAIN

- Published by Bantam Books, Inc.

EMILIE LORING

TODAY
IS YOURS

NEW YORK
LONDON · TORONTO
BANTAM BOOKS

The names of all characters in this novel
are fictitious. If the name of any living
person has been used it is coincidental

The names of all characters in this novel
are fictitious. If the name of any living
person has been used it is coincidental

This low-priced Bantam Book
has been completely reset in a type face
designed for easy reading, and was printed
from new plates. It contains the complete
text of the original hard-cover edition.
NOT ONE WORD HAS BEEN OMITTED.

TODAY IS YOURS
A Bantam Book / published by arrangement with
Little, Brown and Company

PRINTING HISTORY
Little, Brown edition published February 1938
2nd printing .... February 1938
3rd printing .... February 1938
Grosset & Dunlap edition published June 1947
Bantam edition published November 1966
2nd printing
3rd printing
4th printing

Copyright, 1938, by Emilie Loring.
All rights reserved. Including the right to reproduce
this book or portions thereof in any form. For information
address: Little, Brown and Company,
34 Beacon Street, Boston, Massachusetts 02106.

Published simultaneously in the United States and Canada

Bantam Books are published by Bantam Books, Inc., a subsidiary
of Grosset & Dunlap, Inc. Its trade-mark, consisting of the words
"Bantam Books" and the portrayal of a bantam, is registered in the
United States Patent Office and in other countries. Marca Registrada.
Bantam Books, Inc., 271 Madison Avenue, New York, N.Y. 10016.

PRINTED IN THE UNITED STATES OF AMERICA

ABOUT THE AUTHOR

EMILIE LORING grew up in Boston in an atmosphere of writing and dramatics. Both her father and her brother were playwrights, so it is small wonder Mrs. Loring's own novels are filled with a strong sense of drama and with the romance and mystery that give unfailing pleasure to so many thousands of readers.

I

WITH a flash of fiery eyes and a weird crackle a huge shape scuttled into the shrubbery by the side of the road; faded like an apparition in the twilight gloom. Brian Romney jerked the maroon convertible, which his surprise had switched almost into the gutter, back to the highway.

"Lucky I wasn't driving a horse. It would have climbed that tall pine tree in terror," he said aloud. The thing had disappeared so suddenly that he was left only with an impression of discs of flame in something big, unwieldy, brownish. It might have been a stray cow or a bear escaped from a circus, though mid-September was late for a circus in these parts. An explanation so tame wouldn't account for the icy prickles which had broken out all over him. There had been menace in it, something uncanny.

He looked back. There were no houses on the side of the road where the brown creature had vanished. Only woods which ambled downhill to the brook where the old stone mill with its moss-clogged wheel loomed in lonely dignity. Plenty of life on the opposite side. The chimneys of the home of his cousin, Sue Romney Dubois, reared lofty tops on the ridge. He visualized the fury of her face had she caught the mysterious thing prowling about her grounds, and chuckled. He wished she had and that he had been present to see the fun.

He dismissed all thought of the creature as the car shot between entrance pillars topped by urns and up a drive at a pace calculated to relieve his pent-up emotion and crush the memory of that night, a year ago, when he had dashed away from the house on the ridge ahead at an even greater speed than that at which he was now approaching it.

Could it be only one year? It seemed ten since he had left the estate his great-grandfather had developed from three hundred wild acres and had named "Rosewynne," for his wife, Rose Wynne. Toward the east were the chimneys of the homes of his cousins, members of the Romney clan, and toward the west the white village that housed the workers in the family Plant. Beyond that he could see the pinkish haze beneath which roared the furnaces.

The cream stucco house his grandfather had built to replace the homestead which had burned was designed in the Italian manner. On the square tower with its long windows and lacy iron balconies, vines clung and climbed until they reached the roof of the main house where they detoured to straggle over its heavy tiles and drip in festoons from its edge.

Nothing had changed since that night. Nothing but himself, he qualified, as he caught the reflection of his face in the mirror above the windshield. Now there were fine lines at the corners of his dark blue eyes, his mouth was tight-lipped. It was his firm chin and the set of his jaw that made trouble for him. Surprisingly, his hair was still black, without a tinge of silver. Thirty. He felt fifty. If his feelings and business experience were taken into account instead of his age, he was equipped to take on the responsibility of the Romney Plant and relieve his uncle, a widower with no children and a private fortune, who was entitled to a rest from the care of it.

As he stopped the car in the brick court the massive entrance door was opened by the negro who had been his uncle's butler since he had inherited Rosewynne. He was grizzled as to hair but his body was as straight as one of the Lombardy poplars that bordered the drive. With pure-blooded African dignity, in a voice which betrayed emotion, he greeted:

"Proud to see you back, Mr. Brian. You're a sight for old eyes."

"Where'd you get that 'old eyes' stuff, Sampson? I'd hate to have you on my trail now if I wanted to snitch grapes and nectarines for my girl friends as was my custom in times past."

The butler was all gleaming eyes and white teeth.

"I reckon de young ladies did like dem grapes. Other folks is likin' 'em too. You wouldn't b'lieve dey'd dare to when de hothouse is so near dis house, but dey've been a-stealin' 'em so fas' we've had a 'larm put in de hothouse to signal de police in town if dey break in again. Haven't had no trouble since, no sah. Major Willum an' me'll let you have all de fruit you want ef you'll only stay home wid us. He sure done need you somethin' terrible."

"What do you mean? Is my uncle ill?"

"No! Don't you go gettin' frightened 'bout him. He's not sick, jest kinder spindlin'. You leave your car standin' right there. I'll send Tim to drive it to de garage an' carry de bags into your old room in de tower. Major Willum's waitin' fo' you in de lib'ry."

As Brian followed him the sound of trickling water and fragrance drifted from the flower-filled Venetian Renaissance court. Arches separated it from the great domed hall from the middle of which a stairway with lacelike balustrade curved upward to an encircling gallery on the second floor.

"Mr. Brian Romney," Sampson announced ceremoniously.

Brian advanced eagerly toward the man who was standing back to the fireplace above which the portrait of a dark-haired woman with tender eyes and faintly smiling lips was inset like a medallion. His snowy hair waved at the temples, his fine mouth was set hard under the line of his clipped white mustache, his blue eyes—eyes on a level with Brian's own—under bristling brows were piercingly keen, his skin was clear with a touch of healthy color at the cheekbones, he was as straight as when he had worn a military uniform.

That man "spindlin' "! Brian jeered to himself and laughed.

William Romney held out his hand.

"Well, boy, I'm mighty glad to see you're taking with a smile the responsibility I'm dumping on you," he welcomed. "You brought a current of strength and zest into this room which set my blood tingling with renewed vitality. From your letter of protest I expected you'd pull the house down about my ears when you arrived."

Brian returned the pressure of the hand gripping his.

"You may not believe it, Major Bill, but since I pulled my own house down about my ears a year ago, I've learned to ride my hot temper with a curb."

"Sit down. Let's thresh out this matter of the business first and get it behind us. Great Scott, boy, it's grand to have you home."

Brian swallowed an annoying lump in his throat.

"There's no place like it. Something tells me that has been said before." Back to the fire, he faced his uncle. "Shoot! I'm ready to take it. But, why have you picked on me to head the family Plant? What's the matter with Mac or Sam, Major Bill?"

William Romney rested his elbows on the arms of the deep chair covered in crimson velvet which matched the long hangings and the frock of the women in the portrait. His eyes beneath the bushy white brows glinted like blue ice rimmed with snow.

"It will take considerable shooting to present my case, so don't get restless if I go back to ancient history. As you know, I've been president of the Romney Manufacturing Company since my elder brother—your father—and your mother were fatally injured in an automobile accident. You were a small child and came to live with my wife and me. She adored you."

He glanced at the portrait above the mantel. The fragrance of the three crimson roses in a slender silver vase beside it scented the air. Violet dusk veiled the corners of the room. The licking scarlet and yellow flames of the fire cast dancing shadows on the backs of calf-bound books on the wall shelves. From the court stole the sounds of trickling water and the drowsy chirp of birds. A log fell apart with a loud crack and a splutter of sparks. William Romney drew his hand across his eyes.

"The past got me for a moment, Brian. To go on with the family saga. My brother Mac, your uncle, died and left twin sons, Mac and Sam. Your Uncle Dug left a daughter, Sue. As I control the stock, I carried on the business your Great-Grandfather Romney founded. I had to, for the livings of you young people were dependent on it—all but yours, you had your mother's fortune. Young Mac and young Sam each has an office at the Plant and draws a salary, but they are not unduly interested. The girls they married have money. Mac is a sporting gentleman preoccupied to the exclusion of his job with the details of his kennels, stables and collecting Dickensia. Sam wants to be a writer. Mystery yarns are his speciality. I think he'll make the grade—in time. Dug's daughter's husband, Louis Dubois, also draws a salary from the Plant, but he's a mighty disturbing element in it."

"He also draws heavily on his wife for money, doesn't he?"

"He does, and Sue makes plenty in the stock market. She is jealous of him, keeps him on a leash, figuratively speaking. I hear that sometimes he slips it. I forgot for a minute that you were antagonists."

Had William Romney really forgotten why he detested Louis Dubois? Brian asked himself. Forgotten that Louis, already married to Sue, had conspicuously devoted himself to Gabrielle Wainwright at the skating party on the pond, had begun to call her "Gay" within five minutes after meeting her for the first time? That when she was Mrs. Brian Romney he had not attempted to disguise her attraction for him?

"Sue is determined that her husband shall be the head of the family business," the Major went on. "When he married her he was manager of a plant owned by a Frenchman whose products were similar to ours. He's a crackajack salesman but, he's so sleek I don't trust him. Sue and Louis are working on Mac and Sam to help push him into the presidency of the Plant. I haven't inquired into their reactions yet. Fortunately I have sole power to make the appointment. You are the only member of the family in whose hands this great industry will be safe."

"Safe! How do you know? I've made a mess of my own life."

"Not of your business life. You've no idea how much I leaned on your judgment when you were here; you're a born executive. You were liked, respected and admired by our workers, with the exception of foreman Eddie Dobson. He was jealous of your popularity, I presume."

"There was more than jealousy behind his animosity. He was rushing Lena, that nice little maid of ours, and because of his Don Juan reputation Gay got worried and asked me to warn her. I did. He heard of it, I suppose."

"You did right to warn her. Dobson would ruin any woman's life. He's gone wild in other ways since he's been chummy with a Frenchman, Lavalle, whom Louis recommended for a job. On top of that he thinks he should be promoted from foreman to superintendent. To return to business. You made a fine record during the year you've been at the head of our mid-Western branch. As reports of your progress came in, I was profoundly relieved to know that instead of carrying out the threat you flung at me that night a year ago when you told me that you and Gay—"

"That I'd go straight to the devil? Remember your slashing reply? It's burned into my memory.

"'Going to the devil can be accomplished with the greatest of ease, Brian, but don't forget that Satan travels in cheap company. You are twenty-nine and you're still a spoiled kid. With your brains and background you ought to count in the life of the nation. Do you? Go out to our mid-Western branch and think things over. If you still yearn for the devil as a pal you'll find him on the job there, as he is everywhere, beating the tom-tom to summon the faithful.'"

"Did I say all that?"

"You did. I went. I began to think things over. I realized whither I'd been drifting. I drank too much. Pulling myself up by my bootstraps wasn't easy at first, but I did it. I don't drink. I've cut out playing cards for high stakes. Now that you need me I'm back to stay, to be of some help to you who have done so much for me. You may shift your business cares to my shoulders. They're broad."

"That settles it. It's an excellent time for you to take hold. There is a decided upturn in business, bringing with it rising profits. We have established a school to insure a supply of trained workers. We have no trouble from outside organizations because we are doing more for our workers than any one of them can do. After the first of the year we'll be justified in boosting pay and distributing a bonus. Mac, Sam and I will form an advisory board which will be subordinate and not superior to the decisions of the president of the Company. You'll be commander-in-chief with undisputed authority, Brian."

"That puts the responsibility straight up to me. I'll do my darnedest to make good. Won't Sue insist upon Louis' appointment to the advisory board to protect her interest in the Plant?"

"She hasn't an interest. A year ago she begged me to buy her out—she said she could make more money in another investment. I did. The stock is entirely in the hands of the Romneys and will remain so."

"You're telling me. I haven't forgotten that you almost snapped off my head when I suggested that Bee Ware wanted to buy a small block. Sue has colossal nerve to try to dictate the Plant policy, but if she has made up her mind that her husband is to be president of the Romney Manufacturing Company, watch for fireworks when she learns of my appointment. You wrote among other things, that Gay was considering di–vorce," his voice broke on the ugly word.

"Yes. I never understood what caused the break between you two. I thought yours would be one of those ideal marriages which would be time- and world-proof, which only goes to show that I am out of tune with the temper of your generation. Possibly the fact that Jim Seaverns is home from an engineering job in South America is influencing her to want her freedom. He's a fine man and adores her. Whatever is the cause she has begun to realize that if she won't live with you, it is unfair to keep you from marrying."

"But I'm married, Major Bill. Gay is my wife. I love her. It was entirely my fault that our marriage went on the rocks. The first year was—heaven."

Slow color rose to his hair, his eyes darkened, his heart thumped as in that dusky, fragrant room he relived moments of tenderness, ecstasy. He shook off the spell of memory and admitted gruffly:

"After that the gay set of the community absorbed us. Cards. Drinking. Dancing. Round to cards again. A vicious circle. Late at the Plant in the morning with my mind as fuzzy as my tongue. Not keen enough to realize that Gay hated the social treadmill. She didn't drink. Since I've cut it out I realize how infernally boring it is to sit around cold sober and see others drinking and getting more than mellow. We began to differ on trivial matters, on important matters, she turned to ice and because I was unendurably hurt I began to slash at her in private. Think you can stand this true-story confession, Major Bill? If you can, it will be like getting rid of a jumping, stabbing tooth that won't let up. Talking it out may help."

"Go on, boy. You are the biggest thing in my life, remember."

"Well, Gay and I muddled along getting more and more on edge. Why? I've asked myself a thousand times since, why? I adored her but I began to feel she detested me. Then one evening when she, my partner at contract, made a careless play, I thrust at her. For an instant her lovely, contemptuous eyes met mine, her lips went white. Then she laughed and carried off my rotten breach of good manners with beautiful dignity, but, when we reached home—I can see her now, her face pale as a dead girl's as she said in a low voice:

" 'I'm through, Brian. I won't live with you ever again as your wife. When you spoke as you did to me tonight I knew that in your heart you hated me. No man speaks like that to a woman he really loves; he couldn't. When a man and wife quarrel in private it is tragic enough, but when they slash at one another in public it's degrading. It isn't long before their friends dodge them as they would the plague.'

"If only she had flared at me, but she was so quiet, so controlled, I knew she meant it."

He crossed the room to the long windows and stared out upon a garden burning with the autumn fire of crimson, scarlet and gold blossoms, beyond the terrace.

"After that, she told me not to come near her, ever—again."

"You haven't seen her since?"

"No. That night the door of our room was locked. I told her I must talk to her. She didn't answer. I phoned the next morning. She said she had nothing to say to me, repeated that she never wanted to see me again. That I was free, that I needn't worry about testing the Romneys' reaction, she would take the blame for our separation. Never understood what she meant by that. Sounded as if she were quoting. I went West, wrote her that I would deposit money for her every month. She made no response." He cleared his husky voice. "You wrote that she was ready to talk divorce. Paris or Reno brand? She might try Mexico. I hear that Florida also is installing the cash and carry system. Are you encouraging her?"

"Don't be bitter, Brian. I am, if 'encouraging' means that I want to see Gay happy. She is such a choice, such a real person. Mac and Sam married attractive girls but they haven't her heart-warming charm—nor her intelligence. Don't think me disloyal to you—your starved eyes hurt me damnably—but you had your chance and wrecked it. The Romney clan knew Jim Seaverns before you and Gay were engaged, and liked him. He and she were boy and girl sweethearts, held the amateur pair-skating championship at one time. Then you crashed into her life with your whirlwind lovemaking. You know, of course, that Bee Ware closed her house the week after you left for the West?"

"I didn't know it until she wrote to me from somewhere in Europe. What has that to do with Gay and me?"

"Gay didn't say so, but I felt she suspected you were in love with Bee. When the fortune of Bee's first husband went into a nose dive she expertly bailed out of marriage. You and she had played round together before you met Gay and after the death of her second husband—Bee Ware the Widow, they call her now—you advised her about her business affairs, didn't you?"

"I did. If Gay is trying to make anything sentimental—or worse—out of my friendship with Bee Ware it's because she wants her own freedom. Where is she now? What's she living on? She hasn't touched the money I've deposited to her account."

"I begged her to make her home with me. She refused and settled in New York. She had a chance to try modeling for a commercial photographer. A skate-manufacturing firm wanted pictures of an expert skater for advertising. She made good, posed for other ads and now has all she can do. What she earns augments the small income her father left her. She stayed with me while she was closing your house, the furniture of which is stored over the garage. She insisted upon returning the pearls I gave her when she married—said she couldn't feel honest wearing them as she was no longer your wife."

"That sounds final. She must hate me to give up those. She loved them. You gave pearls to Mac's wife and Sam's and to Sue for a wedding present. Can you see any one of the three returning them?"

"I can't. I have the pearls and if things should come right between you—"

"You're an optimist. Ever see Gay now?"

"She lunches with me when I go to New York. I keep an eye on her."

William Romney thoughtfully regarded his nephew's straight back.

"Now she is—"

From the threshold Sampson announced impressively:

"Mrs. Brian Romney."

II

FROM the shadow of a hanging at the long windows Brian incredulously regarded the woman in the doorway. Was he dreaming or was it Gay? She was real, all right. Gay, in a smart brown *tailleur* and a matching velvet beret adjusted at an angle to reveal waves of rich chestnut hair, hair he had rumpled with his cheek. Gay, with that little air of distinction which had had a way of straightening the shoulders of the most bibulous members of their old set; with the same perfect, natural line of brows and gold-tipped lashes which had screened the beauty of her dark eyes from his, eyes which flashed with spangles when she was gay and mirrored the soul of her when she was grave; tender, vivid mouth with its lovely curve which he had kissed till she cried out that he was smothering her and in the second after her release had raised again to his. Gay! Who now wanted her freedom that she might marry Jim Seaverns! Good God! Why had he ever let her go? If only he could go back one year she would open that locked door or he would smash it in.

He watched her as she stood motionless against the background of the lighted hall as if uncertain as to what awaited her in the dusky room. Why was it dusky? Had Sampson been instructed not to snap on the lamps? Was the pattern of this situation of Major William Romney's designing?

After the instant of hesitation she crossed swiftly to the fireplace and held out slim ungloved hands to the man standing straight and tall before it.

"I didn't see you at first, Major Bill. Why the romantic gloom? Not planning dark and desperate deeds are you? Perhaps, though, it's nothing more serious than a light-saving complex."

There was a hint of strain in her laughing voice.

"Talk about magic. You don't have to rub Aladdin's old lamp to get what you want, do you? You write that you're not feeling too fit and need me and I jump the first train —Jim Seaverns wanted to motor me here, but I couldn't wait for him to finish a business appointment—and here I am."

"You're a sweet child, Gay. I do need you," William Romney admitted gruffly.

"Then I'm glad I asked for a few days off from my work. Now that my eyes are getting accustomed to this dim cathedral light I can really see you. You're looking gorgeous. When I dashed out of the car you sent to the station and glimpsed Sampson's face I thought I had arrived too late. With tears in his eyes he told me you 'appeared to be spindlin'.' Old fraud! Two frauds! What's the big idea deceiving a trusting girl from the Big Town, Major Willum?"

Her lovely teeth gleamed between her tender lips as she laughed up at William Romney. He put his arm about her. With a little murmur of affection she pressed her face against his shoulder, but not before Brian had seen the glitter of tears. Time to make his presence known he decided, and stepped within the radius of the firelight.

"Hello, Gay! That's the very act old Sampson staged for me. What is the big idea, Major Bill?"

At his first word she took an impulsive step toward the door but the arm about her tightened. Had he been such a brute that last night that she was afraid of him? Her face was colorless. Her hand flew to her heart as if to still its pounding.

"Brian! You! Here!" she whispered incredulously.

He knew as his eyes held hers that he hadn't been living this last year. He had been caught in a backwash; except for business, he had been paddling aimlessly in a pool of poignant remembrance. He tried to speak. His voice caught in his throat.

Gay twisted free from William Romney's arm. With unsteady hands thrust hard into the pockets of her jacket she turned her back on Brian and faced his uncle.

"Have you, whom I trusted—as I trust no one else on earth —double-crossed me, Major Bill? Did you plan this with— with Brian? If you did—"

The husky strain in the words restored Brian's voice.

"Just a minute, Gay. I was as surprised to see you come into this room as you were to find me here. Had I known you were arriving—"

"You would have been miles from here, wouldn't you?"

"I would have met you at the station. Do you think I'd let my wife—"

"I'm not your wife!"

The icy denial sent a surge of the hottest anger Brian ever had known licking through his veins. How dared she? Was she so sure that she would marry Seaverns? She had no grounds for divorce.

He met his uncle's warning eyes. Was he reminding that only a few moments ago he had boasted that he had learned to ride his temper with a curb? He now had the chance of a lifetime to prove it. He said as lightly as his clamoring pulses would permit:

"My mistake, Gay. I was under the impression you were!"

"I'm not. I never will be again. Now, Major Bill, having put on your act, the show is over. Please have my bags brought down, order the car to take me to the station, and, like the King of France and his forty thousand men having walked up the hill, I'll now walk down again. I—"

"You can't go back tonight, Gay. I'll go." Brian interrupted the lovely, mocking voice.

"Neither one of you will go," William Romney interposed authoritatively. "I've stood here like a dummy and let you two talk. Now I intend to be heard. Snap on the lights, Brian. Sit down, Gay."

With an inarticulate protest she sank into a deep chair beside the fire, dragged off her hat and rested her ruddy head, with its sleek swirl of wave breaking into soft curls, against the tall back. Her skin took on a faint rose color reflected by the red velvet of the chair.

Lamps blossomed into glowing oases of opaline light.

Vermilion, green, crimson and gold flames writhed and twisted on the burning logs. In dusky corners of the room ghostly shadows met and joined and swayed apart. The musical notes of the Westminster chimes stole in from the hall, the sound of the trickling fountain from the court. The air was fragrant with the smell of the wood fire and the scent of crimson roses. Gay leaned forward impetuously.

"Why, why, have you done this to me, Major Bill?" she demanded. "Have you forgotten that for a year Brian hasn't been near me? That it's a year since—"

"Since you told me you were through," Brian interrupted. "Since you walked out of my life, perhaps you'll remember?"

She was on her feet. She brushed back her hair with her left hand, which was ringless. Wouldn't she wear her wedding ring even until she was free? Brian asked himself, bitterly. First her pearls, then his ring had been discarded. Her brown eyes challenged his, her voice was shaken music as she retorted:

"Remember! Do you think I'll ever forget that night when you slashed at me and then said nothing when that hard-boiled Bee Ware cooed, 'Don't be cross with the child, darling, because she hasn't card sense.' Darling! Card sense! How could I have card sense when I felt you and she were critical of every play I made? When I knew—" she caught back a word and hurried on: "I wouldn't, I couldn't be the sort of wife who either slashes back at her husband or cringes like a stepped-on worm."

"My dear, please!" William Romney protested. "No third person should hear these intimate details."

"Perhaps he shouldn't, but this one is going to," Brian declared savagely. "You brought it on yourself by staging this situation, Major Bill. Now you'll have to take it."

With steady eyes on Gay's white face he demanded:

"Perhaps you remember also that as you left the room you flung over your shoulder, 'Don't come near me, ever again.'"

"And what did you reply? 'There are other women in the world!'"

The blood crowded back into Brian's heart and left his head light. Had that been rankling in her memory all this time? Had that fool remark kept her from sending for him? Had she tied up with that the fact that Bee Ware had closed her house shortly after he left town? No wonder she hated him.

"As you two insisted upon an audience you'll have to take the consequences," William Romney declared sternly. "I'm here to stay until we get this matter threshed out. Did you really fling that rotten threat at your wife, Brian?"

"I did, but you can't believe I meant it." Brian met his uncle's eyes squarely. "You know enough about my life before I met Gay, to know I didn't. I was wild with fury, shame, fear that I would lose her."

"That makes it easier for me to say what I brought you two together to hear."

"If it is to suggest that I live with Brian again you've wasted both time and gray matter planning this one-act melodrama, Major Bill," Gay retorted with flippant bitterness. "I love Jim Seaverns and I intend to—to marry him." Her breath had caught as if she were frightened at her declaration.

"Gay, for a naturally sweet girl, you can be maddening," William Romney retorted. His eyes sparkled as blue water sparkles in the sunlight. "Why don't you wait until you hear my proposition before you refuse to consider it? I can see that Brian is set to fight, but he has the sense to wait until he finds out what it's all about."

"Oh, Brian! Brian can do no wrong in your eyes. You idolize him. The sun of your life rises and sets in his shoes."

"You would be surprised if you knew how many times my love for Brian has been used as an argument against putting him in my place as head of the business, Gay."

"Brian! Head of the Romney Manufacturing Company! Do you mean it, Major Bill?"

"There you go, speaking as if you thought me in my dotage. Of course I mean it. Do you think I'd joke about a matter as serious as that? I'm tired of responsibility. I want to play. I want to travel. Why shouldn't Brian shoulder the burden? If he doesn't Mac and Sam and the girls will force Louis Dubois into the position."

"Louis Dubois! You wouldn't let that grand business which has stood for everything honorable fall into the hands of that —well, being a perfect lady I can't say it."

How like her to flash with anger and then end on a note of laughter. It had been one of her lovable traits that had caught Brian's heart the first time he met her.

"I'm glad you appreciate the gravity of the situation," William Romney said. "There are six against me, Sue tells me. She says that Mac, Sam and their wives are for Louis. I understand he has promised to boost their salaries when he takes over. But I still have control and I can put through my plan if you will help, Gay."

"I, how—can I help?"

There was breathlessness in the question, a hint of resentment and more than a hint of fright. Brian's eyes narrowed. What was this maneuver to checkmate the other members of the family Major Bill had up his sleeve? His nerves were taut as he waited for his answer to Gay's question.

"You can help immeasurably by forgetting yourself for the present and coming here to live with me and Brian."

"No! You shouldn't ask it of me, Major Bill. Brian, tell him that it is impossible. That you would hate it as much as I would."

"I couldn't tell him that, Gay."

"You won't, you mean. Why is it necessary for me to—to give up my work and life in the city which I love, all my plans for happiness with—with Jim, to come here and vegetate in this country town just to save that beastly old business?"

"The fickleness of woman! You thought it a 'grand business' a moment ago." Laughter left William Romney's eyes. "One of the arguments Sue has used to push Louis' candidacy, is that the head of the Romney business has always had an ideal family life, that Brian's already has cracked up, that she and Louis would carry on the tradition."

"She and Louis! That's a joke. Sue's a cat and Louis is a—" Gay pressed her face against William Romney's shoulder. "I don't want to come, Major Bill," she said in a hurt little-girl voice. "I like my life as it is."

"Then don't come. Why should you make a martyr of yourself? I'd rather the business would go to thunder than live in the house with—"

"Say it, Brian." Leaning within the security of William Romney's arm Gay prodded, "Live in the house with a woman you hate."

"That wasn't what I was about to say, but we'll let it pass for the present. I would like to carry on the business my great-grandfather founded. Will you help until I am well established—I'm not expecting or asking anything of you but to put on an act of friendliness—I promise—until I can swing the job?"

"I'll stand back of that promise," William Romney concurred gravely.

"How—how long will it take for Brian to become 'well established,' to 'swing the job,' Major Bill?"

"That depends on himself and you, Gay."

"Do you mean we are to live in this house? I couldn't bear to go back—"

"To the house in which we lived together? You can't. It's leased," Brian informed her tersely.

"It would please me if you and my boy would live here, Gay. The house is big. Brian's rooms in the tower are as he left them. So long as you put up a 'happily married' front to the world you two can go and come without meeting, if you prefer. I suppose we would be amazed if we knew how many couples live in the same house on those terms. I believe it is called separation, not divorce. You can do it if you'll forget the yesterdays and remember that today is yours, and the miracle is, it is always today. It will take courage, kindness and good sportsmanship to carry on. How about it, Gay, will you help save the family business?" He managed a hollow cough before he admitted hoarsely, "Sampson's right. I'm spindlin'."

"You're a fraud!" Gay accused with an unsteady laugh. She pressed tender lips against his cheek. "Just the same, I'm crazy about you, Major Willum."

Her eyes were gravely steady as she said:

"I will have to finish posing for a series of ads, but I'll make my headquarters here, on one condition. That you agree to a divorce when I ask for it, Brian."

Old Giant Trouble, who had been resting his entire weight on Brian's heart and brain for the last year, tumbled off. He felt a surge of new power. If he couldn't win her back he didn't deserve her, but it meant watching his step every moment they were together.

"I promise. Do you think I want a wife who 'loves Jim Seaverns and intends to marry him'? Not for a minute. You may not believe it but love and marriage mean something to me, too. I'll promise to help you get your freedom when you're ready and while you stay here I'll stick to the 'separation' compact and keep out of your way unless matters of diplomacy require our appearance together."

"I'll stay. You're witness to this agreement, Major Bill. I'll go now and unpack."

The two men watched her as she left the room.

"If only I could go back one year!" Brian said hoarsely. "Do you realize that by asking Gay and me to live under the same roof as friends only you've created an impossible situation, Major Bill?"

William Romney laid his hand on his shoulder.

"Nothing is impossible. Remember, Brian, that my honor as well as yours is at stake in the promise you've made. If you break it, you discredit me."

III

HAD ANYONE told her when she left New York that she would be sitting in the dining-room at Rosewynne with its royal-blue damask hangings against silver-leaf walls, gowned in last summer's white chiffon, with her one-time husband between her and Major William Romney at the opposite end of the table, she would have suspected that the person was suffering from an acute attack of brain shock, Gay reflected.

She forced her attention to the court beyond the open glass doors. Mother-of-pearl sheen of lilies; dahlias in all the tints of an autumn sunset; chrysanthemums rosy as the lining of a seashell, yellow as the gold of nuggets, white as a snowdrift, bronze as the kid of a lady's slipper, made a fairyland of breath-taking color. She had forgotten how lovely it was.

Her eyes came back to the men in dinner clothes at the table. Brian was cracking nuts and sliding them along the lace cloth to his uncle as she had seen him do innumerable times. As if he felt her eyes on him he looked at her and smiled.

"Can I tempt you, Gay?"

She shook her head. She couldn't speak. She felt like a small child being dropped by a parachute, not knowing where she would land, or if she would land at all but keep blowing along in the winds of the world.

It was all so tragically like the happy days of her engagement and the first year of her marriage. Why had she weakly allowed herself to be persuaded into this impossible situation? It wasn't like any of the "separations" she knew of to be sitting here with Brian near, talking and laughing with his uncle and courteously trying to draw her into the conversation. How could he do it? Didn't he care that he and she had made a mess of their lives? Didn't he know the real reason she had left him? Of course he did. How could he have greeted her with that casual, "Hello, Gay!" after a year's absence? Her heart, which had been frozen to insensibility, was coming to aching, stabbing life. A tempest of emotion shook her. She rose hastily.

"Ex—cuse me. It's—it's so warm," she mumbled and left the room. Not so quickly that she did not see that the two men were on their feet, that she did not hear William Romney say gravely:

"Have we asked too much of the child, Brian?"

Child! The word echoed in her mind. Had her bolt from the table seemed childish in a woman of twenty-four? As she crossed the hall she disciplined a desperate urge to run up the curving stairway to her room and entered the house-depth library.

Going to be a quitter the very first evening? she asked herself scornfully. You'll stay right here and later make a dignified and graceful exit in your best dramatic manner. She turned on the radio.

> "The night is young
> And I'm in love with you,"

a man sang with caressing tenderness.

She snapped off the current as if the voice had been a keen, shining blade-thrust. She curled up in a deep chair beside the fire and tried to bring order out of the chaos of her thoughts.

Suppose she had not been left by the death of her parents in her Great-Aunt Cassie's care when she was ten years old, that great-aunt who was one of the last of the grand old female tyrants for whom New England had been famous? Suppose that instead of growing up in a boarding school and coming to a certain sort of maturity in college she had lived in a home, would she have torn her life to shreds because her husband was irritable and wanted another woman? What else could she have done when Bee Ware had come to her and said:

"You're modern, Gay. So am I. Let's talk this out. I love Brian and he loves me. If you don't believe it, read this."

Hurt to the soul she had taken the note. Its words had been etched in her memory with a red-hot point:

I can't do it. I've diplomatically sounded out the family enough to know that any suggestion of what we talked

*about would bring them down on me like a ton of
bricks. You may try it. Good luck!*

                                        Brian.

Bee Ware's black eyes had been alight with triumph as
she said:

"Well, I've tried it. I've come to ask you to free Brian.
What are you going to do about it, Gay?"

And she had kept her voice steady, had even smiled a little
as she answered:

"Nothing. I'll let Brian do it."

But when that evening he had snapped at her because of
her dumb play at cards she had done something and done it
quite thoroughly.

Someone had said that building a house was the man's
job, that building the marriage for that house was the
woman's. Doubt stole upon her in a thickening cloud. She
forced her way out. Why blame herself? What else could she
have done when her husband was in love with another
woman? Brian's and her smash-up was no worse, probably,
than dozens of others happening all over the country, but
this one had happened to her marriage which she had
thought invincible. Her love for Brian was as dead as a ten-
year-ago problem, but even now the memory of it hurt intolerably. Well, marriage had been too big for them.

Suppose, her thoughts trooped on, she had not come to this
manufacturing village to spend a week-end with a college
friend who had taken her to the Romney ice carnival where
she had met Brian who had proved to be as perfect a skating
partner as Jim Seaverns? Would she have married Jim?

Jim! She had been seeing him frequently in New York
since his return from South America. His companionship had
eased her heartache and restored to a degree her self-con-
fidence which had taken a terrific beating. What would he
think when he heard that she was at Rosewynne? She would
explain. No—she couldn't, couldn't even tell him that Brian
had agreed to a divorce when she asked for it—not only had
agreed but had said he would help her get her freedom. She
had solemnly promised to stand by until he was established
as head of the business. If Louis Dubois or Sue had a suspicion of the real state of affairs, they would make capital of it
and do their worst to oust Brian and that would hurt Major
Bill.

She couldn't tell Jim. She knew exactly how Pandora felt

when she opened the forbidden box and loosed the ills of life on the world. When she had walked out of marriage she had released a lot of trouble which had spread to others and no matter how she struggled to snatch it back she couldn't crowd it within the confines of her own life again.

She would write Jim that she had decided to return to Rosewynne because Major Bill needed her. She was glad now that she had refused to allow him to talk marriage while she was legally if not actually Brian's wife. No one would have been more surprised than he, had he heard her passionate declaration in this very room a few hours ago:

"I love Jim Seaverns and I intend to marry him!"

Did she love him? She loved his tenderness and thought of her—but—could she marry him? She shivered. She didn't want to marry anyone. Divorce might free her from Brian legally but would it black out the memory of their life together? If it didn't, would she ever feel free?

Why consider that question? It had been decided for her. She was here to help Major Bill, whom she loved. That his nephew had been drawn into the compact was unfortunate, that was all.

"Drink this hot coffee, Gay. You left yours untasted."

With a start she looked up.

"I don't care for it, thank you, Brian. Where's Major Bill?"

"Don't get panicky. He's coming to your rescue."

He set the small silver tray on a table and returned to the fire.

"I told him I had something to say to you. Don't go," he protested as she rose hurriedly. "Sit down. It isn't what you think it is. That subject was settled when I swore that I would neither ask nor expect anything of you more than putting on an act of friendliness. You haven't used the money I've deposited for you. Will you, now that you are here?"

"No. Why should I use your money? I don't need it."

"You'll give up studio work, won't you?"

"After I've finished the present series of ads, but I have the income my father left me."

"You will be ostensibly—the wife of the president of the Romney Manufacturing Company. You will be also hostess of Rosewynne. To dress the part will require more than your personal income, won't it?"

"I don't wonder you've made good as an executive if you cross-examine your employees as you do me."

She appealed to William Romney as he entered the room.

"Major Bill, do you think it right for Brian to force an income on me when I don't want it?"

"I don't like that word, force. One would think—"

"Just a minute, Brian," his uncle interrupted. "I was hoping, Gay, that you would wake up this old house and restore it to its one-time place as the center of hospitality in the town."

"I'll love to be hostess for you, Major Bill, but—"

"Then you will need extra clothes. Would you rather I would pay my official hostess a salary?"

The blood stung Gay's face as she agreed:

"Much rather if you insist that the part I am to play requires smart clothes and lots of them. I feel like a worm letting you pay me for helping you but I'd rather feel like that than spend Brian's money."

"Aren't you helping me earn a bigger salary? Why shouldn't you have your share?"

"I'm not staying here to help you, Brian. I'm here because I believe in what the Romney Manufacturing Company stands for—and because I love Major Willum madly." Gay had begun the declaration belligerently but ended it on a note of laughter. Why turn what promised to be an up-to-the-minute drawing-room comedy into a family row?

"Mr. and Mrs. Louis Dubois," Sampson's voice boomed from the threshold.

"Here's where you begin to earn that fat salary, Gay," William Romney reminded with a chuckle, before he advanced to greet the woman and man who had followed the butler's announcement.

Halfway across the room they stopped in surprise and regarded the slim figure in white before the fire. Tall, massive, sharp-nosed Sue Dubois quivered from her red curls, along the curve of her lustrous pearls, down the rippling black sequins of her gown to her sandals. Her eyes, as yellow-green as the eyes of a cat and about as evasive, met Gay's and slipped away. The man beside her, who was an inch or two shorter, thrust one hand into the pocket of his dinner jacket and looked at Gay with smoldering eyes.

She had seen that expression before. She hated it. Louis Dubois was her Private Detestation Number 1. His hair had the gloss of black patent leather, his features were as perfect as those of a marble Adonis and as cold. His left eyelid twitched occasionally. He caressed his clipped dark mustache. His thin lips pinched into a thin smile. Sue, with her arrogance, her corroded estimate of human values, her lack of men friends, had been an easy mark for his suave flattery and undercover courting.

"Gabrielle! Where did you come from?" Sue Dubois exclaimed in shrill staccato. "We knew that Brian had dropped in on a flying visit, but you, my dear! We've understood that you were Reno-bound, haven't we, Louis?" She accented every few words with a hunch of her shoulders. "Brian, aren't you relieved to have her back or did you like being a gay pursuing and pursued bachelor?"

Gay felt Brian go tense. He detested his one girl cousin. Sue's shrill voice and malicious eyes roused her fighting spirit. She slipped her hand under Brian's arm. What use was Major Bill's plan if she couldn't carry through her part in the conspiracy convincingly and act as if she loved the man who had killed her love for him?

"I don't like that word 'relieved,' Sue," Brian protested, "but if you mean, am I glad that my wife and I are together at Rosewynne, I'll say I am."

"You're mistaken on two points, Sue," William Romney corrected genially. "Brian is here to stay, not on a flying visit. And I ask you, what would Gay be doing in Reno with her husband president of the Romney Manufacturing Company?" He smiled as he shot his bolt.

The announcement was more than a bolt. It was a broadside. Figuratively speaking it swept the Dubois off their feet. Louis was the first to recover.

"So, you've picked your successor without considering whom the rest of us want, Major?" he drawled.

"You're so quick to catch onto an idea, Louis. You've expressed the situation in a nutshell."

"I don't know what the other boys will say," Sue Dubois protested. "They planned to drop in to see Brian tonight, not expecting of course to see Gabrielle—here are Mac and Jane now."

Sampson's announcement of the guests had been drowned in her shrill voice.

Tall, heavy, handsome Mac Romney, his red, weatherbeaten face in striking contrast to his blond hair and the white of his dinner shirt, shook hands with his uncle.

"Howdy, Major Bill. Great to have you back, Brian. Well,

for the love of Mike where did you come from, Gay?" There was full-blooded gusto in his laugh. He caught both her hands in his.

"Say, you're looking out of sight! You always were a knock-out." He turned to his dark-haired pretty wife who, in smoky chiffon trailing flame and vivid green, was greeting the Dubois.

"Jane!" he called. "See who's here looking very Big Town-ish with an International Social Set touch."

Mrs. Mac Romney arched her perfect brows.

"Precious girl! When did you arrive, Gay?" she greeted in a silky voice which was in striking contrast to the stri-dency of Sue Dubois'.

"This afternoon. It is grand to be here and—"

"She's come because Brian, the light of Major Bill's eyes, is to be made president of the Company," Sue Dubois in-formed shrilly.

Mac Romney clapped a hand over his ear.

"Pipe down, Sue. Your voice goes through my head like a siren. Is that true, Major Bill?"

"Yes, Mac."

"Well, take it from me, I'm darned glad. 'Fraid you might pick on me for the job. I don't want it. Sam doesn't want it and we believe that someone of the Romney name should carry on and that Brian is the stout-hearted lad for the busi-ness." He joined his uncle and Brian in front of the fire.

Jane said nothing, but Gay noticed that she glanced at Louis Dubois from the corners of her eyes and slightly, very slightly raised her brows. Was she allying herself with him against the Romney men?

"You can always be counted on to shift with the wind can't you, Mac?" Dubois' smile was a hateful thing. "You've changed your point of view since the last time we talked together, what?"

"Perhaps I have, Louis, and then again perhaps I've felt that Brian should have the job but thought it simpler to let you do the talking." Mac's temper was patently at boiling point. "Now that we're on the subject I'll give it a thorough workout. I—"

"Mr. and Mrs. Sam Romney," Sampson announced pon-derously.

Petite, golden-haired Lucie Romney whose skin was as perfect as the pearls about her throat, in a frothy, pale-blue evening frock floated toward the three men standing back to the fire. Her page-boy coiffure made her seem younger than she was. Complacently aware of the charming picture she made, she clasped her white hands in childish enthusiasm.

"Oh, you three wonderful Romneys!" she twittered. "Brian, how did you happen to be such an Indian when your cousins are so fair?"

She beckoned to the tall man behind her whose features were as lean and clean-cut as his brother Mac's were florid and heavy.

"Join them, Sammy. I don't wonder the townspeople call you Romneys the Royal Family. You make me think of those All for One, One for All men, in a movie. I've forgotten the name of it."

"A gentleman named Dumas wrote a story called *The Three Musketeers* which was adapted to the screen, Lucie."

Sam's wife wrinkled a perfect nose in response to his amused correction.

"Thank you, darling, I knew my literary-minded husband would come to my rescue. I want a portrait of you men just as you stand there to hand down to the children."

"That's a good suggestion of yours, Lucie," William Romney approved. "I'll look into it. How are the twins?"

"Not as well as they should be. They won't eat, Major Bill."

"Ever thought to stop them gorging candy, Lucie?" Sue Dubois inquired stridently. "Those two four-and-a-half-year-olds dropped in to see me the other day and stuffed themselves with chocolates. When I told them they had had enough they said you and Sam—I don't approve of their calling their father Sam—let them eat all they wanted."

Lucie raised and dropped her white hands in a gesture of futility.

"But what can I do, Sue? I tell them to stop but they won't."

"Do!" Brian's repetition exploded like a pistol shot. "Make them obey. Going to let those corking youngsters grow up into pests? Can't you discipline them for their own good?"

"Listen to the oracle, Lucie," Sue Dubois gibed. "Bachelors always know how to bring up children. My mistake, you aren't a bachelor are you, Brian-me-lad? But you seem so little married."

"A truce to sharpshooting," William Romney interposed impatiently. "Why can't you and Brian be in the same room two minutes, Sue, without staging a battle? Sam, you and

Lucie weren't here when I announced that Brian is to succeed me as president of the Company."

"Good work!"

"Is that all you have to say, Sam Romney? You've told Louis that he ought to be president."

"Your mistake, Susie, my girl. Louis has told me he ought to be." Sam's smile was bland. "Of course Brian should succeed Major Bill. Even though he's the youngest of the Romneys, he has the family's Number 1 business head and he has the two indispensable I's needed by an executive, Imagination and Initiative. Believe it or not, I don't envy him his job. I hear Eddie Dobson's got a swelled head and a touch of dictator complex since he's been teaming with that Frenchman you wished on us, Louis."

"Wished on you! You're lucky to get Lavalle. He's a skilled workman," Dubois protested angrily.

"Maybe so, but he makes me think of something that's squirmed up from the underworld." Sam dismissed the Frenchman with a shrug. "Going to stand by and see Brian through, Gay?"

"Where did you get the idea she wouldn't see me through, Sam? Gay is as keen to have me succeed as I am to make good," Brian interposed before she could answer.

"Is she really?" Sue Dubois shrilled. "Then I suggest that she get her wedding ring out of pawn or storage or wherever it is, I notice she isn't wearing it. They are still being worn in the best circles. Come, Louis, we have a date for contract with Bee Ware the Widow. That reminds me, she opened her house only two weeks ago. A little bird must have whispered that you were coming back, Brian. How amusing. Lucie, you and Sam are expected at the party. Good night, everybody."

"So are we," Mac Romney groaned. "I'll have to toddle along. I loathe cards but Janey's crazy about 'em. Mighty glad you're back at Rosewynne, Gay." He added in a whisper: "Attaboy! Don't let Sue get you down, gal."

The big library seemed curiously still. Major Bill and Brian were in the hall speeding the departing guests. What a hideous half hour, Gay thought. Sensing an atmosphere loaded with dynamite that might be set off by a spark of malice. Feeling as if her heart had run into nettles each time she glimpsed the pearls about the women's throats. She had adored the string Major Bill had given her. Setting a watch on her tongue for fear some word of hers might betray the true state of affairs between Brian and herself. Betray! That was funny. As if the family didn't know.

"Thank the Lord, that's behind us!" Brian remarked fervently as he crossed the threshold. "Your performance of the devoted wife rates three stars if not four, Gay. It was a good build-up."

"Where's Major Bill?"

"Look here, are you going to have a nervous breakdown each time you and I happen to be alone? If you are, we'll call the deal off."

"Of course I'm not, Brian. I wanted to ask Major Bill something. Never in my life have I been nervous. If I appear so now it's the result of the strain of combating Sue. She's like the beast in a fairy tale, she has us all stiff with apprehension because of her reputation for invincible verbal sharpshooting. She never misses the vital spot."

"Forget it. While I agree that Sue is the world's Number 1 feline, you'll have to admit that she brought up a point to be considered. Where is your wedding ring?"

"In my room."

"Get it, please."

She opened her lips to refuse, thought better of it and raced up the stairs. She lifted a diamond circlet from its white satin lining in her jewel case. No matter what Sue said she wouldn't wear her engagement ring, she declared to herself obstinately as a large emerald-cut stone blinked up at her.

Three minutes later in the library she extended her hand to the man still standing back to the fire. He lifted the sparkling ring from the rosy palm and slipped it on her left third finger. He bent his head, straightened abruptly.

"Sorry you don't like it but you really should wear a wedding ring while you are here," he said with cool authority. "I thought if you had pawned it or left it in storage, as Sue so tactfully suggested, I would get another tomorrow. I'm off to New York tonight as soon as I change my clothes."

Halfway across the room he stopped.

"The next time we are staging a social act together, don't put your hand on my arm, Gay. It isn't necessary and I—don't like it. Good night and thanks for agreeing to stand by."

IV

GAY WAS thinking backward as she sent her shining blue-black roadster forward. It was October. She had come to Rosewynne in September. She had had to learn all over how to live after she left Brian a year ago, to forget the splendor of her dream of marriage with him, her reliance upon his strength and tenderness; had had to shape her own plans, keep her own counsel, suffer for her mistakes, rally from them, and to a certain extent provide jam for her bread and butter.

And this is where that year of heartache and anger and loneliness had landed her, she reflected, back in this town struggling to ignore the ghosts of the past that flitted through her mind. Living at Rosewynne instead of in a house of her own, entertaining at dinner and being entertained; visiting the homes of some of the workers who had been employed in the Plant for a generation or two; sitting beside Brian on Sunday in the church where the Romney christenings, weddings and burials had taken place for the last eighty years, with the cousins in neighboring pews, deceiving them, trying to, as to the relations between Brian and herself; avoiding being alone with him and making herself utterly ridiculous in the process and amusing him—she could tell by his eyes.

She had planned to be so brilliantly charming, always to have something to say that would make his sensitive mouth widen with laughter or his blue eyes darken thoughtfully, and, to be honest, to make him realize what he had lost when he lost her. Instead she was a little breathless and inadequate and if by chance she met his eyes, instead of registering appreciation of her wit and wisdom they were dangerously amused as if it wouldn't take much to blow off the lid of his control and tell her how inane he thought her. No wonder he spent his evenings away somewhere—when they were not invited out together or were not entertaining at home. She presumed he was with Bee Ware. His rooms were in the tower, hers were in the main house.

She had been at Rosewynne four weeks, four lagging weeks, and what had she accomplished? Nothing. Absolutely nothing. The tie which held Brian and herself together was as impermanent at that gold light on the tree tops, as frail as the silken thread of the cobweb on the shrub which glittered with iridescence. Where was the situation leading? What did it mean in the pattern of their two lives? At least she was not on the same old treadmill. She had stubbornly refused to go out every evening and she had days in New York while she finished posing for the series of ads.

She watched the sun slip below the horizon leaving behind a burst of crimson splendor which fringed with gilt a scatter of hyacinth clouds and tinted pink the tower of Rosewynne that loomed from the top of the ridge. Tall trees which still flaunted a few tattered pennants of scarlet and orange caught the reflection and proudly reared tops crowned with red-gold. A three-quarter moon was mounting toward the zenith. Earth and sky mellowed.

The broad, dusky highway which led to the near-by small city was quiet. A drift of late sunlight on a sloping roof faded slowly. Tree branches swayed in drowsy rhythm. The hum and beat of distant traffic was muted to a sound like the susurrus of the tide on a sandy beach. A twilight star glowed in the darkening sky. Another followed. Did those blinking jewels hung in infinite space know or care what happened in the small revolving sphere below them?

As she passed the Plant's park, with its fully equipped hospital, swimming pool, dance pavilion, library and recreation fields, the clock struck six. It was not too late to drop in at the Widow Dobson's and leave the peppermints she had brought for her mother, old Ma Bascom, she decided.

She stopped the roadster in front of a white cottage, complete with garage, lawns and garden, in one of the white-cottage-lined streets which radiated like the spokes of a wheel from the broad road that encircled the iron-railed yard enclosing the boundries of the Plant. A man dashed along the neat stepping-stone path, entered the house and slammed the door behind him.

Eddie Dobson! In spite of the fact that he was a capable foreman, he was the Number 1 trouble-maker at the Plant. Two years ago an indispensable part of a valuable machine had suddenly disappeared. The damage couldn't be traced to him but it had followed close upon Brian's warning to their maid, Lena, that she would be desperately unhappy if she didn't break with him. The superintendent of the building in which it had happened had been sure that he was in some way responsible. He was jovial, with a roving eye and a way with the banjo that drew the women workers as honey attracts bees. They had protested in a body at the injustice of picking on Eddie as the culprit. The Plant was running at high speed to fill orders, the time was inauspicious to push the charges and they had been dropped.

The hurrying figure had radiated excitement. Should she go in? If she didn't she might run into him the next time she came. Better get it behind her.

In response to a cheery "Come in!" she entered a spotless room. It smelled of wood smoke seasoned with the appetizing aroma of a cooking stew rich and racy with onions. It was comfortably furnished with golden oak. Pine logs blazed and snapped in the ample fireplace.

A crone with a face wrinkled and brown as the shell of an English walnut and eyes which sparkled like two jet beads, was huddled in a welter of woolen shawls in a wheel chair near the fire. Mrs. Dobson, tall, muscular, with a face which told a story of disappointment and worry, but which still retained traces of wholesome good looks, straightened a frilled cap on the old woman's head with red, work-roughened hands as she smiled at Gay.

"It's fine to see you back in our village, ma'am," she welcomed cordially. "Ma, here's pretty Mrs. Brian. She's come to see you in a handsome green suit. Guess she remembered you like green."

Mrs. Bascom frowned her face into a new pattern of wrinkles.

"Wish you'd stop thinking I'm deaf, Liza, and yellin' my head off," she fretted. "I kin hear's well as anyone when I want to. Glad to see you, M's Brian." As Gay bent to speak to her, she fingered the sleeve of her jacket. "How soft it is. Like velvet. What's the stuff?"

"Tweed, Mrs. Bascom. I'm glad you like it."

"I like pretty things." Her beady eyes twinkled. "I like pep'mints, too."

"Now just think of her remembering for a whole year that you used to bring 'em to her. Isn't she smart?" Mrs. Dobson demanded in the tone of a mother displaying a prize-winning baby.

Gay untied the gilt cord around a white package. She opened a candy box and laid it in the old woman's lap.

"There you are, Mrs. Bascom. Half peppermints and half wintergreen, your favorite mixture."

The old woman's clawlike fingers fumbled in the waxed paper. She shook her frilled head.

"You take one out, Liza. I can't manage."

Her daughter selected a pink wafer and placed it in her toothless mouth.

"There, Ma. I'll bet it will taste good." As the old woman sucked the sweet her daughter leaned her crossed arms on the top of the wheel chair and smiled at Gay.

"I was pleased when I heard you'd come back, Mrs. Brian."

"Who's wearing black? Who's dead?" inquired Ma Bascom with a quaver of excitement in her croak.

"Nobody's dead. I said—b a c k—not black."

"Don't yell at me, Liza. Jest because I can't hear you mumble, you think I'm deef. . . . Give me another pep'mint."

"Ma's terrible sensitive about her hearing, but land, she's ninety-six, I guess she's a right to be lazy about listening," Mrs. Dobson explained indulgently. "An' I tell her that's all 'tis, just plumb laziness, she can hear well enough when she wants to. I'm glad Mr. Brian is taking his uncle's place at the Plant instead of—"

"Are you, Mum? Guess you won't be when you hear that the new boss has fired me!" advised a drawling voice.

Mrs. Dobson started nervously and turned to look at her son, who leaned against the frame of the door which led to the kitchen. From behind him came the hiss of a boiling kettle, the clink of metal as its cover rose and fell. A felt hat perched rakishly on the back of his head. His wavy light hair was rumpled. His handsome face was flushed; the skin about one bold and rowdy eye was puffed and discolored. He bit at a cigarette with strong white teeth.

"Fired, Eddie? What you done now?" Mrs. Dobson's question was a choked whisper.

"Nothing—to get fired for." He put his hand experimentally to his bruised eye. "They're always pinning things on me at the Plant an' I'm getting sick of it, see?"

"Don't take on about it now, Eddie, don't you see who's here?"

"Yeah, I see, Mum." Eddie Dobson pulled off his hat and flung the cigarette into the fire. He treated Gay to his most ingratiating smile.

"How are you, Mrs. Brian?"

She didn't wonder that the factory girls fell for that smile, it had charm.

"Very well, thank you."

His grandmother peered at him from beneath the frill of her cap.

"For the land's sake, did you say you got fired, Eddie? What you been up to now?"

"None of your business, old girl!" He grabbed a handful of mints. She snatched up the box and held it tight to her breast.

"Shame on you, Eddie, for taking Ma Bascom's candy," Mrs. Dobson scolded. "Mrs. Brian came specially to bring it to her. She's been away a year and she hasn't forgotten your grandmother likes peppermints. Ain't it kind of her?"

"Sure. It's too bad she's married to such a hunk of granite."

"Eddie!" his mother breathed in horror.

"Forget it!" he blustered, snatched more peppermints, tweaked the frill of his grandmother's cap when she whimpered, and swaggered across the room. On the threshold of the kitchen he sniffed.

"Meat-stew night. I'm stayin' home for supper," he said and vanished.

"That means he wants flapjacks," Mrs. Dobson interpreted with the same hint of excitement her voice might have held had she proclaimed that she had been given a ten-dollar bill.

"I'll be running along." Gay rose. "I'm glad to find you so well, Mrs. Bascom."

"Oh, I'm pert. Guess I'll be drawin' my pension from the Plant long after some of the rest of you are dead and gone. The Lord don't seem to have no use for me yet among the cherubims an' seraphims. Come again." There was a twinkle in her black eyes. "I don't care much for pep'mints."

"I can see that you don't." Gay laughed and patted the clawlike hand. "Next time I'll bring something you really like. Good night."

At the front door Mrs. Dobson whispered:

"Please excuse Eddie for what he said about your husband. He's sore because he's been fired. That boy—I can't realize he's a man grown—worries me, not only on his own account but because his brother Joey wants to do everything he does. It's awful hard for a woman to bring up boys these days, they need a man. You know boys will get mad about nothing."

"Yes, I know, Mrs. Dobson, that's all right, don't worry."

"If Eddie'd thought first he wouldn't have come in with that black eye while you was here. Sometimes I think it's bad for him that he's so smart, he was made a foreman so young and then the girls spoil him. Goodness me, I don't know why I'm whining out my troubles to you. When you're so good to come and see Ma."

"You weren't whining, Mrs. Dobson, we all have to let off steam occasionally. Good night."

"Good night, ma'am. God be with you!"

"God be with you!" The words echoed in Gay's heart as she opened the door of the roadster. Did God concern himself with an individual? If He did—

"Snappy car you've got, Mrs. Brian."

The voice came from a shadow which separated from a tree trunk and stepped toward her.

"It is a nice car," Gay responded.

Dobson laid his hand on the door of the roadster as she closed it. He smiled and wheedled:

"Say a good word to Mr. Brian for me, will you? Ask him to take me back."

"Sorry, but I never make suggestions about the management of my husband's business, Eddie."

"Oh, you don't! Well, you tell him from me that everyone knows he's had it in for me ever since he's been boss—he butted in on my private affairs before—an' they ain't going to stand for it. Everyone knows, too, that I ought to be boosted to superintendent. If he doesn't take me back and promote me there'll be others that will quit and that'll kind of cramp production he's speeding up. Tell him to chew over that for a while."

Eddie Dobson had delusions of grandeur if he imagined he had sufficient power with the workers at the Plant to cause them to give up their jobs, Gay thought, as the roadster shot ahead. Only two years ago they had signed a document pledging their loyalty and their faith in the fairness of their employers' decisions. He thought she could influence Brian! That was a joke. Brian was becoming more and more remote. When she spoke to him she felt as if it were an effort for him to drag his thoughts back from a distant country. Country! That was a joke too. Probably from a woman who wasn't so far distant.

Why think of it? How cool the sky was. How thickly spangled. Like a backdrop in a Christmas pantomime. The moon was as brilliant as a new penny, a badly nicked penny. It would be a starry night. She loved starry nights. They set her spirit a-tiptoe.

She listened to the chime of the deep-toned bell in the church steeple. Half after six. She had time to stop at Sam's and see the twins. They were apt to be at their riotous best after their supper. She had brought stuffed dates which would be better for them than the chocolates of which Sue Dubois complained.

Sue! She wrinkled her nose in disdain. Sue was the family critic-at-large. But, she was right, the children shouldn't gorge on chocolates. Sue was so often hatefully, maddeningly, entirely right, darn her, Gay thought as she caught the glitter of the circlet on her left hand. The sight of the ring brought with it a vision of Brian as for the second time he slipped it on her finger.

That memory and its ramifications occupied her mind until she stopped the roadster before the Italianate house Sam Romney had built after his marriage six years ago.

A maid opened the door in response to Gay's ring. A look of relief banished the frown from her round, Irish face:

"Sure it's glad I am to see you, Mrs. Brian. An' me about out of me mind from the noise."

"I came to see the twins, Bridget. Are they still up?"

"Up is it? Listen!"

High childish shouts punctuated with, "Get up, there! Hi!" and a hoarse cough drifted down the stairway.

"Come in, Mrs. Brian. Them kids have been yellin' like that for the last ten minutes. Nurse Wickes come runnin' downstairs wringin' her hands an' askin', wouldn't I go up an' stop 'em. Me, tryin' to stop 'em! I'd as soon step into an airplane propeller whirlin' at full speed. An' me tryin' to get the table ready for a dinner party."

"Where is their mother?"

"She hasn't come from the city yet an' their father's in his den writin'—it's as much as your life's worth to go near him whin he has one of them writin' spells."

A crash shook the house. An ominous silence followed.

"Mother of God!" Bridget muttered piously. "Somebody's killed!" She raced up the stairs.

Gay, scarcely less breathless, dashed into the nursery at her heels. She swallowed an able-bodied laugh as she looked over the maid's shoulder.

A white-capped nurse was wringing her hands as she stared at a tangle of overturned chairs from under which emerged a curly golden head and two wildly waving childish hands. On a dilapidated couch, feet spread, clothesline reins clutched in one chubby hand and something which looked suspiciously like Sam Romney's pet trout rod in the other for a whip, balanced William Romney Second, Billy to his familiars. His naturally cherubic face registered indignant amazement. His hair, usually as yellow and curly as that on the head protruding from under the wreckage, was dark and matted with perspiration. The sole adornment of his perfect body was a crumpled white towel knotted about his waist.

He turned eyes as deeply blue as Burma sapphires on Bridget and Gay who were on their knees extricating the little girl as the nurse lifted the chairs from the struggling, coughing child.

"Look at Sister!" he growled. And Gay thought how true he ran to masculine form to scold when frightened. "Ol' meanie! We were playin' char'ot like in the picture book Cousin Brian gave us an' she was the lead horse an' I tole her to go slow roun' corners but she said she had to 'pwance,' she just had to 'pwance.' Now see what she's done!"

He dropped the reins and the precious rod. Perched on the edge of the couch, elbow on his dimpled knee and chin sunk in his rosy palm in the attitude of one of Raphael's celebrated cherubs he scowled at the coughing, gasping little girl, clad only in her original birthday suit, whom Gay, seated on the floor, had lifted to her lap. The trappings which supposedly had caparisoned the lead horse remained in the wreckage of chairs.

"Hand me Sister's bathrobe, Nurse, quick. Isn't it in that pile of clothing at the foot of the couch? Thanks. Give Billy his. We won't need you, Bridget, go back to your work. There, that's better."

She kissed the top of the curly head against her breast and smiled into the blue eyes fringed with long wet lashes.

"All right, now, angel?" she asked tenderly.

"Hmp! Angel!" snorted Billy. "I'm bigger'n she is an' if she's an angel I guess I'm God."

Gay disciplined a chuckle and suggested:

"Better put on your slippers, Billy."

Hands in the pockets of his gaudy red and green and white striped bathrobe, William Romney Second frowned down upon his sister in lordly superiority.

"What you cryin' for, Sister? Hurted?" Anxiety tinged his disdain.

"I'm not hurted. I—I just want to see my muvver."

The boy's worried eyes sought Gay's. She said quickly:

"My goodness, children, I forgot. Where's that box I dropped when I came into the room? All right for the kiddies to have a stuffed date or two, isn't it, Nurse Wickes?"

"They'll eat 'em whether it's right or not," grumbled the long-suffering woman.

With whoops of excitement the children pounced on the package. They brought it to Gay still on the floor, and dropped to their knees beside her.

"We'll let you open it," Billy announced magnanimously. "It's more polite, 'sides you'll do it quicker."

"Looks as if you'd given up modeling for a nurse-maid-by-the-day job, Gay."

Gay stared unbelievingly at the man beside Lucie Romney in the doorway. She scrambled to her feet, held out her hands and welcomed fervently.

"Jim! You dear! Why Jim Seaverns, what brought you here?"

V

"I BROUGHT him, Gay," Lucie Romney explained. "I needed an extra man for my dinner tonight, so I phoned Jim and picked him up at his club. He's staying with us for the week-end. Why, Brian, when did you come in?"

Gay freed her hands as if those gripping hers had suddenly burned red-hot. In the hall behind Seaverns loomed Brian Romney. The blood rushed to her hair as she met his eyes. Had he heard her say, "You dear!"?

"Brian! Bwian!" the children shouted. They seized his hands and dragged him into the middle of the room.

"Now we'll play char'ot again. Brian'll be lead horse an' you can be the little dog an' run behind, Sister," Billy announced with lordly patronage.

"Don't want to be little doggie." The child clutched Brian's hand and rested her face against it. "Don't want to be little doggie," she repeated hoarsely. "My fwoat hurts."

He lifted her and brushed the yellow hair back from the flushed forehead.

"You needn't be a little doggie," he consoled tenderly. "Lucie, this kid is feverish. She ought to be in bed."

"I know it, Brian, the doctor told us to keep her there, but she wouldn't stay. What can I do?"

"I'll make a try at it. You'll stay tucked in to please Brian, won't you, Sister?"

The child slipped an arm about his neck, cuddled her hot face against his and asked hoarsely:

"Will you wock me first, Bwian, and tell me Muvver de-ar, Muvver de-ar?"

"Just a teeny, weeny rock, Sister. You'll be better off in bed."

He looked at Gay and Jim Seaverns standing at the door. "Gangway!" he said. With the child in his arms, mother, nurse and Billy following, he passed into the hall.

"That seems to be that," Gay laughed. "Come on, Jim, you and I are useless here."

"Where are you going now?"

"Home."

"I'll go with you. We have something that must be talked out, Gay."

They went down the stairs without speaking. He picked up his hat. As he opened the front door she protested hurriedly:

"We'll have that talk some other time, Jim. Don't come with me. You came here to dine with Lucie. I have the roadster—"

"You mustn't drive around after dark, Gay. Lucie says that Sam suspects trouble is brewing at the Plant."

"Suppose it is? No one would harm me."

"Probably not, but just the same I'm taking you home."

"I'll take my wife home."

Startled, Gay looked up at Brian. When had he come down the stairs?

"Your wife?"

The implication in Seaverns' voice flooded Brian Romney's face with dark color. His left hand clenched.

"What do you mean by that?"

Without appearing to move, Gay maneuvered herself between them.

"Please—Jim. I prefer to go with Brian."

White to the lips, his eyes glowing like coals, Seaverns laughed.

"I suppose the farce—it is a farce, isn't it—must be kept up —for a while. But our talk is only postponed, Gay. I'll be seeing you. Good night."

In silence Gay stepped into the shining roadster. In silence Brian slipped behind the wheel. The spicy air was frosty. The road blanched by moonlight flowed by. Wayside shrubs blurred into silvery shapelessness. An out-of-season moth winged through the light from the lamps like a luminous wraith of the night. The somber tips of hemlock branches flashed into crystalline beauty and were left behind.

Brian beside her—but miles away in spirit. Curious that two who had been so much to one another now found no words to bridge the chasm of separation, Gay thought. Well, it couldn't last much longer—they were in the drive of Rosewynne.

He unlocked the massive entrance door and stood aside for her to enter.

"Come into the library, Gay. I have something to say to you."

"It's late. I have barely time to dress for dinner."

"I won't keep you but a moment. Come."

Blazing logs sent dancing shadows on the booklined walls as they entered the room. Lamps softly lighted it. Crimson roses scented it. Gay looked hopefully toward the large chair by the fire. Perhaps Major Bill would be there and then Brian couldn't bring up the subject of Jim Seaverns. He wasn't.

"Relax, Gay. You make me think of that statue of someone or other poised for flight."

Brian was smiling. After his furious flare at Jim Seaverns it was unbelievable. As if he read her thoughts he apologized:

"Sorry I lost my temper at Sam's. There was no reason why Seaverns shouldn't drive you home, but I was annoyed that he had told you there is trouble at the Plant."

Was that the true explanation? Why question it? Why should he care with whom she played round so long as she kept to the outer conventions of their life together?

"Is it serious trouble?" she asked.

"No. I had to fire Eddie Dobson and—"

"I know, I saw him."

"Where?"

"At his mother's. I went there to take candy to Ma Bascom."

"Did Eddie speak to you? What did he say?"

When she had finished telling him she asked:

"Couldn't you promote him to be superintendent and avoid trouble?"

"No. He's a good shop foreman and that's all. He can't rise because increased mechanization in industry calls for graduates from technical schools to fill the top-place jobs that demand something besides experience. He is bright enough to know that but the realization only increases his grouch against me."

"Can he cramp production? Has he that much influence?"

"Time will tell. At present strikes seem to be this country's fastest growing industry but our workers never have been affiliated with an outside organization; they haven't needed to be. A strike of workmen which is the sole object of compelling the employer to re-employ a discharged fellow-workman is a strike for an unlawful purpose. Not that court decisions have had much effect, lately.

"However, I still demand the right to hire and fire as I see fit. Dobson is a crackajack foreman but he has attracted the worst elements among our workers and I've heard rumors of a secret society that he and the Frenchman, Lavalle, whom Louis brought to the Plant, have organized. He's not only ugly because I won't promote him, he has an added grievance in the fact that I warned Lena against him. Of course, I haven't had it in for him; he's so good at his job that I've turned a glass eye on some of his deviltry, but I can't do it any longer, it is too dangerous for the other workers. Whether he has or has not the power to cramp production, he won't be taken back. He beat up a man in his department—he was working off a personal grudge. Please don't drive about the village alone after dark, Gay."

"Do you realize what that would mean? I'm always coming home from teas or contract or the club or New York in the late afternoon at this time of year and in the winter. You don't want me to stay at home, do you?"

"I do not. There are two chauffeurs on the place eating their heads off. If you won't have one of them, have Tim O'Brien, that red-headed brother of Lena's, drive you. He doesn't have enough to do in the house to keep him busy."

"It's too silly. I won't do it."

"There's only one other thing to be done, then. That's all. I won't keep you any longer."

Gay felt as if she had been dismissed by a coldly displeased schoolmaster. In her boudoir, whose walls were gay with stripes that shaded from pale yellow almost to orange, she faced the girl in the mirror, noted that the light brought out gold and bronze tones in her chestnut hair that harmonized with the walls.

"Can you go through with this farce of marriage?" she asked that girl. "Sometimes it seems easy, like taking part in a play, and sometimes you loathe being a cheat and would like to run and run and run till you put the whole world between you and the Romney clan, wouldn't you?"

Her thoughts returned to Brian's "There's only one other thing to be done." What had he meant?

Her question was answered the next afternoon when in the dusk she approached her roadster at the Country Club and saw the red glow of a cigarette and the outline of a figure at the wheel.

"Brian! What are you doing here?" she demanded.

"Hop in."

As the car slid smoothly forward he reminded:

"I told you not to drive alone after dark, didn't I? Did you think I said it just to hear myself talk? If you won't have Tim I'll take over the job."

She glanced at his profile cut like a cameo against the dark sky, noted the set of his chin, the hard line of his mouth. She might as well beat at steel bars for freedom as to try to combat his determination, she told herself, and immediately made the attempt.

"I'll feel like a prisoner if I can't drive about alone, Brian. If you insist upon being chauffeur for me I'll stay at home."

"Not such a bad idea. You've been going at a pretty fast pace since your return to Rosewynne besides keeping up with the New York job, haven't you? Do you good to slow down for a while."

"I shan't slow down. I shall keep going and I shall drive alone, too."

"Sure?" he said.

After that they maintained a bristling neutrality, more bristling than neutral. The rosy afterglow faded into warm amber, the slender branches of white birches waved like silver wands to the rhythm of a soft wind stirring the dark pines and balsams behind them. A flock of geese in wedge formation honked and winged westward. The sky burst suddenly into starry splendor. Venus, the lovers' star, glittered like a great diamond set in purple enamel. In serene majesty the moon regarded them with its one and one-half eyes.

"Ever wonder if the moon has a face on the other side?" Brian asked. "Perhaps, instead, it has a page-boy haircut like Lucie's. That reminds me. Sister's a pretty sick little girl. Do you ever remember that her name is Rose? I don't."

Gay promptly forgot her grievance.

"She had a horrid cold. Is she having proper care? Did you 'wock' her yesterday and what did she mean by 'Muvver de-ar, Muvver de-ar'?"

"Funny kid. I walk home from the Plant across lots and

I've gotten into the habit of dropping in at Sam's. I like children and the twins are tops. Sister was feeling low one day, Billy had been teasing her. She asked me to 'wock' her and tell her a story. Not having a fund of bedtime yarns all I could think of was Three Little Kittens. I rendered 'Oh Mother dear, Oh Mother dear, our mittens we have found' in my best dramatic style. So now she asks for 'Muvver de-ar, Muvver de-ar.' "

"I'll look up a book of nursery rhymes for you."

"That will help. See that tall pine? Whenever I pass it I think of the huge, brown, eerie thing that scuttled into the shrubs near it the afternoon I came back to Rosewynne. Probably it was a cow but it had me haywire for a minute. I could feel my hair rise. Scared as I was it handed me a laugh when I thought of Sue's reaction had she caught it prowling in her grounds across the road. Apropos of nothing at all, Lucie phoned the office and asked me to invite Jim Seaverns to Rosewynne for the rest of the week-end as her household was upset by Sister's illness."

"But you didn't?"

"I did. Why shouldn't I?"

"He won't come."

"Sure he'll come. Why shouldn't he? He accepted with enthusiasm."

"You might have consulted me, might have inquired if I wanted him as a guest."

"It didn't occur to me that you wouldn't. You said you—loved him, didn't you? Except for yesterday you haven't seen him since—since you decided to help me out, have you?"

"I haven't but I don't need anyone to plan my life, Brian. I can manage it very nicely, myself, thank you. Leave me at the side door, please."

Sampson met Gay in the hall.

"Mr. Jim Seaverns 'rived 'bout ten minutes ago, Mrs. Brian. I put him in de green room in de tower. He say he come for de week-end. Has you seen anything of Mr. Brian? Mrs. Ware she been—here he come now." He took Brian's hat.

"Dat M's. Bee Ware she been telephonin' an' telephonin' fo' you, Mr. Brian. She say tell you she need you to fill in fo' dinner dis evenin', dat she has a lady f'om Hollywood fo' you to meet. I tol' her Mr. Seaverns was here fo' de week-end. She say you could leave him easy. She say you's to phone her soon as you come in."

"I will, Sampson. Sounds like a good party and I feel the need of a good party. If Seaverns has you and Major Bill he won't need me, Gay. I'll take your car."

He crossed the hall and took the three steps to the tower door in one jump. Terribly happy that he was to have an evening with Bee Ware the Widow and a Hollywood glamour-girl, wasn't he? How characteristic of that woman to invite a man without his wife, Gay thought bitterly. But a woman who would ask that same wife to give up that same husband that she might marry him would do anything to get him, wouldn't she?

"What are you muttering about, Sampson?" she asked.

"Mr. Brian went so fas' he didn't give me a chance to tell him Major Willum's gone to New York fo' de week-end."

VI

BRIAN ROMNEY found himself noting little details about Bee Ware tonight with unusual clarity. The faint lines at the corners of her eyes, the two sharp cuts etched deep between the thin penciled line of her brows, the too heavy perfume. Had her skin coarsened in the year since he had been away, had her eyes hardened, or was Gay's delicate yet vivid face so imprinted on his heart that she looked slightly over-blown in comparison? How old was she? Twenty-five as she claimed? She looked a more likely thirty-five at this moment.

Even as these thoughts occupied his mind he told his hostess that it had been a good party, that the dinner had been perfect, the glamour-girl from Hollywood a knock-out—although for himself he preferred beauty with a dash of brains—that gold lamé did wonderful things to her own dark hair and eyes and that he really should be on his way now that the other guests had gone.

Beatrice Ware shook her head.

"Too smooth. Your voice sounds as if you were hitting the high spots but your eyes look as if your heart had been simonized. Is life—at home very hard, darling?"

"Life at home hard! Where did you get that crazy idea, Bee?"

"Oh, I'm psychic." She pressed her lips against the gardenia in his coat lapel. He quickly removed it.

"If you like it so much you'd better take it."

She stuck the flower in her dark hair and nodded approval at her reflection in a long mirror. In the hall she solicitously adjusted the collar of his topcoat.

"Don't jerk away, Brian. You don't wear it turned up about your ears, do you? Sometimes I think your heart has begun to ossify. Hope for the sake of the Plant that your mind won't turn to stone. You look worried. Is it business? I've heard that the workers are getting restless, that there is likely to be a walkout or a stay-in or a sit-down, or whatever is the latest style in strikes."

"Who told you that?"

"Louis Dubois. He dropped in for cards one evening when Sue was patroness at some charity affair."

"Dubois talks too much. Ours is not a 'key plant.' Besides, our workers do not belong to an outside organization. If there is trouble it will be entirely a family disagreement, which will be adjusted amicably as the differences of opinion between the Romneys and their employees always have been adjusted."

"You Romneys have a Royal Family complex, haven't you, darling."

Her second use of the endearing term sent dark color to Brian's hair even as he told himself that the word was in such common use that it had lost its one-time tender significance.

"Where'd you get that silly idea?"

"Don't go savage about it, though you're irresistible when you're savage. I hear that Jim Seaverns is week-ending with Gay and you."

"So what?"

"Don't bite, darling. Jim is fascinating and—"

"Good night!"

"Come in for cocktails—tea for you—to-morrow—"

Brian chopped off the sentence with a smartly closed door.

He'd better take a turn around the Plant before he went home, he decided as he started the roadster. Of course everything was all right there but the rumors of restlessness among the workers made him uneasy. What an expert at innuendo Bee Ware was! His blood was pretty near boiling point.

Well, he deserved all the annoyance she had handed him. He knew from his experience when he was trying to help her with investments that he'd better keep out of her way, and hadn't he been cutting across lots to Rosewynne to avoid her cream-colored roadster, which seemed always to have business on the highway between the Plant and home in the late afternoon? But when Sampson had repeated her invitation he had seized the chance to show Gay that he wasn't afraid to leave her with Seaverns, to apologize in that roundabout way for his flare of temper at Sam's.

Evidently Louis Dubois was behind the stories of friction at the Plant. Was he craftily encouraging it to make conditions difficult for the new president of the Company to handle? Was he figuring that he might be called in to arbitrate and in that way gain power and prestige among the workers?

If he is, he has another guess coming to him, Brian's thoughts trooped on. Looks as if I'd have to fight Dubois as well as Dobson with Lavalle thrown in for good measure. A hot fight is right down my street. It will keep me from thinking of Gay.

He drove slowly around the iron railing which enclosed the Plant. The sky was pink above the foundries. There were lights in the windows. The night shift was on the job. Nothing wrong there.

He thought of his great-grandfather, the son of a country parson, who had angered his father by neglecting his studies to tinker on gadgets of steel and iron. One spectacularly successful invention had been the beginning of the Romney Manufacturing Company. The crude bench at which it had been worked out was enshrined in the office of the Administration Building.

Beginnings interested him tremendously, Brian reflected. When he met a person who had been distinguished for accomplishment he was always tempted to ask eagerly: "How did it begin? From what acorn did your great oak of achievement grow?"

Mac had been given a copy of *Pickwick Papers* when he was a kid. It had fired him with ambition to own all the books of Charles Dickens. One of the finest collections of Dickensia in the country had grown from a present made to a small boy. Sam had—

The sight of three men close together on a street corner had the effect of a bomb dropped in the midst of his thoughts. He recognized them. Dubois, Eddie Dobson and Lavalle.

As the roadster came abreast of them two turned and walked quickly down the street. The other stepped into the shadow of a tree. Brian stopped and called:

"Taking a look-see about the Plant, Louis? Evidently you and I had the same hunch. May I give you a lift?"

Dubois emerged from the shadows.

"No, thanks. Out for a constitutional. I left Sue at Rose-wynne performing an act of family devotion. She felt she must stay with Gay until you came home."

"Gay! What's happened to her?"

"Nothing *has* happened," Dubois' laugh mocked. "Sue and I dropped in at Rosewynne after dinner. Gay and Jim Seaverns were in the library alone so Sue sent me to look you up. She will stay with them until you get there. Not that she wanted to, but she thought it would look better if some of our crowd were to drop in."

Brian resisted a furious impulse to take a crack at the man's perfect features, wondering how his face would look toothless, before he inquired smoothly:

"How long since Major Bill hasn't been a sufficient chaperone for any woman of the Romney family?"

"I ask you—how can he be in New York and Rosewynne at the same time?"

"The Major isn't in New York!"

"Isn't he? You'd better beat it home and find out. Tell Sue to come along in the sedan. I'm walking."

The Major couldn't be in New York—he would have told him if he were going—wouldn't he? Brian demanded of himself as he let in the clutch. Why hadn't Sampson told him that his uncle was away? Of course he wouldn't have gone to Bee Ware's if he had realized that Gay would be left alone with Jim Seaverns. He wasn't that crude. His heartbeat hadn't yet returned to normal after the shock of Dubois' "She is staying with Gay until you return." For one horrible moment he had thought— Why live over that? Nothing tragic had happened to her.

He paused at the door of the library. The room was like a stage setting for a modern comedy of manners. His aunt's portrait above the mantel was the focal point in the room itself. Beyond open glass doors the pink-walled court was a blaze of color. Gay, in a bouffant frock of net which shimmered into golds, yellows, brazen oranges and rusty coppers as the firelight struck it, was snuggled into Major Bill's deep chair. Seaverns in dinner clothes, looking unutterably bored, was standing back to the fire smoking. Sue Dubois was on the broad couch at right angles with the fireplace. Her silver-sequined costume glittered like a coat of mail with every movement of her body as she nervously trotted one foot.

As Brian entered she rose with a little shriek of relief. She patted jeweled fingers over her painted lips as if to suppress a yawn, hunched her shoulders and shrilled:

"Here you are at last, Brian! Did Louis find you at Bee Ware the Widow's? I told him you were probably waiting until the other guests had left. You and she always have so much to talk about. When I found that Major Bill was in New York and that Gay and Jim were alone in the house—"

"Would you call it being 'alone' with Sampson and five servants, Sue?" Gay demanded. "Jim, do help her with that silver fox cape. She must be fairly worn out with her arduous duty of chaperone."

"My dear girl, why get mad about it? I'm always glad to help. You know this village is a hotbed of gossip, Brian. And even though I knew that Gay and Jim wished me in Tophet, for the honor of the Romneys, I stayed."

"My wife is quite capable of guarding the honor of the Romneys, Sue."

"Good gracious, what have I said now to turn your face ghastly, Brian? I never can please you. Did you see Louis?"

"He's walking. Said for you to come along in the sedan."

"Alone? I can't drive alone at this time of night. You'll have to come with me."

"I'll drive Mrs. Dubois home with—pleasure, Romney." If Jim Seaverns' voice and facial expression were to be believed he would also with pleasure run her head-on into a stone wall.

"Will you really, Jim? Perhaps it would be better than to take Brian away again. Good night, Gay. Your gown is ravishing but rather too strong in color for you; it washes out your skin. I'm afraid you'll think I'm a pest, Jim, but—"

The shrill voice diminished to a murmur. A door closed with a bang.

"That is Jim registering rage. It has been a rare evening. Never a dull moment." Gay's laugh was brittle. "Good night."

"Wait, please. How long has Sue been here?"

"Don't be worried. We found her here when we came out from dinner."

"I'm not worried, Gay. I am infernally sorry that you

should have had to endure her for a whole evening because I didn't know when I accepted Bee Ware's invitation that Major Bill had gone to New York."

"You're not trying to make me believe that if you had known it would have made any difference in your running out on me, are you?"

"Use a little common sense. Why should I run out on you? You and I are putting on an act of—of marital felicity—that phrase must have boiled up from my subconscious, doesn't sound like me, does it? Do you think I would turn it into a flop by leaving you to entertain Seaverns had I known that Major Bill was away?"

"I wouldn't know about that."

"Major Bill was right when he said that for a naturally sweet girl you can be maddening, Gay. You're darn flippant and here I am practically on my knees in apology."

For an instant she met his smiling eyes in tense passionate protest. Then as if her spirit had soared on the wings of laughter, her brows lifted, her eyes shone, her lips curved in an enchanting smile.

"I'm surprised at you, Mr. Romney. Why stop at practically? Why not make it literally?"

Her grace, beauty and provocative charm drove him to smash through the barrier she had reared between them.

"Gay!"

A backward step, an outflung hand warned him. Her friendliness had gone straight to his head. Lucky he hadn't seized her in his arms. Could she hear his heart racing its engine? His laugh was a major accomplishment.

"If you insist on your pound of flesh I will go down on my knees—but if you've noticed, I'm wearing my swankiest evening clothes and—"

"Terribly careful of your precious clothes, aren't you? You wouldn't do the Sir Walter Raleigh act and throw your cloak in the road for a lady to walk on, would you? That's merely a rhetorical question, no answer. Now I really am going. Good—"

"Just a minute!" a rough voice interrupted.

Eddie Dobson stood between the crimson velvet hangings at the terrace windows. He had been with Dubois and Lavalle near the Plant. How had he gotten here so quickly, Brian wondered before he demanded:

"What do you want?"

The man swaggered forward. His light hair was rumpled. His blue eyes—one darkly rimmed—were cold. Freckles on his cheekbones looked like a sprinkle of brown dust on his colorless face. Brian said sharply:

"Go, Gay."

"You don't have to worry. She's safe." Dobson's mouth twisted in a sneer. "It's you I have business with."

Gay's heart flew to her throat and beat its wings as Brian turned his back to pick up the cigarette lighter on a small table. A little chill shivered down her spine. Was he stark, staring mad to take such a risk? Couldn't he see that Eddie was here to make trouble? She took a step nearer.

"If you will stay, sit in the Major's chair, Gay. Who left that window unlatched for you, Dobson?"

"I'm not telling. Want to know why I'm here?"

"Why you're putting on an unlawful entry act? It's a pretty serious offense. Can't say I'm interested. I'll leave that for the sheriff to find out."

Gay, seated on an arm of the chair, clasped her hands tight in her lap. If only Brian would smile, use a little tact, get Eddie out of the room, she thought feverishly. He wasn't bad —he couldn't be all bad with a mother like his. Brian could manage him if he would talk to him instead of standing there with his eyes burning black in a face which looked as if it were carved from marble. He took a step forward.

"Get out, Dobson, and get out quick."

"Not till I've said what I came to say. You did me dirt, you put me in Dutch with the only girl I ever gave a damn for and now you've fired me for no reason at all." He stopped as Brian looked at him over the lighter he was applying to a cigarette. "Well anyway, it hadn't nothing to do with the Plant. I'm one of the best foremen you've got, I ought to be superintendent, you know it, and take it from me my private life ain't got anything to do with how I do my job."

"I've heard that somewhere before. I don't talk business here, only in my office. Out you go, Eddie."

"I'm stayin' till I say what I come to say an' if you don't hear me you're goin' to be sorry."

Brian crossed to the doorway that opened on the hall.

"Get out, Dobson. Because of that fine mother of yours I'd hate to call the sheriff, but you can't get away with walking into a man's house and threatening him."

"All right. You're hard enough to bite nails. You win—this time!" The last two words were ground between clenched teeth. "But if you don't give me back my job—I'll—I'll—well, you'll be sorry."

"This way out. Better not act again on the advice of the person who sent you here."

"No one sent me here! Can't I think for myself?" With a muttered imprecation Dobson swaggered from the room.

Oh, why, why does Brian go with him? Eddie may attack him, Gay told herself frantically. If Jim would only come back, he might help. The mere thought of him warmed her heart. How still the house was. How loudly the hall clock ticked. What was that bang?

The stiffening left her knees as Brian returned. To prevent their folding up entirely she sank to the edge of the Major's chair.

"The next time I tell you to leave the room, Gay, leave it," he said curtly.

"But, I couldn't. He—he might have—have done something terrible to you if you'd been alone."

"Oh, no. It wouldn't be Eddie's racket to attack openly. He's an undercover guy."

"Why wouldn't you let him blow off steam? Why wouldn't you listen to what he had to say? What did he mean, you'd be sorry?"

"That's some of his theatric mumbo jumbo. Melodrama is Eddie's dish." His low laugh hummed along her veins, something glowing behind the cool amusement of his eyes set her heart beating like a trip hammer.

"Business for business hours. I won't have it intrude when I am about to tell my wife that I think the gown she is wearing is perfect. Your color washed out! Sue's crazy. Good night. This time you'd better go, Gay."

VII

"KNOWING as I do that the Romneys are rooted deep in tradition and that keeping up family customs is a fixation, I still wish Major Bill wouldn't persist in having dinner at two o'clock on Sunday because his father had it served at that hour. Old Morpheus will get me if I don't watch out," observed Brian Romney. He stifled a prodigious yawn.

Gay, seated at a table set in the middle of the mosaic floor in the center of the warm, fragrant court, was pouring coffee into silver-mounted porcelain cups.

"I know how you feel, I'm sleepy too," she admitted. "Dinner following that soporific sermon this morning—if it hadn't been for Sam's glorious voice soaring in 'Once to Every Man and Nation,' I would have gone sound asleep in church—the drip from the mouths of those stone dolphins into the pool and the scent of that bank of gardenias have reduced me to a comatose state. The cook's plum pudding and hard sauce, fluffy as whipped cream, which is also a Sunday custom handed down through the ages, hasn't helped. Coffee, Jim?"

Seaverns was looking up at a Gothic window on the second floor. A profusion of nasturtium vines jeweled with shades of gold, topaz and ruby cascaded from its balcony over the soft pink and cream walls.

"No thanks. The beauty of this court tightens my throat whenever I come into it."

"It does things to me too," Gay confessed. "Major Bill had it designed for his wife, who was an invalid. The balustrades of the eight Gothic windows, the stone stairs mounting on each side of the pool to the small gallery above it were brought from a Venetian palace. The space between the dining-room and library seems to have been divinely designed for it."

"It's a knockout. Come for a hike, will you, Gay? You'll have to change from that crepy rust wool frock—it looks paper-thin to me. It's a perfect autumn day."

"I'd love it. The air will wake me up and by suppertime I'll be little bright eyes. Will—will you come with us, Brian?"

"Nice of you to include me in the marathon but I promised to drop in on a party. Show Jim the spot we've selected in the stream for a swimming hole for the kids. Remember the old stone mill with the water wheel below the dam?"

"Yes."

"Sam and I plan to make a pool between the boulders opposite that. The sun shines directly on it and warms the water. The old grain chests in the building can be used as lockers. It will be much more thrilling for the twins than a stereotyped pool in the garden. They are keen for adventure. You're an engineer, Jim, perhaps you'll give us pointers on construction. Where's the Sunday supper to be tonight, Gay?"

"At Mac's."

"That means grand eats. It means, also, that there will be at least two dogs per person watching with furtive eyes and dripping jaws each mouthful consumed."

"But they are such perfect dogs. I never see one of Mac's French poodles without wanting to hug it. I'd adore having one of my very own. Will you go directly to Mac's from your party, Brian?"

"I'll come back here and drive you and Seaverns to Dingley Dell. I wonder what his father would think if he knew Mac was so Dickens-minded that he had renamed the old place for the favorite haunt of the Pickwickians? Hope Major Bill will be back in time to join us. He's keen for the Sunday fests, another time-honored family custom."

Whistling the latest song hit, Brian ran up the marble steps bordered with ferns and giant salpiglossis, purple, yellow, red, and vanished into the library. Gay listened until the last musical note thinned away. She thought of his burning eyes and stony face last night when he had ordered Eddie Dobson out of the house and she thought that a moment ago he had looked as if he hadn't a care in the world.

"You'll never give up all this beauty for the home I could offer you," Jim Seaverns remarked bitterly as his eyes lingered on the towering acacias that flanked an arch.

"Don't be foolish. I lived a great many years without a Venetian Renaissance court in my life," Gay laughed. "How about it? Are we walking?"

In the wooded ravine an hour later, seated on a mossy log which might have been dipped in the same dye pot as her green knit frock, Gay listened to the splash of white water foaming over the dam into blackish green pools, to the purl and ripple as it lapped into curves where it dozed in the shallows. Late sunlight gilded the stone mill, with its moss-clogged water wheel, which stood out sharply against the gloom of the woods and seemed to give her back look for look with its shutterless windows so like staring eyes.

A little chill crept to her finger tips. She glanced furtively over her shoulder. She had the haunting sense of an unseen presence. Silly. Why should that old building give her the jitters?

With an effort she broke its hypnotic spell and glanced at her wrist watch. Each time she looked at it she experienced the same thrill which had tingled through her veins the evening Major Bill had given it to her as an engagement present. Five o'clock. The patch of sky visible between the tree tops resembled nothing so much as a huge turquoise streaked with a matrix of cloud tinted pink by the slanting sun.

"Isn't the air glorious, Jim?" she called to the man leaning against the rail of a rustic bridge. "All spiced with spruce and hemlock, balsam and pine. What's your verdict on this location for the swimming pool?"

"Don't like it. Treacherous. The spot between the boulders will wash, and one day, when it wasn't expected, it would be too deep for the kids. I'll take a look at the stream lower down. There may be a pool somewhere that could be reached easily from the mill."

Gay thrust her hands into the pockets of her green cardigan, dug the heels of her heavy shoes into the moss and dried pine needles and watched him as he picked his way through a tangle of tall blackberry bushes whose reddened stalks clawed and clung as he passed.

Two days ago, at Sam's, he had said that he and she must "talk out" the situation. She had agreed to his suggestion that they walk this afternoon, that she might get the talk behind her. Last winter in New York they had drifted into the affectionate friendliness which had existed between them before she had met Brian, had entered a few pair-skating contests together. She wasn't sure that she didn't love Jim enough to marry him when she was free. But that wouldn't be for months, it might take a year for Brian to "swing the job," more, if Eddie Dobson made trouble.

Tomorrow she was going to New York to pose for the last time. After that her apartment would be sublet. She had been lucky to dispose of it. She had enjoyed the work. She had been stimulated and inspired by her contact with the business world. Her present life was narrow and colorless in contrast, though the men and women who kept their residence here because of business interest in the near-by small city were forever on the social merry-go-round, forever on the move. . . .

She had fought against being swept along with them after she married, but Brian had liked it and she had tried to keep pace. She had broken loose—rather, he had broken loose from her—and here she was back again doing the same old senseless things, though now she had her evenings at home. She had adopted a program of systematic reading of American history, and tuned in on her boudoir radio on subjects in which she was deeply interested. To a slight degree she was carrying on her education, as the president of her college had begged the members of the graduating class to do.

Why go over all that? She would much better concentrate on what she would say to Jim Seaverns. Though she had made light of it she had been startled by his reference to the home he could offer her. She hadn't liked it. It had made her feel that she was being party to something dishonorable. She would ask him not to come to Rosewynne again until— Could she trust him with the truth about the pact between Brian and herself and say, "Until I am free"?

The ravine was weirdly still, almost as if it were holding its breath to listen to the splash and tinkle of running water. A soft green gloom was stealing through the woods. She called:

"Jim! We ought to start for home. It's getting dark."

He waved and crashed through the blackberry tangle. Gay met him as he stepped from the bridge. His hands were scratched and torn.

She pulled her handkerchief from her pocket quickly. The clasp of her watch bracelet caught and drew a long green thread of wool from her cardigan. She broke it before she tenderly dabbed at the bleeding fingers.

"Jim," she crooned, "how did you do it?"

"It's nothing. I've slashed my way through jungles as were jungles but for sheer torture that blackberry patch has them beaten to a standstill. It had a million claws. Come on!"

The woods hummed with sounds as they climbed the trail, spooky sounds that stole from the gloom which was changing from green to purple under the trees. Was the weirdness getting on Jim's nerves? Gay was aware that he kept turning his head from side to side quickly as if he expected a monster to leap from ambush. Had he the feeling of an unseen presence?

His alertness must be contagious, she decided, for her nerves were taut as she heard uncanny rustlings in the underbrush, the sibilant hiss of a breeze through the pines and an eerie "Whoo! Whoo! Whoo!" Strange. She couldn't remember having heard the hoot of an owl in these woods. Black wings flapped overhead to the accompaniment of a raucous "Caw! Caw! Caw!"

Out of the woods at last. Serene and russet-gold lay the smooth lawn, and beyond rose the walls of the house, tinted soft pink by the afterglow. Jim Seaverns caught her arm.

"Just a minute, Gay. What are we going to do about it?"

She didn't pretend to misunderstand him. She asked wistfully:

"Need we do anything, Jim? Can't we just go on being friends as we were?"

"No. We were more than friends, my dear. We were getting back to where we were when Brian Romney crashed into our lives. I can't go on like this. Seeing you. Loving you. Not knowing if you love me or if—tell me what it's all about. You owe me that. Why did you come to Rosewynne? You seemed happy with your work, with our, well, call it friendship. You don't love Brian, do you?"

If she told him she didn't she would not be living up to the agreement made that night in the library. Brian was keeping his promise.

"I'm married to him, Jim. And I told you in New York, that if you and I were to remain friends you must not even hint at anything more while I was another man's wife. So let that settle it and please, please, don't come to this town again. We'd better hurry, it's getting late."

They crossed the lawn in silence. Without having spoken, entered the hall. At the foot of the curving stairway Seaverns caught her hands and raised them to his lips.

"You couldn't say you loved him, could you?" he demanded. His eyes were alight with triumph as he declared:

"I don't understand why you are postponing your divorce, but I'll wait! We'll wait, darling."

"For me, Seaverns?" Brian Romney inquired lightly as he came down the three steps from the door of the tower. "You won't have to. I got home earlier than I expected. Let me know when you're ready to drive to Dingley Dell, Gay. I'll be in the library."

At the window of her boudoir Gay regarded the tower thoughtfully. Brian's rooms occupied the entire first floor. Had he seen her cross the lawn? Had it been chance or intuition that had brought him to the hall at the moment of Jim Seaverns' impassioned, "I'll wait. We'll wait, darling"?

Had he really thought that Jim meant that he and she would wait for him to drive them to Dingley Dell? Or had he suspected that he had referred to her divorce?

If the last, he would think she wasn't playing fair. Suppose he did? Was he keeping up to the letter of their agreement when he paid conspicuous attention to Bee Ware the Widow? Perhaps he couldn't help it. Perhaps she was insisting, "We *won't* wait, darling." Dining with her last night.

A party with her this afternoon. In comparison Jim's devotion to herself was what a summer shower was to a tornado.

Impatiently she turned from the window and glanced at her wrist. Her heart stopped. Her watch! Her precious watch! Gone!

"Now don't get panicky, you know you always find things," she said aloud, as with eyes searching the rust velvet carpet she crossed to the door. She went slowly down the stairs and across the hall trying to remember when she had looked at the watch last. In the ravine! She had pulled her hand from her pocket and the bracelet had caught. The strand of wool she had impatiently broken off was dangling from her cardigan. Had she loosened the bracelet clasp then?

She must hunt for it. It would be ruined if left out all night. She might ask Jim to go with her. He was dressing in his room in the tower. No. One solo with him in a day was enough. Going alone would be excellent self-discipline. When it came to poky dark places she was a coward.

She noiselessly opened the front door, tiptoed across the terrace and down the steps. As she crossed the lawn she looked back to get her bearings. She and Jim had approached the house in a direct line with the tower windows. She remembered thinking that they shone like brazen copper in the sunset.

She walked slowly, poking the turf with the toe of her heavy shoe. She mustn't overlook a chance of finding the precious watch before she reached the ravine.

She stiffened her courage and plunged into the dusky trail. A loose stone hopped and skipped downhill with the clatter of a machine gun in action. Hoping against hope that the diamonds surrounding the watch would blink up at her, she slid, slipped, dexterously avoided holes.

Purple dusk had increased by an hundredfold the weirdness of the sounds she had heard on her way up. Rustlings in the brush were more sinister. They conjured a close-up of a war-painted Indian slithering from tree to tree. The breeze whined through the woods. The owl hoot had become the wail of a disembodied spirit floating on noiseless wings and the crows flapping overhead were black witches of the night.

Thank goodness! She could see the end of the trail, the rustic bridge and the glitter of glass in the old mill, could hear the rush of water over the dam. Its roar and splash obliterated the spooky noises of the woods.

What was that "tum—tum—tum"? A drum? Muffled! Sounded

like a dirge! He throat gripped her breath in a stranglehold. Lights floated past the stone mill! Twin lights a few inches apart! Two more passed. Two more! A line of them! They blinked! They blinked horribly! Could they be eyes?

She stood in trancelike stillness. What did those fitful lights mean? Something secret? Something sinister? They were crossing the bridge! She could see the outline of the rail. She listened. No sound of tramping feet on the planks. Ghosts, maybe, faring forth on a haunting expedition. That thought helped. No more lights! Ghosts or men, were they coming up the trail?

What was that? That eerie sound in this fearful solitude? A stone rolling! Someone creeping down from above. Had she been seen? Were the light carriers closing in on her?

VIII

"GAY! GAY!" The voice was a mere whisper.

Jim! For a split second her mind spun like a top. Steadied. Jim was looking for her. His foot had loosed the stone. He must not be seen on the trail.

"Sstt! Sstt!" she warned and blinked as a light blinded her.

"Gay! Gay! What are you—"

"Don't ask questions! Put out the flash! Is the trail clear above?"

Seaverns seized her arm.

"Have you gone completely haywire?" he demanded.

"Don't talk!" she whispered. "I've seen things! Quick! Let's go!"

Hand in hand they groped up the trail. When they reached the edge of the lawn on which trees were casting purple shadows she shivered.

"Just a minute before we go on, Jim. The stiffening has come out of my knees."

He put his arm about her and she leaned against him.

"Will you tell me for what darn-fool reason you went

down that trail, Gay? From my window I saw you enter it. I had just stepped from the shower. It took me years to get into clothes enough to follow you."

She told him briefly.

"What does it mean?" she asked breathlessly. "I'll never hear the muffled beat of a drum again without my blood turning to ice. It was weird. It was terrifying. What's going on there, Jim?"

"Nothing but foolishness. I suspect that some youngsters are using the old mill for a clubhouse. When I looked in I saw a lot of stuff like stage props lying round. Probably Brian has given them permission but I'll tell him what I saw when I report about the pool."

"Of course that's the explanation. Imagine my getting so wrought up about a lot of moving lights." She laughed. "You look like a movie menace in that brocade lounge coat, Jim. I—"

"If you intend to make Mac's in time for supper you'll have to hustle, Gay," reminded Brian Romney icily.

Gay stared incredulously at him. Where had he come from? She put her hand to her tight throat before she said with an attempt at flippancy:

"Cultivating the Jack-in-the-box act, Mr. Romney? You have a way of popping up at the most unexpected moments."

"Unpleasantly unexpected, perhaps?" he inquired and let it go at that.

Gay walked across the lawn with Jim Seaverns on one side of her and Brian grimly silent on the other. She felt like a prisoner between guards.

As they entered the hall Seaverns said lightly:

"Just a minute, Romney, I'd like to explain my part in the situation you interrupted."

"I wasn't aware there was a 'situation' so no explanation is necessary," Brian countered frigidly and crossed to the library.

"Wham! That seems to be that!" Seaverns shrugged.

"We'd better dress or that great big bear will charge out of the library and bite our heads off, Jim. We'd look pretty going round with them under our arms, wouldn't we?" Gay chuckled at the vision her imagination had conjured. "And after all the excitement I haven't found my adorable watch," she added sadly.

Brian couldn't be so brainless as to think that she and Jim had planned to meet again on that poky trail, she fumed, as she raced up the stairs. He had seen them come back earlier, had spoken to them in the hall. She had started to explain as the three had crossed the lawn but the rigid set of his jaw —she knew that expression of old—had roused her resentment. He could think what he liked, she never would explain, never.

As she entered her boudoir a figure in a chair by the fire snapped her attention to the present. There was only one person in her world who sat as if nature had equipped her with a pillar of granite in place of a spine.

"Aunt Cass," she breathed. "Are you real? Where did you come from?"

Madam Cassie Wainwright regarded her great-niece with snapping black eyes whose pupils were set in milky rims. They and the many jeweled rings on her bony fingers were like sparks which lighted her gray monotony.

"Hmp! If you'd been at home on the Sabbath instead of gallivanting when I arrived you wouldn't look as if your wits had gone wool-gathering. My doctor in Boston told me yesterday I needed a change—a few days in the country—so I phoned to you. You weren't at home and your husband answered—as you are living here I presume he's still your husband—and told me to come along, so I chartered a plane and here I am."

Gay dutifully pressed her lips to the top of the gray transformation. "I hope there was someone here to show you to your room. Most of the servants get off early Sundays."

"That pert piece, Lena, who was your waitress when you lived in your own house, unpacked my bags. Never did like that girl. How did she happen to come here?"

"When I—when we—"

"Don't stammer. I know you left your husband. I suppose you call it being modern—that word modern has a lot of deviltry to answer for—to walk out on the man you married."

Gay conquered an almost unconquerable urge to throw something at her aged relative and clenched her hands behind her.

"Lena had difficulty finding a place. As she needed work Major Romney engaged her as a sort of ladies' maid. Many of his business guests have their wives in tow."

"Hmp! That girl has a weak face. She's been crying her eyes out. Over some worthless boy, doubtless. I offered to mix some aromatic spirits of ammonia for her but she refused to drink it. She told me we were to have supper at Mac Romney's. I like that man, he's a real person but his wife's a featherbrain if ever there was one. Do you intend to wear that dress bristling with moss and twigs to supper?"

"I do not. I'll change at once. Why don't you join the men in the library while I'm dressing, Aunt Cass?" Gay suggested in a wicked spirit of revenge on Brian for not telling her that he had invited Madam Wainwright to Rosewynne.

"Don't tell me what to do, Gabrielle. I'll go down when I'm ready."

Why is it that persons who are everlastingly giving advice resent it for themselves, Gay wondered. She leaned against the closed door of her bedroom and let the soft whiteness of the room flow over her spirit. It was so cool, so peaceful, so simple. White Venetian blinds, slightly off-white walls, white hangings, silver-gray carpet. The soft green lacquer of the furniture, French in design, and the iridescence of peacocks in the panels of a folding screen framed in dull silver supplied the accents of color.

A black-frocked, white-capped maid with a pile of towels over her arm came out of the dressing-room. Her heart-shaped face flushed with sudden color, her red-rimmed Irish blue eyes brightened.

"I thought I heard you come in, Mrs. Brian. Have you seen your aunt?"

"Yes, Lena. Get out my blue velvet afternoon frock and matching maribou cape, the silver bag and sandals and my three rhinestone bracelets. Wait around. I may need you. I'm terribly late."

Aunt Cass was right, Lena has been crying, Gay thought as she shivered under an icy shower. Crying about a worthless boy? For a time while the girl had lived with her Eddie Dobson had been her steady company, but Brian had stopped that—he thought. Eddie! Had she gone back to him? Had she let him into the house last night?

Later, as the maid laid the cape over her shoulders, Gay asked:

"Anything wrong that I can help about, Lena?"

"Oh, Mrs. Brian, I'm so worried!" she wailed. "I—I—don't know which way to turn."

"At one time or another we all reach crossroads and think and worry about which turn to take, Lena. Tell me what is troubling you. I may be able to help."

"I haven't anything to tell, really I haven't, Mrs. Brian. It's just that I get jittery about my brother Tim sometimes. It's dumb of me, I know, but he's getting so—so hard-boiled. Guess I'm just low because it's my Sunday evening in."

"Does Eddie Dobson come to see you now?"

"Eddie Dobson! That trouble-maker? Oh, no. That foolishness was done with after Mr. Brian talked to me. But he's kept Tim under his thumb. To spite me, I suppose. Tim believes whatever Eddie does is right. That's why I asked Major Romney if he couldn't find a place for him here as houseman. I—I've been going steady with Willie Watts, Mr. Mac's head hostler, for over a year. He's a fine man, Mrs. Brian."

"I'm glad to hear that, Lena. I wonder who let Eddie into the house last night."

"Let him in here? I wonder—" the sentence died in a frightened whisper.

"Don't repeat that, Lena. Can I trust you?"

"You can trust me always, Mrs. Brian. I'll never forget what you did for my mother, never."

"Then that's all right. Don't wait up for me. Good night."

She is loyal, Gay thought as she ran down the stairs, and I did so little for her. Just getting the dying woman into the hospital and paying Lena's wages while she looked after the children at home. I wonder if she suspects that Tim let Eddie into the house last night? Perhaps I'd better have him drive my roadster after dark and watch him. If I don't Brian will persist in doing it. Poor Lena! She's carrying a terrific load. Her beau, Willie Watts, must be a good sort or Mac wouldn't have him about his horses. Willie Watts! What a Dickensian name for a hostler. From the threshold of the library she announced:

"Here I am. Alone, Jim? Where are the others?"

"Major Bill returned, was disturbed that we were late, so he and Madam Wainwright and Brian went along to assure our hostess we were coming. You're worth waiting for, Gay. You're breath-takingly lovely in that color."

"Good heavens, don't stop to pay compliments. Let's get to Mac's before supper is quite over. I'm hungry."

As the roadster skimmed smoothly along the highway she drew a long breath.

"This is the first moment I've relaxed since you and I started on our hike after dinner, Jim."

"Why didn't you let me know you had lost the watch? I would have hunted for it."

"Because the mere thought of going down to the poky ravine gave me the shivers I decided that my courage was getting soft, that I needed a dose of self-discipline."

"Better explain that to Brian. The indications are that he thinks you went there to meet me."

"He couldn't think I would be so stupid."

"Thanks for the orchid."

"I suppose you consider that a snappy comeback, Mr. Seaverns. I don't. Why spoil this perfect evening getting miffed, Jim? Look at the blues in the sky. Delicate way, way up; deepening as it comes earthward, green-blue, strong blue, purple-blue where it fuses into that strange hot red on the horizon. The moon looks as if it has gone in for food control and sliced off one of its curves. Those stars broke through as suddenly as sparks from a rocket bomb. Here we are at last."

Mac Romney was waiting for them on the steps of a rambling brick house almost smothered in vines turned scarlet. He was dressed like a hunting squire from a page of his favorite *Pickwick Papers*, slightly modernized.

"The effect of that fluffy thing you're wearing is stunning, gal," he complimented as he opened the door of the roadster. "You look like a million. Come on. Supper in the gameroom."

Gay cordially returned the welcoming pressure of his big, warm hand. She had a deep affection for him. She liked his superb carriage, his friendliness, his boyish exuberance, his honesty, his loyalty to his wife who was always restless, always dissatisfied with his country interests.

In the hall he inquired in a hoarse voice he fondly believed to be a whisper:

"When did the old battle-ax arrive? That woman's in her dotage, she tried to make me take a tablet because my voice was husky."

"Aunt Cass has a remedy for everything and everything in it," Gay replied under her breath.

As Mac's laugh boomed she shook her head and put a finger to her lips before she entered a long room equipped with one black and one white poodle on the hearthrug, only their dark, keenly intelligent eyes in motion. Its air was freighted with the scent of countless cigarettes; its walls were lined with glassed-in shelves laden with silver cups, blue and red ribbon rosettes and other sports trophies; its occupants were such as would be found in any gathering of socialites in a country community within motoring distance of a big city.

Jane Romney, gowned in billowing net the shimmering green of a pheasant's plumage, was directing two black-uniformed maids who were placing small tables before her guests. The sequins on Sue Dubois' brown frock twinkled like a thousand knowing eyes as she indulged her incurable urge to advise and told Lucie Romney, who looked like a golden-haired Fra Angelico angel in light blue, how to bring up her children. Cassie Wainwright was a wash of shadowy grays, except for her eyes which were shining black beads of suspicion as they watched Louis Dubois who was saying something in a low voice to Jane. Sam's face, as keen and intellectual as Mac's was red and fleshy, was aglow with enthusiasm as he talked to Major Romney who stood back to the fire.

All present and accounted for except Brian. Where was he? Gay wondered. Jane Romney turned and saw her standing in the doorway.

"Oh, you and Jim have come at last, Gay. Now we'll have something to eat."

"Sorry to have kept you waiting, Jane. Hello, everybody! The late Gabrielle Romney speaking, feeling dashing and dangerous."

"Come here and tell me what you've been up to since I've been away," William Romney commanded. "If it isn't mischief I'll forgive you for having kept a starving man waiting for his supper."

Gay slipped her hand under his arm with the sense that here was something solid to which to cling in a tempestuous sea. Her brown eyes were warm with love and admiration.

"No mischief, cross-my-throat-an'-hope-to-die." A hint of emotion tinged the gaiety of her voice. "I've missed you terribly."

That was Brian's laugh! Who was with him in the garden-room? Guests were not encouraged to drop in on the Romney Sunday suppers. Was the Major wondering too? His arm had stiffened. She said hurriedly:

"I'm going to the Big Town myself tomorrow. What shall I see at the theater? Did you take in one of the new shows, Major Willum?"

"No. I went over in response to a sudden call for a meeting of my Regimental Club than which there are duller but also more blood-stirring occasions. Didn't have a chance to get in touch with Brian to tell him I was going. Well, boy, have you decided to join the family?"

His white brows drew together in an annoyed frown, the color deepened on his cheekbones as he regarded Brian who stood in the doorway of the garden-room. Bee Ware, in a trailing red frock, had linked her arm in his. She tilted her head until the shining dark waves of her hair touched his sleeve.

"Have you been looking for me, Major Bill?" Brian asked with the affectionate consideration he always showed his uncle.

Before the Major could answer Bee Ware had deserted the younger man and was looking up at the elder with assumed terror.

"I shake in my shoes when you frown like that, Major Bill. Don't scold Brian because I am here. It isn't his fault. He had a date with me this afternoon and when he didn't keep it I was afraid he was ill—he always keeps his dates with me. I waited for a message and when none came I was almost out of my mind with anxiety so I drove to Rosewynne and Sampson told me that he was having supper at Mac's. Then I came on here to make sure he wasn't suffering from amnesia and had lost his way."

"Lost his way! Brian! That's the funniest thing I ever heard," Sue Dubois shrilled.

Mac clapped his hands over his ears and opened his lips to protest.

"Mac!" his wife reminded under her breath.

He shrugged his shoulders and turned to Cassie Wainwright who sat straight as a granite shaft behind him.

"Hear that? My life is one 'demd horrid grind.' I'm henpecked," he confessed theatrically.

"Henpecked!" Something which might have been a smile twitched at the corners of Madam Wainwright's lips. "Scarcely a man is now alive who isn't, if you mean that your wife is everlastingly trying to make you over to fit her pattern, only after a year or two the husbands don't acknowledge it even to themselves! But that's neither here nor there. Well, Brian," she had raised her voice. A gasp like a wind-blown sigh fluttered in the room as the others stopped talking to listen. "Where were you this afternoon when you should have been keeping a date with a woman who says you always keep your dates with her?"

"I'll tell you where he was, Madam Cassie," Mac Romney answered in a stage whisper. "That nephew-by-marriage of yours routed me out, spoiled my after-dinner nap and dragged me to the kennels while he fussed over the selection of a poodle for a lovely lady."

"A lovely lady! The plot thickens. Did he tell you who the lady was?" Bee Ware asked. She smiled self-consciously and fluttered a fringe of black lashes.

"He said it was Gay and as Brian never lies, I guess it was," Mac Romney responded promptly. "She's to have one of those dogs on the hearthrug, note the smart English trim. He pays his money and she takes her choice."

"One of those poodles for me!" Gay exclaimed after an instant of hesitation. "I'm all excited! Thanks a million, Brian. I choose the black one. What's his name, Mac?"

"Her name is Mrs. Fezziwig. Doesn't her mouth suggest 'one vast substantial smile'? I'll send her over tomorrow."

"Not tomorrow, please. I'm staying in town overnight and I want to be at home to welcome Mrs. Fezziwig and present her with the golden key to my heart. Send her Tuesday afternoon."

"I suppose your husband stays in town the nights you do, Gabrielle?" Sue Dubois inquired in a voice which intimated that she supposed he didn't.

"Sure I do," Brian anticipated Gay's answer. "The Brian Romneys are getting to be high lights in café society. Always seen at the best and most swanky night clubs. That's us. You really ought to get Louis to show you the Big Town after dark, Sue. A gala night at one of the top spots is the all-time high of the Manhattan scene. Jane, if I don't have something to eat soon I'll begin on Lucie. She looks like a peach."

IX

PERCHED on a corner of the mahogany kneehole desk in the library at Rosewynne, Brian Romney thoughtfully regarded Gay curled in a deep chair near the fire. Darting scarlet flames cast dancing shadows on her face, on the toe of one silver sandal, and brought out the high lights of her blue velvet frock. After Mac's announcement in the game-room at Dingley Dell that one of the poodles was for her, he had read her mind as if it had been a printed page. Incredulity had been followed by protest, then, realization that refusal to accept the dog from her husband would betray the fact that their reconciliation was only expediency deep; next well-feigned enthusiasm as she made her choice.

He glanced at Jim Seaverns resting crossed arms on the back of her chair. Had he heard the man's husky "I'll wait—we'll wait, darling," seen her leaning against him at the entrance to the trail before he had spent hours selecting the dog for her, would he have turned down Bee's party to go to Mac's? Gay had declared that she intended to marry Seaverns. Did she love him? "He can't have her," he told himself savagely. "She's mine." A surge of passionate protest brought him to his feet. He couldn't endure the situation an hour longer. He wouldn't.

He met his uncle's eyes regarding him from beneath frowning white brows. Had Major Bill sensed what he was thinking? He had been gruff during supper, ever since he himself had appeared at the garden-room door with Bee hanging on his arm. It had been in rotten taste for her to barge in on the family supper. She had left early with Louis Dubois as escort. Looks had passed between them that had made him wonder if theirs was more than friendship. It was a crazy suspicion. However rotten Dubois might be, Bee was decent if indiscreet.

The quiet of the room was stirred only by the purr and snap of the fire and the sound of water dripping in the court. Why didn't someone speak? They were all masked. Each one had different aims and tastes and human emotions held in check by social convention behind the mask. Each one was streamlining along a trail of thought. Would it end in a blind alley as his had ended? Even Cassie Wainwright, sitting bolt upright on the edge of a chair, was staring straight ahead in tight-lipped absorption.

"Louis Dubois is trying to seduce Mac's wife." Her voice slashed through the silence with the swish of a keen, shining blade.

"I'll be darned!" Jim Seaverns muttered. The Major regarded her with startled eyes.

"Aunt Cass!" Gay breathed in horror. "How can you say such a thing?"

"I say it because I think it. Do you mean to imply that you haven't seen which way that wind is blowing? Hmp! I'm going to my room. I presume, Gay, that you, being a modern young woman, breakfast in bed. I'll have mine downstairs."

"No such luxury for me tomorrow, Aunt Cass. I'm taking

the seven-thirty train to the city. Mondays and Tuesdays, I'm a business woman," her niece reminded with gay importance.

"Do you mean that you stay overnight in New York? Alone at an hotel?"

"I have had an apartment for a year." Gay hurriedly sidetracked a tirade. "I'll go up with you to be sure you have everything you want, Aunt Cass."

"Everything I want. That's promising a lot. But that's neither here nor there. Good night, Major. You'd better wake up to what's going on in your immediate family. Dubois isn't the only wolf on the prowl." She pinned Jim Seaverns like a butterfly to a board with her sharp, pitiless eyes. "Come Gay, if you're coming."

"Good night, everybody!" Gay followed her aunt into the hall.

"Is she a terror! Boy, is Aunt Cass a terror!" Jim Seaverns exclaimed and snapped open an enameled cigarette case. He held it up.

"I'm always apologetic about this gaudy thing. It was presented by the men under me on my latest engineering job. I could stand the red enamel but that flamboyant J. S. in diamonds sends a blush of embarrassment to my cheek whenever I produce it."

"Gaudy is right but it will be better than a Social Security card for identification. I'll bet there isn't another of its kind in the world," Brian commented lightly.

"Do you believe that stuff about Dubois and Mac's wife, Brian?" William Romney demanded anxiously.

"Just a minute, Major," Jim Seaverns interrupted. "This family powwow isn't my dish. Let me make my report about the swimming pool and I'll vamoose. You've selected a treacherous spot, Brian. I located a better one farther downstream. Do you know what the old stone mill is being used for? From a bit of regalia I saw sticking from a one-time grain bin and the brass safety pins scattered in the dust on the floor I'd guess for some kind of secret organization. Perhaps it's all right. Perhaps you've given permission for its use?"

William Romney and Brian said "No!" emphatically and in unison.

"Then you'd better check up on the place. I didn't investigate, thought I'd better get Gay home. Later, she went back for her watch she thought she had dropped near the bridge. I didn't know she was going, didn't know she had lost it. From my window I saw her crossing the lawn towards the woods. Couldn't believe my eyes for a minute, then remembering what I had seen in the old mill, I grabbed my lounge coat and ran. When I came up with her she was white with excitement. She had heard a muffled drum, had seen mysterious twin lights flit from the stone building and cross the bridge. She's a grand sport, but even a grand sport might contract the jitters after that. When we emerged from the trail she had an attack of shivers. That was why I had my arm around her when you *surprised* us, Romney."

"I had no intention of surprising you." The roughness of Brian's voice betrayed his inner fury at the insinuation. "Sampson reported to me that he had seen Gay cross the lawn and a short time after you ran towards the woods. He thought there must be trouble somewhere. I agreed with him and hot-footed out to see if I could help. I wasn't spying on you and my wife."

"Then that's all there is to be said on that subject, but there is another which needs clearing up." Seaverns steadied his voice. "I'll lay all my cards on the table. I don't know why Gay came back to you, Romney, but I do know she left you, that she doesn't love you and will marry me when she is free. You took her away from me once, but you won't a second time. You needn't catch his arm, Major, I'm going. I didn't accept your hospitality with the idea of making love to Gay. I felt that I must find out where she and I stood. I know now. I won't see you again as I'm leaving for New York by the seven-thirty in the morning. I'll breakfast in town. Good night and thanks for a delightful week-end."

William Romney and his nephew stood motionless until the faint sound of a door closing drifted in from the hall. The elder man watched the blue smoke of a cigar curl upward.

"Seaverns' challenge would have been called flinging down the gauntlet when knighthood was in flower. Going to pick it up, Brian?" he asked.

"Do you think I won't? That I will let him walk off with my wife?"

"But if he is right? If Gay loves him?"

"She's out of luck, that's all. I'm banking on the certainty that honor will prove mightier than love to her. Where is her apartment in New York, Major Bill?"

"That's something you'll have to find out from her, boy. I'm pledged to secrecy."

Brian knocked his pipe against the great brass knob of the poker among the fire irons with a force that broke the stem.

"You're for her, heart and soul, aren't you?" he demanded furiously.

"And shall be as long as you play round with Bee Ware the Widow. You say you love Gay and yet you humiliate her by letting that malicious, lying woman drag you at her heels."

Should he tell Major Bill that he had accepted Bee's invitations partly to escape from the house in which Gay was living and largely with the fool idea of rousing her jealousy? Better not admit that. Well, possession still was nine points of the law. She was his and he would keep her.

"There's something wrong with that picture, Major Bill. I can't see myself being dragged at any woman's heels. It's Bee's line to try to make her crowd think she's the heartbeat of every man who speaks to her. Now that the subject of my private life is disposed of for the present, what do you think of Seaverns' discovery at the stone mill?"

"Don't like it. Sit down. Let's talk."

William Romney sank into his own special seat beside the fire. Brian, hands clasped behind his head, eyes on the ceiling, stretched out in a chair near him.

"I hear that you discharged Eddie Dobson," the Major said gravely. "I promised that if you would take over the presidency of the Plant, I would keep hands off. I'm not asking you to take him back, but do you realize that he's one of our most capable foremen, that he inspires almost fanatic devotion in the other workers, especially in the female of the species?"

Indignation, like a springboard, shot Brian to his feet. Hands in his coat pockets, feet planted squarely apart on the hearthrug, he retorted:

"Can't help it if he trails every worker in the Plant after him. I won't tolerate him. His infernal insolence burns me up. He's obsessed with the idea that he should be a superintendent. Superintendent! Even if he were fitted for the job—which he isn't—nice going it would be with his temper. A couple of days ago he knocked out a man who protested against his attentions to his sister, not before—I am pleased to add—he had taken a right to the eye himself. He staged the row in the yard so that his hangers-on could see what a he-man he was and govern their actions accordingly. I won't take him back. His present pal, Lavalle, will get his walking papers too. I don't trust him."

"You're the doctor. Be sure you are right, that's all. Louis will raise the roof if you discharge his protégé, the Frenchman. I'll stand back of you whatever move you make, only be careful. Ever since he was suspected of tampering with a machine Eddie has been waiting for a grievance. He's a showman. Now he'll hop on the band wagon and lead the others out.

"Even though our workers have all the privileges, all the money they have ever asked for and more, trumping up a grievance is in the air," William Romney continued thoughtfully. "In all the years I have been in business I have had problems but not like the one I feel is threatening."

"Nothing is quite so dead as the problems of production and personnel of even five years ago. Now, a manufacturer has to be on the alert every moment to keep ahead of a workers' walkout or sit-down or what have you."

"You're right, Brian. Added to that we have the menace of Louis Dubois. I suspect he's the man who can and will apply the fuse that will make trouble for us."

"I'll bet my convertible he is and that Lavalle is his go-between with Dobson. Ever since I became president of the company I've had the same sense of security I would feel if I were living over a rumbling volcano which might blow me sky-high at any moment. And speaking of blowing up brings us back to the bomb dropped by Aunt Cass, as blunt-tongued a female as ever made up for deficiencies of hair by a transformation. I hold no brief for Jane Romney but I credit her with too much hard sense to fall for Louis' cheap line."

"Jane isn't falling for Dubois because he is Dubois, Brian. Any man with his 'line,' as you call it, would capture her interest. She isn't wholly to blame if she's listening to the song of—what would a male siren be? She married a man much older than herself who isn't sufficiently intuitive to realize that he can't drift into old fogyism and keep his eager-minded wife interested in him. Mac is the salt of the earth, he'd give his last cent to help a friend in trouble, but if he has thoughts beyond dogs and horses and the works of the late Charles Dickens he doesn't give them the air. His conversation is limited entirely to the subjects in which he is interested, he never thinks that the other fellow may want to talk about his hobbies. Minor faults, I grant you, in a character of major strength, but Jane doesn't sense his bigness."

"Mac may have a one-track mind at times but he's my favorite of the Romney clan—always barring the chief—and he's a gentleman, which is more than can be said of Dubois."

"True. Louis may have no sense of good taste but he has

brains—and worldly experience. He knows when a woman is
an easy mark for a smooth worker like himself and he is
greedily aware that Jane has a fortune of her own. I
wouldn't put it past him to toy with the idea of blackmail. He
has a surface knowledge of art, music, theater, sports and
books which—except for his Dickens fixation—Mac has not.
He makes Jane think she is wasting her brilliant self on a
man who can't appreciate her. I know his kind. He bitterly
resents the fact that you have been put ahead of him. He
knows we know that Gay detests him, he can't attack you
from that angle, so he'll turn his attention to stirring up
trouble in other ways. But, he's Sue's husband, and to avert a
family break we stand for him. I've dropped a heavy burden
on your shoulders, boy."

"I can take it. Mark my words, we won't stand for Louis
forever. Fighting him will keep me from going haywire about
Gay. Sure you won't give me her New York address?"

"Sorry, I can't, Brian. But," the Major drew a notebook
from his pocket and dropped it to the desk. "I made no
promise about a telephone number. I'll drive to the Plant
with you in the morning and we'll decide on the best way to
investigate the activities at the stone mill. It may require
caution. Good night."

"Good night, Major Bill."

Brian waited until his uncle's footsteps on the flagged
floor of the hall died away before he copied Gay's New
York telephone number. He broke the flaming logs with the
heavy poker and set the brass screen in front of the fire.
Snapped off the lights. From the threshold he glanced back
at the room which was touched with enchantment and mystery by the rosy glow from the heaped up bed of red coals.
His eyes lingered on the chair in which Gay had been curled.
He visualized her lovely face from the charming hair line to
her dimpled chin.

A passion of revolt seized him. Why should he stand aside
and let Seaverns win her? They would be off to the city in
the same train in the morning. She would be there two days,
lunching, dining, dancing with him. Why should he let her
go? Suppose he had promised to ask nothing of her?

He stopped in the hall. How quiet the house was. "Today
is yours." Major Bill's words flashed in his mind like a neon
sign. Longing, desperate, driving longing, surged in his
blood like an irresistible tide.

"Sure, it's mine," he said under his breath and took the

stairs two at a time. He walked softly along the gallery to the door of Gay's boudoir.

Before he could knock a key clicked sharply and her startled voice demanded from inside:

"Who's there?"

X

"WHO'S THERE?" Gay repeated breathlessly. Heart pounding, tense, she stood braced against the door of her boudoir and listened. No answer. She regarded increduously the sparkling wrist watch in her hand. She had found it on her desk only a moment before. She read again the crudely printed words on the soiled slip of paper fastened to it with a huge brass safety pin:

KEEP AWAY FROM THE RAVINE

What did it mean? A warning of course. Had she been seen on the trail by a pair of those weirdly glittering eyes? Had her sense of an unseen presence as she sat on the log opposite the old mill been induced by fact, not imagination? Had the watch been smuggled into the boudoir while she was in the dressing-room? A moment ago she had heard a sound outside this door. Like someone breathing. Had the person who had returned the watch lingered in the gallery to listen?

She couldn't know it but her startled "Who's there?" had restored Brian's emotional balance. Furious at his own weakness he whipped back to the stairs and ran lightly down.

Five minutes later his convertible was coasting to the highway. A thousand stars winked understanding in response to his upward glance. The frosty breeze of a perfect October night made music through the trees and laid its quieting touch on his rebellious spirit.

> " 'I could not love thee, dear, so much,
> Lov'd I not honour more,' "

he quoted and laughed grimly at his own sentimentality.

When Gay entered the breakfast-room the next morning color warmed his face. Did she suspect who had been outside her door last night when she had turned the key in the lock? That click still echoed in his memory.

William Romney rose and looked at her in surprise as she approached the table dressed in velvety brown tweeds, with a green hat pulled low over one eye and with matching gloves and bag in her hand.

"See who's here, Major Bill," Brian exclaimed. "Thought you left for the Big Town on the seven-thirty, Gay. Breakfast?" He drew out a chair.

"Thanks, yes. Isn't this a grand morning-room? The sunshine and those gay orange-king calendulas in that blue bowl send my spirit ballooning into the stratosphere. Aren't you two boys early?"

William Romney threw back his head and laughed, such a young laugh.

" 'Boys!' Hear that, Brian? Gay puts me in the class with you!"

Brian, who was filling a glass with orange juice from a crystal jug on the buffet, looked over his shoulder and grinned.

"She's wrong. You're years younger than I am. Major Bill dragged me down early, Gay. He was a brave man under fire, but—"

"I understand. He's dodging Aunt Cass. I don't blame him. She is unbearable at times with her prescriptions and her suspicions. But why waste precious minutes talking about her? I have something exciting to show you. It's a secret. Is anyone near who might listen in?"

Brian closed a door which led to the pantry and looked into the sunroom with its white wicker and scarlet geraniums.

"Okay. Sampson knows when that door is closed that Major Bill and I are in conference and are not to be disturbed. Shoot."

Gay produced the soiled slip of paper from which dangled a brass safety pin and laid it on the polished maple table. "Read that!"

William Romney adjusted his eyeglasses. Brian leaned over his shoulder as he read.

"Looks to me like the trick of a kid who has been gorging newspaper headlines. Was the watch returned?" the Major asked.

"There it is! On my wrist."

"Must have been an honest kid or he would have kept it. 'Keep away from the ravine.' Motion-picture stuff." Brian's comment registered amusement but his eyes were grave as they met William Romney's. "When did you find it, Gay?"

"A cup of coffee would help sustain me while I tell my story," she declared with a glint of laughter in her voice. " 'Listen my children and you shall hear.' After I left Aunt Cass last night I changed to pajamas and lounge coat, then went to the boudoir to collect some papers I wanted to take to town. I thought I must be dreaming when I saw my precious watch blinking its diamond eyes at me from the desk. This dirty paper—which looks as if it had been to the war and back—was attached to the bracelet by that four-teen-carat brass safety pin. I heard a sound in the gallery. A furtive sound. My heart zoomed to my throat. Had the person who left the watch returned to impress the warning on my mind? It was an instant before I could produce a voice, then I gurgled close to the door:

" 'Who's there?' "

Coffee overflowed the cup Brian was filling. With a mut-tered execration he set it aside and held another under the spigot of the silver coffee urn. He wondered if his ears were betraying him. They burned red-hot. That key had not been clicked against him, he realized jubilantly.

"Was your question answered?"

"No, Major Bill. I don't know how long I leaned against the door as motionless and brainless as a leading lady in a waxwork show, listening, clutching my adorable watch, star-ing at that dirty slip of paper. I was aroused from my coma by the sound of an automobile."

Brian placed the coffee beside her plate, twirled the Lazy Susan until sugar and cream were within her reach and de-posited a silver plate of crisp *brioche* in front of her.

"Was the car coming or going?" he inquired.

"Going. I knew by the sound that it was coasting down the drive, the way you always start from the house, Brian."

Brian was aware of the Major's quick look at him.

"Have you told Seaverns about this paper, Gay?"

"I haven't seen Jim since, Major Willum. I sent word to his room that I couldn't make the seven-thirty. I wish now I had taken it. Apparently you men think I've had a rush of imagination to the head because I got excited over what you consider a practical joke. I've wasted valuable time. I must keep my date at the studio. I can get a train at the junction if Tim will drive me over."

"I'll get you there, Gay."

"No, Brian. You should be at your office."

"In the breakfast-room? I'll find it myself," announced a stentorian voice in the hall.

"Aunt Cass!" Gay breathed. "Darn! She'll insist on knowing why I didn't take the seven-thirty, put me through the third degree and—"

Brian caught up her bag and gloves, pulled her hat a bit lower over one eye and seized her arm.

"Scram! We'll beat it through the garden! Sneak round the house. My car is there. I'll be back for you, Major Bill."

"I'll do my good deed for the day and engage the enemy, boy, while you two make your getaway.

"Up so early, Madam Cassie? Yes, Gay has gone. Yes, I presume Seaverns went on the seven-thirty. I—"

His voice trailed away as Gay and Brian dashed round the corner of the house.

"I thought you always coasted down this drive," she observed as the convertible started full speed ahead.

"Can't waste time, this morning." He wondered if she would have recognized it as the sound she heard last night if he had coasted.

The car skimmed over a moist black highway, under a sky pure turquoise, between stark, stripped trees and borders of skeleton shrubs, through air which sparkled and stung. Gay drew a long ecstatic breath.

"Gorgeous day. It shimmers. My spirit is soaring on wings of silver gauze."

"Too gorgeous to spend in the city. How long do you intend to keep up this business career, Gay?"

"Why do you ask? I haven't neglected Major Willum or my duties at Rosewynne, have I?"

"No. You're doing fine. But there's a man named Brian—"

"Who never breaks a date with Bee Ware the Widow. He doesn't need me. If you drag along like this I'll lose the train."

"Like modeling, don't you?" he asked as coolly as if her bitter reference to Bee Ware had not sent hope licking through his veins. "What sort of place do you work in? That's a side of life of which I know nothing."

"You really should get around more," she flouted. "We pose in a studio. It's an enormous place, partitioned as needed. There are huge spot and flood lights. According to the picture being made, it is a lovely garden; a snow scene;

a gaily furnished porch room that will make the ad readers grind their teeth in determination to acquire one like it; perhaps a kitchenette which would make the most eating-out-minded woman yearn to cook in it."

"Sounds interesting. How long do you work?"

"Sometimes all day."

"What do you do the evenings you spend in town?"

"Go out with friends. Any reason why I shouldn't?"

"Of course not. You don't think I am checking up on you, do you? Sue was right again. I put up a bluff last night, but I knew she didn't believe me when I said that you and I were hitting the night spots. Let's make it true. Let's start a forget-the-past movement. Go on a party with me one of the evenings you stay in town, if only to keep up appearances, will you? Saw a statement the other day that one of the movie glamour-girls is seen often in café society with her 'ex' who continues to be her greatest admirer and friend. I'm not legally your 'ex' yet, but why can't you and I step out together?"

"Oh, no! No! You're not my greatest admirer and friend."

"Who is? Seaverns?"

She didn't answer. Brian kept his eyes on the road, his lips clamped for fear he would say more. When they reached the junction the train was ready to pull out.

"Thanks again for the adorable Mrs. Fezziwig and for getting me here so quickly," Gay flung over her shoulder as she dashed for it.

Brian dropped her week-end bag to the step.

"Have yourself a time!" he called.

She was breathless as she sank into a seat in the Pullman coach. Brian's proposition that they step out together in town was the complication that topped all complications. He was putting on his act to perfection. It would cramp his style some if he knew that Bee Ware had shown her the note in which he had told the gay widow to try her luck at getting him free. Suppose she had told him? She couldn't. It had been too humiliating. Why, oh why, had she agreed to live at Rosewynne? During the past year she had adjusted her life to loneliness. When she had gone through the agony of separating from a husband, why hadn't she stayed separated?

The subject occupied her mind to the exclusion of all else as the train clanged steel on steel, clicked, banged, rattled and rumbled a fitting accompaniment to the tumult of her thoughts. Memory raced to it. Heart throbbed to it.

Blood leaped to it. Pulses beat in rhythm to its incessant clang. Once she had heard a symphony ingeniously composed and orchestrated to make music of those same sounds.

The Grand Central! At last! Now she could think of something else.

She rose impetuously at the moment that a woman in the seat ahead stood up.

"Jane!" Gay exclaimed. "Have you been sitting there all this time?" Was it her all-black costume and her pearls that made Mac's wife look so washed out and colorless? There was confusion and indecision in the dark eyes which were usually cool and determined. What had happened to her?

"Louis Dubois is trying to seduce Mac's wife."

Cassie Wainwright's harsh statement slashed through Gay's memory and brought with it a close-up of Louis saying something in a low voice to Jane last night as she listened with downcast eyes. Was she keeping a date with him? It couldn't be possible—and yet—

"I thought you were taking the seven-thirty this morning, Gay," Jane Romney observed in a voice which, it was evident, she was trying to keep steady and controlled. She threw her silver fox cape over her shoulders.

What shall I do? Can I do anything to stop her? Gay was demanding of herself feverishly, even as she said:

"Lost it. Have just time now to make the studio. You didn't say last night you were coming to town."

"I didn't decide to come until this morning. I intend to stay until I get fed up with fun," Jane declared defiantly.

What shall I do to stop her? Gay asked herself again. In a moment they would be in the concourse. She might lose her. That mustn't happen. It shouldn't.

"Where are you staying?" she asked.

"I—I—haven't decided."

"Come to my apartment, will you? I hate being alone there. Plenty of room. You can come and go as you like and take time to pick out the ritziest, gayest spot at which to stay. If you feel as I do when I come from the country, that's what you want."

"That is a suggestion. Won't I crowd you?"

"No. There's an honest-to-goodness bed in the bedroom and a day couch in the living-room. You pays no money and you takes your choice."

They were crossing the concourse now under the great dome at the heels of their bag-laden red cap. Gay was barely aware of the hurrying crowds, the distant surge and beat of

a huge city, the loud megaphoned announcements of departing trains. She was being swept along on a strong tide
of determination not to let Mac's wife out of her sight.

"If you really want me, give me the address of your
apartment, Gay. I'll take my bags there and—and then
I can get in touch by phone—with the friends I want to
see."

"That's a grand idea—wait a minute. Ever seen a commercial photographer's plant in action? You haven't? Then
let's express the bags and you come along to the studio
with me. It will be something to write home about. You
might even have your picture taken for the files. Let's make
it a celebration! Two country girls at large in the Big Town.
We'll lunch, take in a movie, got to the Ritz for tea, then
home to dress and phone our friends. The mere thought
sets my pulses tingling. You're not the only one fed up with
long, peaceful days in the country."

"I'd love it," Jane agreed eagerly. "And I will have those
camera shots taken. Who knows, I might get a chance to
model. Wouldn't that be exciting?" She said to the red cap
"Boy, we'll express our bags."

Good heavens, what have I started? It isn't what I've
started, it's what I hope I've stopped. That suggestion about
the photos was divinely inspired. While she is posing I'll
phone Brian, Gay decided.

At the studio she left Jane talking to the dapper youth
at the desk whose hair always made her think of the wet
back of a seal, while she made up with the newest and
smartest cosmetic *pour le sport* and donned the gayest, latest model in blue and scarlet ski costumes.

As she posed against a background of pine trees glistening with mica-frost and stood in a drift of something which
would have a perfect snow effect in a photograph, she felt
as if a dynamo were churning inside her, driving her on.

The shutter clicked. She was free. While she was supposed to rest and Jane, thrilled and glowing with excitement, sat before the camera, she dashed for the telephone. Her heart pumped as she put in her call for the
Plant. Her breath caught as she waited. Suppose Brian were
not there? What would she do next?

XI

BRIAN ROMNEY thoughtfully regarded Louis Dubois seated on the other side of his office desk. The man was sleek and glossy from the top of his black head to his shining shoes. Beneath his suavity he simmered with eagerness and hatred.

Since he had seen her board the train Gay's eyes and voice had persisted in getting between Brian and a competent consideration of the morning's problems, but so startling had been Louis' proposition to buy the Plant's entire equipment and good will, so skilled his manipulation of figures to prove that the price offered was magnificently adequate, so adroit his intimation that if the offer were turned down the Romney Manufacturing Company would face a strike which would permanently cripple it, that all thought of Gay had been driven from his mind.

William Romney, who had been standing by the window from which he could look out upon the village where the roofs of countless thrifty white cottages shone in the sunlight, seated himself beside his nephew. He glanced at the old workbench in an alcove behind glass doors. What would the man whose invention had started the Romney Manufacturing Company think of selling out to a person like Dubois, he wondered before he reminded:—

"You made the statement, Louis, that our workers are preparing to strike. Do you realize that many of them are of the third generation, that their parents and grandparents were employed in the Plant before them, that some of the elders have been retired on pensions? That we have a banking system to encourage them to save, that we hire experts to advise them how to invest? Never since the business was started have we had a walkout. When there were differences of opinion their leaders met us around this very desk and we adjusted matters in friendliness and co-operation. That can be done again."

"Not this time, Major. You forget you are living in a changing world."

"That changing-world stuff has been done to death, Louis," Brian interrupted impatiently. "Anyone who wants to get away with murder uses it as an excuse. Has there ever been a time when it wasn't changing? You're a member of the Romney family. How do you know what's going to happen? Why should our workers take you into their confidence any more than the Major, or Mac, or Sam, or myself?"

"I've been wondering about that. What's the answer, Louis?"

Dubois examined his glossy fingers nails critically and smiled smugly.

"The answer is this, Major Bill. I keep in touch with—well, call them the third generation. I attend their dances, umpire their ball games, help organize their—their clubs. Naturally they come to me with their problems, naturally look upon me as one of themselves. For instance, there's Eddie Dobson—"

William Romney and his nephew rose as if catapulted from their seats by the same spring.

"Leave Dobson out of this." Brian controlled a furious urge to bang the head of his cousin by marriage on the desk and hear it crack. "The conference is ended. We decline now and forever to sell the Plant to you, Dubois."

"Does that 'we' go for you too, Major?" Louis Dubois inquired smoothly.

"It goes double for me," William Romney confirmed.

Hands resting on the desk, Dubois leaned forward.

"You Romneys would like to get rid of me altogether, wouldn't you? You've ditched Lavalle and next you'll diplomatically ease me out. Believe me, you're going to need me, and need me bad. Wait till pickets walk in front of the closed gates calling, 'This Plant unfair to organized labor!' 'Don't be yellow!' 'Join us and help win!' "

"We'll wait. As I said before, this conference is closed. Washed up. Over," Brian reminded curtly.

"I'm not beaten yet. Sue and I want this business and intend to have it," Louis Dubois persisted. "You 'Royal Romneys' are puffed with pride and I have a fact up my sleeve which will prick that pride like a pin in a balloon. Of course, I'll give you another chance to accept my terms before I prick, Brian. Think it over. I'm off to New York this afternoon to keep a date—an important date with—a lady."

As his footsteps dwindled to silence in the corridor Brian looked at his uncle.

"So this is what you get for having risked your private fortune like nothing at all to keep the Plant going, Major Bill. At least we've blown the lid off Louis' pretence at friendliness. He's out for blood. What did he mean by that last nasty crack? Is he planning to spread some lie about Gay?"

"Gay! He would have a hard time cooking up a yarn about himself and Gay. It's common knowledge that from the time he first met her he's been crazy about her and that she has lost no opportunity to snub him."

"He might make capital of her friendship with Jim—Seaverns."

"He'd have to go some to do that. No, it isn't Gay. Remember Madam Cassie's explosion into words, last night?"

"About Dubois and *Jane?*"

"Sit down, Brian. You make me fidgety when you walk the floor. That's better. I've noticed an if-only-I'd-met-you-first expression in the irresistible Louis' eyes when they met Jane's but I thought it would blow over. Last evening Cassie Wainwright's one sentence crystallized my shadowy suspicion into conviction."

"Good Lord, do you suppose his important date in New York this afternoon is with Jane? It can't be! She wouldn't be such a fool! Good old Mac. I can't bear to see him hurt, neither can I see the Romneys being forced out of business by scandal spread by a cheap guy like Dubois."

"Better get Mac here presumably to tell him about Seaverns' discovery at the old mill and the warning to Gay to keep out of the ravine. Then we'll tactfully inquire if Jane is at home."

"Louis drove that mill stuff out of my mind. Do you think he is mixed up in that?"

"He may be. We'll take but one person into our confidence about it. I've been thinking over the matter since breakfast. I've decided Mac is the person."

"I agree. I'll tell him we want him." He touched a button on the mahogany box beside his desk.

"Not in his office?" he replied to a voice. "Tell him I want to see him here as soon as he comes in."

"You're convinced that the warning on that dirty slip of paper is more than a kid's trick, aren't you, Major Bill?"

"I am. I don't like it. We must watch our step, boy. Did you notice Louis' hesitation when he referred to a workers' club? It may have headquarters at the old mill. If we find that Jane is at Dingley Dell and Louis' date has nothing to do with her, you and Mac would better investigate the place. It will be easy while you and he are together to lead into Dubois' threat of a Romney Scandal. Let's forget it for the present and attend to business. We haven't decided what price we'll make on the morning's orders."

A few moments later Mac Romney, dressed in checked tweeds, loomed in the doorway.

"What's up, Brian? You and Major Bill look as if you were stand-ins for Atlas and had had the world dumped on your shoulders."

"Come in and close the door, Mac. We want your advice."

Beginning with the after-dinner walk of Gay and Jim Seaverns Brian outlined the events of the following hours. He produced the warning.

"What do you make of it? Are we crazy to pay any attention to it?"

"I'd think you were crazy if you didn't." Mac Romney frowned at the slip of dirty paper. "Had any rows with the workers?"

Brian told him of Eddie Dobson's discharge and of his appearance in the library at Rosewynne. Mac whistled.

"He's tough, ma'am, tough is E. D." he paraphrased, "but I didn't think he was that tough. The more I look at this slip of paper the more I wonder. If the 'club' does meet in the mill who would give it away by sending this to Gay? Why not return the watch and let it go at that? Looks to me as if they'd let in a fella who couldn't stomach their program."

"You and I'll go for a game of golf this afternoon. Poke around the old mill and take a look-see. By the way, is Jane at home? Gay left a message for her," Brian said as casually as if he were not holding his breath for the answer.

"No. She went to New York this morning. Mad because I wouldn't take her over for a few days. I couldn't leave. My prize mare is likely to foal any time now. Women are so darned unreasonable."

"Mac—"

"Just a minute, Major Bill," Brian interrupted.

He answered the telephone.

"Who? Gay! Where are you? Yes. I'm listening. Take it easy. You're breathless. Who? Yes. Yes, I get you. He's sitting on the corner of my desk now. I will if I have to chloroform him. White tie and tails if I have to stuff him into them my-

self. I'll phone at once for tickets to a show. Dinner first.
Dress early. Sounds like a good party. Sure, I'm taking it
seriously. Your apartment—how should I? You've never told
me. I'll get the address from Major Bill. Steady, lovely,
steady. I don't think you're silly—I think—

"She shut off."

"Was that Gay?" William Romney inquired anxiously.
Mac's usually ruddy face was colorless.

"What is it, Brian? Is it Jane? Has anything happened?"
He ran his fingers under the collar of his shirt as if its
tightness had choked off his voice.

"Nothing has happened to Jane—yet, Mac. Sit down.
Listen."

XII

IN THE late afternoon Gay unlocked the door of her
apartment, set down the long florist's box the elevator boy
had handed her and switched on the lamps which glowed
like great opal beads.

"How charming!" Jane Romney exclaimed. "The wall cov-
ering looks like a wash of mauve over silver. I like the
mauve and pink chintz. I like the absence of doodads. It's
restful."

She dropped her black hat and fox cape to a chair, stopped
in the process of kicking off her patent leather pumps as
Gay opened the box and lifted out a mass of crimson roses
which flooded the room with fragrance.

"My word, how gorgeous, Gay! Two dozen! Look at the
length of the stems! I've heard that red vibrates. Now I
know it. Each one of the roses is broadcasting a message.
'Better Times,' their name is. Pretty subtle I calls it." She
laughed and hummed:

"Somebody loves me,
I wonder who?"

"Whoever it was forgot to enclose a card," Gay answered

lightly. As she arranged the flowers in two tall silver vases she thought, "Better Times." Jim sent them of course, though it is rather subtle for him.

Jane Romney flung herself on a chaise longue and wriggled her shoeless toes.

"I'm dead. I wouldn't get out of this chair if all the kings and former kings in the world commanded my presence. What a round! The studio!—the photographer said I was a natural for modeling. Lunch at Pierre's. Radio City. The movies. Tea at the Ritz. Do you keep up this breakneck pace every day you're in the city, Gay?"

"Of course I don't. How could I with my work? I was trying to give my little country cousin a time, that's all."

She set a match to the kindling in the fireplace and dropped into a low chair. She wondered if nerves ever snapped like violin strings. Could she keep cool and casual while her ears were on the alert for the ring of the doorbell? Suppose Brian couldn't make Mac come? For all his genial kindliness he was an obstinate soul. She closed her eyes and intoned to herself: "He will come. He will come! He will come!"

"Asleep, Gay?" Jane asked. "I don't wonder. I'm dead to the world. I'm so tired that even thinking of the country is restful. I can bear to imagine the cocks crowing and the poodles barking."

Gay rigidly controlled a nervous urge to laugh.

"My dear, this is but the edge of the evening. I have a date. You'd better call your friends and tell them you are here, hadn't you?" I'll cut the phone cord, before I'll let you do it, she added to herself.

"I'm not phoning friends. Keep your date. I suppose it's with the 'Better Times' lad. I stay right here. You're a grand actress, Gay, but you haven't deceived me for a minute. You knew, didn't you, that I had planned to meet Louis Dubois? He has been suggesting for some time that we take a little fling together. So when this morning Mac and I had a row because he refused to give me a whirl in New York for a few days, I decided that this was as good a time as any to go modern, and phoned Louis I would meet him at the Plaza for tea. Hiking along with you cleared my brain. I began to realize what a darn fool I'd been. So much for Case History Number 1. I wonder what Louis thinks has become of the simple little country lass. How did you know I'd gnawed my rope?"

"Something in your manner made me fear you had started

out to be reckless, merely reckless, dear. I suspected it was with Louis. I was scared—scared stiff because I wouldn't trust a woman with him after he'd been the rounds of a few night spots. The drinking habit is tightening its octopus-like tentacles. He hates the Romneys since Brian has been made president of the Plant. Nothing he would like better than to have a bit of scandal with which to trade for advancement. I thought if I could keep you with me, after a while you would realize that coming to New York alone, and being seen about with a man other than your husband, was foolish to say the least."

"You kept me, all right. It wasn't hard. The minute my anger at Mac cooled I knew I'd been having pretty cheap, shoddy thoughts lately. But I don't understand why you picked on Louis?"

Jane mustn't suspect that Aunt Cass had suggested it, Gay decided.

"I just felt it was he. He has such a—a line with women and he is a sneak. His love—if it can be called love—like some fashions, has no survival value. He's the sort of man who would try to snitch another man's wife."

Jane fumbled in a crystal box on a small table, produced a cigarette and lighted it.

"That goes for Jim Seaverns too, doesn't it?"

"How can you compare those two men?"

"Don't get peeved. Jim isn't subtle. It's common knowledge that he wants to marry you."

She swung her feet to the floor and sat on the edge of the chaise longue.

"Was what I was tempted to do any different from what you're *doing*, Gay? Say what you like about modern standards, the world still gabs about women who leave their husbands and go twosing with other men. You did leave Brian, didn't you?"

"Yes."

"And this last year you have been playing round with—"

"Jim and I have been friends, nothing more."

"I believe you—now—but I'll tell you this. From the moment I first saw you, I admired you tremendously. I was eighteen. I thought you perfect. You were the nearest thing to a storybook Princess I'd ever met. There was a Prince utterly in love with you—I thought. You're beautiful. You have infinite chic. I copied your clothes, your way of speaking, tried to be gracious as you were. My idol crashed in a heap when you separated from Brian and when I heard that

you and Jim Seaverns were being seen together again—I—
I—well, Mac was immersed in his interests for which I didn't
give a tinker's darn and I began to wonder if it would be
exciting to go modern as you had—"

"Jane! Please! You're breaking my heart! I'm not modern
in that way. I'm not! I did separate from Brian because I
knew he no longer loved me. We were forever at cross-
purposes. It seemed wrong for us to live together. I had
no thought of divorce then—I wasn't thinking. I was just feeling. I was adrift and when Jim came into my life again as a
friend—I clung to him. Don't let any foolish resentment or
another man come between you and Mac. He adores you.
I'll confess honestly—anything to make you stop, look, listen
—that after my heart stopped burning and aching and froze
there hasn't been a moment when I haven't realized that
I couldn't just walk out of marriage without paying a tre-
mendous price for my freedom, and that price has been a
constant battle with my inner self, my spirit, which has
fought an unending fight for my return to the standards
which were my inheritance. Now do you understand, Jane?"

"I understand that you have a nineteenth century be-
havior engine in your twentieth century streamlined body.
I've grown up in the last twelve hours. If ever again I'm
tempted to slip my leash I'll remember this day and your
face and voice as you laid your very soul open to me."

She brushed her hand across her eyes.

"My word, I shall be crying in a minute and I thought I
was hard-boiled. Imagine sitting in an apartment in New
York at this hour of the day wasting time, when lights are
flashing on, bands are playing, everyone is getting ready to
go somewhere. It just isn't done!"

She sprang to her feet.

"What do we do next? I'm all rested and refreshed. I
want to go somewhere. I forgot, you have a date and mine
is—" she made a little face—"I wonder where Louis thinks I
am? I must have had a brainstorm—he was a man, an escape; he's nothing but a surrealist nightmare now. Is that
the doorbell? Your date? And you're not dressed."

Gay thought Jane must hear her heart thumping as she
whispered:

"Hustle into the bedroom before I open the door. I'll ar-
range to take you along on the party. Don't stop to protest!
What will you wear?"

"White satin."

"Then I'll wear my silver mesh, with the camellia pink slip. Hurry, I've got to dress too, haven't I, silly?"

Jane paused on the threshold.

"Look here, Gay, it's none of your business, but I can't help warning you. Bee Ware the Widow has gone very *femme fatale* since her return from Europe and points South. Just in case you care, she's betting her square-cut emerald that she'll be the second Mrs. Brian Romney."

Speechless, Gay stared at the door Jane closed quickly behind her. Her throat ached. Her lids smarted. How dared Bee Ware make such a bet? Why shouldn't she? Hadn't Brian given her encouragement and then plenty? "Don't be cross with the child, darling, because she hasn't card sense."

Bee Ware's mocking words flashed through her mind. She had known Brian was in love with her as long ago as the afternoon the woman had shown her that note, hadn't she? Why was she standing here dazed with fury as if she never had suspected?

Someone was holding a finger on the bell. She had forgotten she had started to open the door before Jane dropped her bomb. Brian and Mac, of course. She mustn't let them see her angry, it might upset her plan for Jane. She forced a smile as she answered the bell which was still ringing.

"Where's the fire?" she demanded.

"Jim!" Amazement gave way to resentment raised to fever heat by the red-hot coals of her recent anger. "Why are you here? I told you never to come."

Seaverns' lean face flushed. He closed the door.

"I know you did, but I had to, to find out what you meant by the snippy note you sent me before I left Rosewynne this morning."

He flung his hat on a chair, lighted a cigarette and dropped his gaudy enameled case to the table.

"Sit down and let's talk this out or shall we go to dinner somewhere?"

Gay's mind was in a tumult. Suppose Brian and Mac arrived and found Jim here? Would they believe her when she told them that he had never been in the apartment before? They would not. Suppose they didn't. Thousands of fine women entertained men at dinner or late supper in their apartments. It just happened that she hadn't and, what was more, she didn't intend to begin now. She must get rid of him. His being here might upset the rescue party she had planned.

"I can't talk with you now, Jim. You must go, please hurry!"

"Why the excitement? Another date? With the guy who sent those red roses? Is that why you wouldn't take the train with me this morning?"

Jim hadn't sent the roses! Who had? She snatched a look at her watch. She must get rid of him no matter if she hurt him horribly.

"I have another date. I must dress. I have barely time now to keep the appointment."

"Where and with whom are you going?"

"Am I accountable to you for what I do?"

"So—that's how it is! Another man! I'll go." His face was white. His eyes were pools of fury. He snatched his hat. "If ever you want to see me you know where to find me. Until then—good-by!"

Gay regarded the violently closed door. Had it shut Jim Seaverns out of her life forever? Would she call him back? She loved him in a way.

She filled her lungs with the fragrance of red roses. Who had sent them? Brian? She must be losing her mind to think they had come from him. Wasn't Bee Ware boasting that she would be the second Mrs. Brian Romney? Better not think of that tonight, nor of her growing conviction that she herself had been an easy mark when she had read the note the woman had shown her.

She thought of what Jane had said about copying her clothes and her manner of speaking and "going modern." It was a terrific responsibility to be admired. It made one to an extent one's brother's keeper. Her separation from Brian had ramifications more extensive than she could have imagined. Did all matrimonial crack-ups touch other lives as theirs had done?

The bell again! Had Jim come back or was it—she fairly flew to the hall door. Opened it.

"Brian! Where's Mac?" she whispered.

"Is old Mac my admission ticket? Can't I enter without him?" There was humor and bitterness in the twist of his smile. He handed her a box. "Orchids for the girls with all our love."

"How grand! Come in! Come in!"

Gay forgot her recent attack of fury. Her spirit unfolded silver wings and mounted to her eyes. Brian wouldn't smile if he had failed to persuade Mac to come. She watched him deposit his Inverness and top hat on a chair. He was magnificent in evening dress, all the Romney men were.

"Where's Jane?"

"Dressing. Is—is Mac coming?"

"Sure. Don't be so breathless. We changed at the Club. He fussed with his white ties till he reduced them to strings and had to send out for others. I came ahead to ease your mind and to give you a preview of one of your snappy escorts."

"I don't like to talk about myself but—" Gay mocked. Brian had always been the best fun in the world until—she hurriedly switched that train of thought.

"Swell little place you have here. Stunning roses. From your greatest admirer and friend?"

He had sent them! She knew by his voice, by the laugh in his eyes as they met hers above the cigarette he was lighting. Why couldn't she think of something casual and debonaire to say?

As he dropped his gold case back into his pocket he glanced down at the table. Her eyes followed his. Her heart went into a nose dive. Jim had forgotten his gaudy cigarette case.

"When did you commence to smoke, Mrs. Romney?" He no longer smiled.

"I don't smoke. A—a friend left that. I'll take it and return it."

He slipped the case into his pocket.

"Suppose I save you the trouble. I've seen it before. I know where it belongs."

She could have stamped her foot in annoyance, had she been the foot-stamping type. Lot of good it had done to fairly drive Jim from the apartment. Brian knew now that he had been here and she was behaving as if she'd been caught stealing.

"Why are we spending time talking about an old cigarette case when I'm cracking up with excitement about Mac's coming," she protested. "How much did you have to tell him to lure him here?"

"I told him that he was a fool to let his wife get the idea that she could have a rattling good time, perhaps a better time, with another man than her husband."

"You—you didn't mention Louis Dubois?"

"I didn't have to. Old Mac's not dumb. He turned as white as a dead man and said, 'What time do we start, Brian? Order orchids for the girls.'"

"I'm so—so happy, I could cry."

"Don't! This is to be one grand party, remember."

"I won't. There's the bell! It must be Mac! Let him in. I'll send Jane out."

"Hold on! I don't want to be here when they meet. Where can I go?"

"Through that door. Dinette!" Gay whispered and dashed into the bedroom.

Jane, in a white frock that complemented her dark beauty to perfection, was outlining her lips before the mirror. She met Gay's eyes in the glass.

"Did the 'Better Times' roses date come? I needn't ask. You're all twinkle, twinkle."

"I'm not twinkling because of my date. I'm all excited because he's brought someone for you and orchids in that box for both of us. Take them out, will you? This will be a party. Why am I chattering while the men are waiting for us? Go out and entertain them while I make myself gorgeous." Gay opened the door of the dressing-room.

"Wait! What are their names?"

"The name is—" A torrent of water from the shower drowned the rest of the sentence.

Hours later sitting beside Brian in a café Gay watched Mac and Jane dancing in the midst of a perfumed, jeweled maelstrom of bare shoulders, brilliant eyes, crimson lips and white shirt-fronts to the rhythm of a Rhumba band of Cubans with ruffled satin blouses and eyebrow-thin mustaches who sang to the accompaniment of guitars.

"What did Jane say when she walked into my living-room and saw Mac?" Gay asked hurriedly to break the silence which was becoming strained.

"She stopped on the threshold and said breathlessly, 'Mac!' and I melted into the dinette."

"She appears happy now and every little while she looks at him as if she had found someone new and rather wonderful. I've never seen Mac so handsome. He looks like Sam. As if his face had been put through a refining process. I'm so glad, so *glad*, that all is right between them."

"Then I take it you don't believe in broken marriages, Mrs. Romney. Why devote all this talent for getting results to the preservation of Jane's marriage? Why not—"

Jane dropped into a chair beside him. Her eyes were radiant.

"That was wonderful, Mac. It's a crime for a man who can dance as you can not to love it."

"I'll make a deal with you, Janey," he said gravely. "Love my dogs and horses and I'll love the things you love. How about it?" He held out his hand.

As his wife stretched hers across the table to meet it, he said:

"Jane and I will go back to the apartment with you to pick up her bags, Gay, then we'll check in at the Ritz for a week, while we do the town."

"Mac! Really?" His wife's eyes were stars of excitement. "If you will, I'll—I'll—"

"Don't make any promises, Janey. This isn't a trade. It's a party. Better stay here and make it a foursome, Brian."

"With Eddie Dobson on the warpath? I'm going back tonight or rather this morning. Dance, Gay?"

The smart foreign *maître de café* touched Mac on the shoulder.

"A telephone for you, Mr. Romney. It was so urgent I brought the message, sir."

Mac took the slip of paper. He laughed and explained:

"It's time for the prize mare, Mrs. Micawber, to foal. After Brian had made our reservations I told Willie Watts, my head hostler, where I would dine, the show we were going to and the night spot later. Left our table number at the desk here. If the Blessed Event came off safely, he had instructions to get in touch with me by phone. I have a pot of money invested in that hoss."

The color drained from his face as he read the message. Gay caught one arm, Jane the other.

"What is it? What's happened?" they whispered.

"It's Major Bill. He's been shot."

XIII

IF SHE lived to be a hundred and twenty, the allotted span of life with which the scientists had replaced the Biblical three score years and ten, she would never forget this night, Gay told herself as Brian's convertible sped toward Rosewynne beneath infinite heavens sewn thickly with stars which quivered like diamonds on a lovely woman's neck.

Time and the frost-whitened road whirled by. No one spoke except when Mac or Brian would burst out:

"Who would shoot him?" "Major Bill hasn't an enemy in the world." "Why didn't someone get hold of Sam?" "Perhaps they did!"

Rosewynne at last. Brian caught Gay's hand and drew her into the dimly lighted hall. Mac and Jane followed on tiptoe. He touched a button and flooded the place with light.

Grizzle-haired Sampson, who had been dozing in a big gold chair, roused with a yell and brandished an army pistol.

"Stay where you are! Or—or— For de Lawd's sake, what you young folks come home for?"

Brian seized the pistol.

"Drop that, Sampson. Where's Major Bill. Is he—is he—"

"Fit as a fiddle!" assured a voice from the stairs. William Romney stood halfway down. His white hair had been clipped about a long strip of adhesive plaster, another white patch was high on his cheekbone and another on his throat under one ear. The left sleeve of his crimson brocade lounge coat had been slit to accommodate a sling. He was pale but he smiled at the four who surged toward him like an irresistible tide.

"What are you doing here? I thought you were in New York on a binge."

Mac made a sound that was a cross between a sob and a groan. Brian twisted his neck in his stiff white collar to loosen the tension of his throat.

"What happened, Major Bill? Who shot you?"

"Take it easy, boy. Where'd you get the crazy idea I'd been shot? Last evening I couldn't get to sleep so went down to your bookroom for one of those mystery stories you had recommended. After I selected it I stood looking out at the stars, hoping and praying that all would be well with my young people, when something smashed through the window and hit me on the head. Glass flew and nicked me more or less as you can see. I had sense enough left to shout for Sampson. When he found me I was a huddle on the floor beside a big stone. He phoned Sam. Sam phoned the doctor who, when he arrived, asked in the jocular manner so peculiar to doctors if I'd been in a razor fight. He gave me a sniff of something, took a few stitches, patched me up

and here I am, fit as a fiddle and raring to go. . . . How
about an early breakfast of scrambled eggs and bacon,
Gay?"

His words had tumbled over one another, his eyes were
unnaturally bright. Feverish color had driven out pallor.

"Nix on the bacon and eggs. It's bed for you, Major Bill,"
Brian announced.

"Perhaps I have been ambitious. The slash on my wrist
just missed an artery. You'd better move to the second floor
of the tower, Brian, if there's a lunatic around who's gone
stone-minded. How did you four happen to come home tonight? Sampson, did you phone after I told you not to let
a word of the—we'll call it an accident—get out?"

"No, sah, no, sah, I did not, Major Willum. I phoned Mr.
Sam. How could I phone Mr. Brian an' Mr. Mac? I didn't
know where dey was, did I?"

"Never mind how we heard, we are here to get you to
bed, that's all that matters. Where's Sam?"

"In your room. Here he is," William Romney said faintly
as Sam opened the tower door. He was tenderly wrapping
something in a white handkerchief as he came down the
steps.

"Are the stairs going round or—" William Romney
clutched at the balustrade.

"Mac! Sam! Quick!" Brian called.

His nephews caught the Major as his knees buckled.

Two weeks later as she drove her roadster along the village road in the late afternoon, through clear, icy air, Gay
relived those tense moments in the hall. She pressed her
cheek against the woolly head of the black poodle sitting in
aristocratic dignity beside her.

"Are we happy that Major Willum's wounds healed so
quickly and that he is up and about again? I'll say we
are, Mrs. Fezziwig."

The dog regarded her with "one vast substantial smile"
and tried to lick her cheek. She expertly dodged the rough
pink tongue.

"You're a honey but I don't like that. Have you been
a comfort these last two weeks? I'm telling you. With Aunt
Cass driving the invalid almost out of his mind with her
remedies and the Romney men alternating between frozen
anxiety for their uncle and a grimly silent hunt for the man
who threw that stone, I would have blown up emotionally
if I hadn't had you to talk to."

Even though Sam had reached the Major quickly it was lucky that Lena's present heartbeat was the hostler at Dingley Dell, Gay reflected. When Sampson had frantically summoned the maid, she had assumed, because of the blood trickling down the Major's face, that he had been shot and had phoned Willie Watts to tell Mac to come at once. It was a break that the man had known where his employer would be in town, otherwise they would not have heard of the Major's injuries for hours. Now, Mac was giving Jane the promised week in New York that had been shunted one side when the news had come of what his uncle called "my accident."

Street lamps leaped into light. She had left home in broad daylight intending to be back before dark. She hadn't thought to take Tim along. Anyway it was an absurd precaution. It was time Brian realized she didn't need a guard every time she stepped out.

The setting sun shot up long, jagged, crimson spikes which melted into violet in the blue above. The glow spread to the treetops and touched them with unearthly beauty. A gold peephole broke through the sky like the slit in a stage curtain through which the actors squint at the assembling audience. From some cottage along the street drifted a radioed voice singing with male gusto, "On the road to Mandalay, where the flying fishes play." Lavender smoke spiraled from chimneys and the air was scented with the clean smell of burning wood and the appetizing aroma of cooking meat.

The poodle sniffed, whined, wagged the pompon of her tail, and laid a reminding paw on the gloved hand on the wheel.

"Hungry, Mrs. Fezziwig?" Gay asked. "We'll leave the peppermints for Ma Bascom after which we'll drop in to see the twins, inquire for Lucie and Sam, and then dash for home and supper for you. Here we are. I won't be a minute. Coming?"

As she stepped from the roadster a thick voice greeted: "Well, see who's here! Now I won't have to thumb a ride home. I'll go along with you."

Louis Dubois! He'd been drinking. Gay's pulses picked up the hard throb of her heart and shot the vibration through her veins. She looked straight into his eyes and detected a sinister hint of triumph behind their smile. That steadied her. She shook her head.

"Your mistake, Louis. I'm not going your way at present. After I leave here I'll stop at Sam's to see the twins."

"That will take you by our place. I'll wait."

Gay locked the engine, dropped the key into her bag.

"Not for me. I shan't take you home, Louis. To be honest I don't care for your company."

He gripped her wrist. In the dim light his face was greenish white.

"Why don't you care for my company? I'm crazy about you. I—"

She wrenched her wrist free.

"Don't try the cave-man stuff with me, Louis. Can't you see that I detest you? Can't you realize that if you weren't in the family I wouldn't speak to you—ever?"

Fury lighted red flames in his eyes. His face was livid.

"So you wouldn't speak to me!" he repeated harshly. He brought his head close to hers. "Get this. You'll do more than speak to me. You'll be eating out of my hand before I get through with you."

Gay's laugh was a triumph of will over fright.

"Louis, you've missed your vocation. You'd be the gangster-menace answer to a picture director's prayer. Good-by. Come on, Fezz."

Her heart was hammering as she ran along the stepping-stone path with the black poodle at her heels. She released her breath in a long sigh as the sound of footsteps on the gravel faded into the distance. Louis had gone.

Mrs. Dobson radiated welcome as she opened the door in response to Gay's ring. The poodle followed his mistress sedately as she entered the room where a cheery open fire crackled and flamed and the white-capped old woman huddled in a wheel chair near it.

"Come close to the fire, Mrs. Brian. Think of you coming to see us this cold night. Where's all your pretty color? You look pale. Did you get chilled driving? Let me take your fur coat. If you keep it on you won't feel it when you go out." She laid the leopard swagger tenderly over a chair.

"Here's Mrs. Brian to see you, Ma, and look what she's brought with her! It's one of them queer dogs Mr. Mac raises. Foreign, ain't they, ma'am?"

"Very foreign. Definitely old family. They were introduced into Europe before the Christian era. The Romans gave them their first hair cut. How are you today, Mrs. Bascom?"

"Spry as usual."

There was an eager question in the sharp old eyes that

peered at Gay from below the frill of the cap. She answered it by laying a white box on the shawled lap.

"Here they are."

"How's Major Romney?" Mrs. Dobson inquired anxiously as she opened the box and slipped a peppermint between her mother's lips. "Now, ain't that dog cute! Look, Ma, he's sitting up begging. Shall I give him a piece of candy?"

"Well, just one," the old woman consented grudgingly.

"You've had your candy, now come here and lie down," Gay commanded as Mrs. Fezziwig moved nearer the wheel chair and laid a beguiling paw on Ma Bascom's lap.

"The critter minds well, that's more than I kin say about some folks' children," the old woman mumbled as the poodle dropped to the floor beside Gay.

"She was brought up in kennels but she has developed luxurious tastes since she came to Rosewynne, haven't you, Mrs. F.?" Gay demanded of the dog who whined in answer. "It's a constant fight to keep her off my bed. I try not to spoil her but it is a temptation, she's such a dear."

"What's the matter with Major Romney? Liza ain't never told me he was sick," Mrs. Bascom inquired in a voice which creaked from age.

"Now, Ma," protested her daughter patiently while Gay debated what answer to make. The family had decided that the cause of Major Bill's confinement to the house should not become known if it were humanly possible to keep it off the record.

"What'd you say was the matter with Major Romney?" Mrs. Bascom persisted. "He's a fine man. I worked for his father at the Plant. Ain't dying, is he? 'Twould be just like Liza not to tell me."

"Dying! I should say not," Gay answered lightly. "Curious how that detestable flu can flatten out a big strong man, isn't it? Mr. Sam Romney, his wife, and the children's nurse are down with it."

A red-headed freckle-faced boy flung open the kitchen door.

"Hi, Mum! Eddie just drove out of the garage. Said to tell you he won't be home for supper. He says it's so cold there'll be skatin'. He told me to bring—"

He stopped in tongue-tied embarrassment as he saw Gay. He pulled off his cap and shuffled his feet. A fifty-fifty mixture of admiration and fright tinged his gray-green eyes as he looked at the black poodle who was giving a realistic imitation of distant thunder.

"Joey, come in like a gentleman and speak to pretty Mrs. Brian," Mrs. Dobson prodded.

He twitched his head from under her tender work-reddened hand as she smoothed his rough hair.

"Let me alone," he protested sulkily. "Gee, Mum, can't you quit treating me as if I was a kid? Eddie says I'm big and husky enough to cut loose from your apron strings and be on my own. He says if I do what he tells me, p'raps he'll let me into his club. Eddie's an awful smart fella." His eyes glowed with admiration.

"Drat Eddie and his club!" Mrs. Dobson was on the verge of tears. "He—"

Gay didn't hear the rest of the sentence. Eddie and his club! In a flash the room faded into a dim wood trail. Somewhere a drum beat eerily. Lights moved.

In an instant she was back in the Dobson room. She shivered. I know exactly how Alice felt when she fell down the Rabbit Hole. My body was here but the real me left this room for a few seconds. Was Louis here to meet Eddie? her thoughts trooped on. Mrs. Dobson was haranguing her younger son. In her excitement she reverted to the brogue of her girlhood.

"Mind now, ye're to stop yer foolish talk about clubs, Joey, an' ye bein' big enuff to cut loose. Ye—who still wants yer Mum to tuck ye into bed of a night! Yer brother's got out of hand an' he's goin' to pay for it, you watch —but, ye're nawthin' but a boy, an' ye ain't joinin' no clubs if I have to paddy-whack ye to stop ye. Ain't ye ashamed to make this fuss when we have comp'ny. See the dog sittin' there lookin' at ye as if ye was some quare animal he'd never seed before. Now, get away wid ye, an' set the table fer supper an' don't let me hear no more nonsense about clubs."

The boy flung out of the room and banged the door behind him with a force which shook the house. His mother drew her hand across eyes suddenly flooded with tears.

"Children are one tough problem, ma'am," she said sadly. "The girls in the Plant ruin Eddie—they follow him if he crooks a finger—there ain't no fella in the movies they like as much as they like Eddie—an' they say that if Mr. Brian don't take him back an' make him superintendent they'll walk out every one of them, some of their folks will walk out with 'em. An' then there's Joey, he used to be such a perlite little kid an' now he can't be told nawthin'. I hope you'll excuse his bad manners, Mrs. Brian."

"Joey will find himself, Mrs. Dobson," Gay encouraged. "He can't help it with a fine mother like you."

"Joey's spoiled," declared the cracked old voice from the wheel chair.

"Why, Ma, I thought you was asleep."

"Sleep! How's a body goin' to sleep with you an' Joey rowin'? Please give my respects to Major Romney, M's. Brian, an' tell him I hope soon he'll be feelin' as young an' spry as I feel."

Her black eyes twinkled and her thin hunched shoulders shook with mirthful appreciation of her joke.

"I'll tell him, Mrs. Bascom. He will be pleased to know you thought of him. Good-by. Anything you'd rather have than peppermints, the next time I come?"

"No, thank you. I like 'em. They warm my stomach. Liza, don't stand at the front door an' talk. You cool off this room."

Gay tiptoed along the stepping-stone path to her roadster as cautiously as if she were walking on eggs. Suppose she had been mistaken? Suppose those fading footsteps had not been Louis? Suppose he were waiting for her? What would she do?

Her eyes tried to pierce the dusk as she pushed the poodle ahead of her into the car, unlocked the engine and kicked in the clutch. Not until she reached the highway did she draw a steady breath. She rubbed her cheek against the poodle's cold damp nose.

"Looks as if we had ditched Louis, Mrs. Fezziwig." She went on as if the dog understood what she was saying:

"He wouldn't have lost his head if he hadn't had several drinks. Ugh! He was beastly."

The drinking habit was growing on Louis, while Brian had cut it altogether, she reflected. After her return to Rosewynne she had been surprised at first when he refused any sort of liquor, but she had been thankful, profoundly thankful, Not that she had even once seen him unsteady but he used to drink too much.

She shook off memory as she drove through a frosted world, tinted from the afterglow till it sparkled rosy pink, instead, she thought of Mrs. Dobson's shamed eyes as she had apologized for her son and wondered if in the long run a parent's love balanced the heartache and anxiety even the best of children cause. Ma Bascom fretted at her daughter but where would she be without her now? Mrs. Dobson was worrying herself sick about Eddie but even with her eyes full of tears there had been a proud note in her voice as she had proclaimed his popularity.

A mother's love and pride in a child was born with the child, wasn't it? It might ebb and flow like the tide, surge in great waves of emotion, recede until not even a trace of it seemed left, but like the tide it always swept back.

Bridget, the waitress at Sam Romney's, opened the door.

"Oh, Mrs. Brian! I'm glad you've come! Mr. and Madam are down with the flu and Nurse Wickes is flat on her back and two hospital nurses are here an'—"

"I know, Bridget. Where are the children?"

"Having their supper in the nursery."

The twins, gaily attired in pajamas and bathrobes of torrid coloring and blinding stripes, tipped over their chairs at the low table in the toy-strewn room, and dashed for Gay when she appeared.

"Come to play with us?" Billy demanded.

"Bwian come too?" Sister asked in her wistful voice which, in spite of the fact that she knew her to be the more mischievous and daring of the two, always made Gay think of a grieving angel—if angels grieve.

She sat on the couch and cuddled a small figure in each arm.

"Brian isn't here, Sister, but I have a perfectly grand idea. Suppose I come for you two tomorrow and take you to Rosewynne to stay with me until Father and Mother get well? Major Bill is having guests at dinner tonight or I would take you back with me now. Would you like it?"

"Would you let me play with Mrs. Fezziwig?" Billy cannily queried before he committed himself. "Where is she now?"

"She's taking care of the roadster while I'm here."

"Would Bwian wock me?" Sister inquired cautiously.

Gay's enthusiasm for the plan was slightly dampened.

"We'll have the time of our lives," she evaded. "We'll drive in the car and we'll have all sorts of fun in the game-room and we'll play badminton in the court and—"

"Will we have ice cream every day?"

"Yes, Billy, and if I say it, who shouldn't, we have luscious ice cream at Major Willum's."

The boy rubbed his yellow curls against her sleeve.

"All right. We'll go. Won't we, Sister?" He blinked both eyes at her. " 'Member what you said you'd like to do that last time we were at Uncle Major's?"

"Oo—o—o! Billy! Can I?" A beatific expression lighted the little girl's face.

"Sure."

"Okay. I'll go."

What particular bit of mischief had the twins up their sleeves? Gay speculated even as she approved:

"That's grand. I'll talk with Mother and persuade her to say 'Yes' to our plan. You'd better pack up the toys you want to take with you. Mrs. Fezziwig and I will come for you directly after breakfast. Nightie-night, kiddies."

Ten minutes later as Gay, with the black poodle sitting erect on the seat beside her, drove the roadster along the tree-bordered road toward Rosewynne, she wondered if her invitation to the twins had been an inspiration or an attack of brainstorm. It had not been necessary to persuade Lucie. She had received the suggestion with tears which were fifty per cent weakness and fifty per cent gratitude.

"You're a dear, Gay," she had whispered hoarsely. "The children have driven the hospital nurses almost out of their minds, by pretending they were bandits and jumping at them when they came along the hall with trays. I heard dishes crash this morning. They are always perfect angels with you and they adore Brian."

Perfect angels, Gay repeated to herself, as she watched the road ahead. I wonder. Billy's voice when he reminded Sister of what they had planned to do the next time they went to Uncle Major's sent a premonitory tingle along my nerves. "What mischief do you think they are planning, Mrs. Fezziwig?" she asked aloud.

But the poodle was too intent on peering ahead to answer. She hitched forward uneasily and thrust her nose around the side of the windshield. Her growl was deep. Ominous. She let out a blood-curdling howl which sent Gay's heart into a tailspin. What did the dog see?

She bent forward. What was that? Near the tall pine? By the side of the road? That huge thing? Fiery eyes! Shifting eyes! Wings! It hopped. Hopped horribly. The poodle howled.

Gay fought off panic. It was flapping hideous wings! A signal for her to stop? Was fear paralyzing her? Brian had told her not to drive alone after dark. Had he known that this menace was loose in the world? The roadster was creeping. Would the creature grab her? Was it spook? Devil? Fiend?

She gripped her mind. Steadied it. What should she do? It was a situation the creator of Fu Manchu might have thought of. A wing beckoned. Did the monster intend to kidnap her? If it got her it would get others. She'd stop that. The wing beckoned again peremptorily. The thing hopped forward. Into the road. No doubt now. It wanted her. All right! It would get her. At a price.

XIV

TEETH set hard in her lips Gay stepped on the gas. Swung the wheel. Shot straight for the hideous shape.

"Look out! You crazy—"

With the yell the frightful thing crashed into roadside shrubbery. Vanished. The roadster's hood missed a tree by a miraculous inch. With frenzied strength Gay swung back to the highway. The creature had a man's voice! That made it more of a menace. Her body shook. Her throat parched. The car shot ahead. Skimmed up the drive at Rosewynne. Skidded as the brake jammed on. The suddenness of the stop sent the poodle over the door.

Gay raced up the steps. Into the house. Across the hall. Conscious of nothing but a furious urge to warn the Major and Brian. The evil thing might mean danger to them.

She plunged into the library. Stopped. Brian was near the fireplace back to the door. Bee Ware glanced over his shoulder. Her eyes met Gay's. She put her hand on his arm. Protested provocatively:

"Don't kiss me again, darling, until you are free."

Gay clutched her throat to strangle a sob. Too late. Brian wheeled.

"Gay! Gay! What is it?"

His voice came through a fog. A whirling fog. If only she had someone to hold to. If Jim—Jim—

An instant later a savage voice rasped:

"No. Get out!"

The fog closed in again. Cleared. She was in the library at Rosewynne. Who was stroking her hands? Brian? Brian on his knees beside the chair, his head clear-cut against the firelight behind him. It couldn't be Aunt Cass holding a glass to her lips. There were tears in this woman's eyes. Aunt Cass never cried. That was Major Willum looking down at her. Her world steadied.

She freed her hands and pushed away the glass. Sat as erect as she could with her head feeling as if it were a lighter than air ship which would float away from its mooring if she moved quickly.

"If you tell me I fainted—" she fought to keep her voice steady—"I won't believe you. I never fainted in my life."

"Gay! What happened?" Brian demanded hoarsely. He was standing now. She had forgotten how tall he was. His eyes burned into hers, even his lips were colorless.

"What happened to send you bursting into this room like a cyclone, darling?"

Darling. Gay puckered her brows. She had heard that word before the fog caught her. Someone had called somebody darling in the library. What had sent her bursting into the—

Memory returned in an overwhelming tide. She sprang to her feet. Her eyes widened in terror. She shivered. Stammered brokenly:

"It was—it was—"

Brian had her in his arms. Said with his lips against her hair.

"Steady, lovely, steady. Don't talk. Wait!"

"I'm all right now, see?" She pushed him away. "I'm not shaking. It was something in the road. Something hor—rible."

"Sit down in my chair before you tell us anything more, Gay. Brian, make her drink that stuff in the glass."

It was a super-daring person who would rebel when William Romney gave an order in that voice.

"Brian needn't apply the thumb screws. The Emperor speaks! His slave obeys," Gay conceded with an unsteady gaiety which sent Brian's head down on his arms crossed suddenly on the mantel. When she had drained the glass of the last salty drop he was facing her again, his hands thrust hard into his pockets. She shrugged distaste.

"What is that stuff, Aunt Cass?"

"Never mind what it is, Gabrielle, it will steady your nerves."

"Nerves. Don't be foolish, Aunt Cass. I haven't any nerves. I'm perfectly calm, see?" She held out one hand.

Frowned as it trembled and clasped it tightly over the other in her lap. She looked up at William Romney.

"Why am I wasting time when I tore home to tell you what I saw?" She rigidly controlled a shiver. "It was— This ought not to go beyond the family. Wasn't someone here who doesn't belong when I came in? I have a hazy recollection."

"That Ware woman slunk out the front door when I ran down the stairs in answer to Brian's shout. The Jezebel's gone." Cassie Wainwright clamped grim lips.

"I remember. It's all coming back now. She told you not to kiss her again until you were free, didn't she, Brian? Too bad to keep the lady waiting. We'll have to see what we can do about your freedom."

"Gay! You—"

"Just a minute, Brian," William Romney interrupted his nephew's husky protest. "Let's get Gay's story of what happened in the road. There's no one in the room now, my dear, but us four."

"There won't be but three, Gabrielle. I'm going. Come up as soon as you've told your story. Bed's the place for you." Cassie Wainwright left the room with a rustle of taffeta.

"Bed! She's crazy," Gay protested. "We're having a dinner tonight."

"Are you sure you are equal to presiding—"

"Now you're being foolish, Major Willum. Don't make an invalid of a perfectly fit, sound person, because her head went merry-go-round for a minute. Of course I'm able to preside. Now listen.

"I was driving home from Sam's—by the way, the twins are coming tomorrow to make us a visit—when the poodle began to howl. I looked ahead and saw—" With ragged breathlessness she described the creature and its yelled response to the roadster's charge.

"Was the brown thing near a tall pine?" Brian asked. When she nodded he said quickly:

"Try to forget the nightmare, dear. Rest before you dress for dinner."

The next day, during the brief intervals when her attention was not occupied entertaining the twins, Gay wondered what the Major and Brian had thought of her story. During the evening they had treated her as if she were a bit of spun glass which might drop to pieces if not delicately handled. Did they think she had had an hallucination? Did Brian—

Always at that point in her reflections, she shrugged disdain. Poor Brian, who couldn't kiss seductive Bee Ware the Widow until he was free.

She was pouring tea for the Major in the fire-lighted library when the thought again took possession of her mind. The glass doors had been thrown wide to give a vista of the court, yellow with acacias, green with glossy palms towering against pink and cream walls which were broken by arches and balconies, musical with the sound of dripping water.

"I don't take sugar, Gay."

She dropped the tongs with a little crash and met William Romney's amused eyes.

"Sorry. It's a wonder I even remember you like tea. I'm a rag. I've been at the heels of the twins all day. Among other hair-raising stunts I rescued Brian's precious baseball, the one dated with the last Harvard-Yale game he pitched. They were rolling it downstairs for Mrs. Fezziwig to retrieve. Later I snatched the thickly lathered poodle from the court pool in which Billy was holding her while Sister scrubbed. She's now flat on the floor of my boudoir, the poodle not Sister, dead to the world! I don't wonder Nurse Wickes wrings her hands.

"Listen! Mrs. Fezziwig is yelping! As if she were frightened. Has anything happened to—"

The sentence died on her lips as she reached the hall. Her body turned to ice. Sister, in a periwinkle-blue frock, was walking on the gallery balustrade with arms outstretched as if she were balancing on a tight rope. Billy, in matching blue linen, was kneeling at the top of the stairs, hanging on to the barking dog's collar. His face was one broad grin of delight as he watched the little girl.

What shall I do? Gay asked herself. If I move I may frighten her and then— She tried to swallow her heart which was fanning its wings in her tense throat. One sound from her might startle Sister and send her crashing to the flagged floor. She was halfway round! A false step—

She bit her lips to keep back a cry of surprise as a hand gripped her shoulder. Brian! His face was as white as hers felt. She saw him measure the distance between where he stood and the floor beneath the child.

It seemed hours that they stood rigid. Hours before Sister reached the stair balustrade, straddled it and tobogganed. Billy and the poodle catapulted down the stairs in an effort to keep pace.

Brian caught her as she reached the newel post. He swung her to her feet.

"Sister!" he cleared his hoarse voice. "Sister, if you ever do that again—"

She put her finger in her mouth and looked up at him with eyes as blue as forget-me-nots. Her underlip quivered.

"Why can't I, Bwian? I wouldn't have come to Uncle Major's if Billy hadn't pwomised I might walk the wailing. I want my Muvver! I want—"

"Don't scold Sister, Brian! She does that all the time at home," Billy championed.

"Well, she doesn't do it here, understand? Go upstairs now—"

"I want my Muv—ver! I—"

"There's Lena with your supper," Gay interrupted Sister's sob as the maid crossed the gallery with a laden tray. "I know that cook made some little pink frosted cakes and ice—"

The twins shouted and pelted up the stairs with the poodle hopping up two steps at a time behind them.

"Well, that seems to be that." Brian ran his fingers under his collar. "I thought you were a stone girl when I came in and saw you in the hall, Gay."

"I had reverted to the ice age. When I heard Mrs. Fezziwig yelping I dashed out of the library and when I saw Sister," she shivered, "I didn't know what to do."

"Doing nothing was what saved her. Come on. We need tea to steady our shattered nerves."

"What was the excitement?" William Romney inquired as they entered the room.

Gay told him.

"It's always a wonder to me how children manage to grow up," he laughed.

"It's more of a wonder how parents manage to survive. My knees have turned to jelly." Limply Gay sank into the chair behind the tea table.

William Romney rose. "Gay, give Brian his tea. He looks as if he needed it. The thermometer has dropped thirty degrees in the last two hours. This cold snap will freeze the pond solid and we'll be able to stage one of our old-time skating parties. What's new at the Plant, boy?"

"Nothing. Mac's back after a New York whirl which, I judge from his description, satisfied even Jane's jewels-and-ermine taste. He's no slouch when he starts on a party. He and I tramped through frozen trails to take a look at the old mill. We've had an idea we might use it for storage as Seaverns didn't approve of our swimming-pool plan."

Major Romney's eyes met his.

"I understand. Come to my study after you've had your tea and tell me what you found."

The quiet of the great room was stirred only by the diminishing sound of his footsteps on the marble flags in the hall, the snap of the fire and the trickle of water in the court.

From somewhere in the house came the melody of Schubert's "Serenade." A violinist was playing, sensitively, beautifully, with embracing tenderness and warmth. Major Bill had tuned in on a concert.

"Tough having this scare about Sister come on top of yesterday's fright. Feeling all right, Gay?" Brian inquired anxiously.

"Of course. I can't understand why I should have gone to pieces as I did in this room. I didn't really lose consciousness." She wondered if the disagreeable skirmish with Louis had contributed to her emotional upset. It wouldn't do to tell Brian, he detested his cousin-in-law sufficiently without adding that.

"If you didn't you gave an imitation that frightened us out of a year's growth."

"Have you found out what the—the horrible thing was?" Memory reduced her voice to a shaky whisper.

"Not yet. Try to forget it, will you?"

"It hasn't borne heavily on my mind today. I've been entertaining the Romney twins. Perpetual motion. A thousand or two decibels of sound. What you saw in the hall was top flight but there has been plenty almost as good. I'm going up. The children may be in mischief this minute."

"Not while they are eating their supper. Don't go. I want to talk to you."

She settled back in her chair. Did he intend to explain that "Don't kiss me again, darling, until you are free"? All right. She'd let him try. It would give her the chance to tell him that the sooner he was free the happier she would be. Had she better refer to the note Bee Ware had shown her? No. If she did she might get furiously angry and she wanted to appear coolly sophisticated.

She was poignantly aware that the space between them vibrated with electric currents. As if attracted by a magnet her eyes met his. Not blue now but black, they held hers by the indomitable purpose in their depths.

"About that fool remark of Bee's in this room, yesterday," he began. "I found her here when I came home from the Plant. Sampson had told her that you would return at any moment and she was waiting for you."

Words, just words, Gay thought. Aloud she said:

"And you kept her from being too bored while she waited. How exciting. Don't try to explain. As has been said before, your freedom can't come a moment too soon for me, or for her for that matter. Sure as she is, it must be something of a strain to fear she'll lose her square-cut emerald."

"What has Bee Ware's emerald to do with you—and me?"

"As if you didn't know she was betting her ring that she would be the second Mrs. Brian Romney!"

"The second Mrs. Brian Romney! If I can't hold the first do you think I will ever try again? I've never kissed—"

"Don't think I mind. While you're waiting for your freedom you may kiss any woman you like as often as you like."

"You mean that?" His reckless laugh set the pulse in her throat hammering. "Then I'll begin—"

"A man! Help! He—lp!"

The shrieks rang through the house.

XV

"IT'S LENA! The children! Kidnapers!" Gay breathed in horror.

Brian grabbed the brass-knobbed poker and charged up the stairs. She seized the fire shovel and followed in a breathless, gasping run.

"Oh, Mrs. Brian! There's a man in your room! I went in to open the bed, and—"

"Keep out of this, Gay," Brian flung over his shoulder as he plunged into the boudoir.

Curious how quiet the twins are in this hullabaloo, sitting as still as two little mice over their supper, Gay thought as she dashed by them.

She crashed into Brian standing on the threshold of her bedroom staring at the bed. Her eyes followed his. The white satin coverlet had been thrown back. A black head reposed on the pillow. Sheet and blankets were tucked snugly about shoulders encased in white pajamas, polka-dotted with blue.

Brian shouted with laughter. Gasped between bursts: "Look!" He flourished the poker. "Observe the—the bandit! The kidnaper! In my silk pajamas."

"Mrs. Fezziwig!" Gay exclaimed incredulously.

The poodle regarded her with one beady dark eye as she bent over the pillow, drew a ragged sigh of content and snuggled deeper under the blankets. She caught the dog's collar.

"At last you're where you want to be! Come out!"

As the poodle landed not too gently on the floor Brian seized the pajama jacket.

"And out of this! Quick!"

With the blue and white garment in his hand he strode into the boudoir and towered over the children.

"Did you kids put Mrs. Fezziwig in Gay's bed? Did you take these pajamas out of my room?"

The twins pranced gleefully.

"You scowl like the Fee Fi Fo Fum giant, Brian," Billy shouted.

"We fooled you, didn't we, Bwian? We took the pajamas out of your woom before I walked the wailing, didn't we, Billy? An' we made Lena scweam," gurgled Sister.

Still clutching the fire shovel, Gay dropped into a chair.

"The end of a perfect day. I hope it's the end though something tells me I'm too optimistic. You'd better reassure Major Bill, Brian. He may have heard Lena's scream."

He looked down at her with quizzical eyes.

"I'll go. Later we'll resume discussion of the matter we were threshing out when so rudely interrupted."

At midnight Gay was thinking of that discussion as stretched flat in bed she watched the slanting moon. Through her weary mind queer disconnected thoughts of love and duty were flashing on and off like a traveling electric sign. She had given Brian no opportunity to return to it. He and Major Bill had attended a Cup Presentation dinner at the Country Club while she and Aunt Cass had had a tray supper by the fire in the library. Aunt Cass rarely dined with the family. Shredded wheat and milk was her usual evening diet. After that she had bathed the twins, had knelt beside them as they said their prayers, had tucked them into beds in the guestroom connected by a door with hers. Billy had been asleep before his golden curls touched the pillow, but Sister,

heavy-eyed as she was, had sniffed and murmured something about "Muvver."

Good heavens, is the child going to have an attack of
homesickness? Gay had wondered. But the little girl was in
the Land of Nod almost as she asked herself the question.

She stretched luxuriously. The relief, the blessed relief to
be flat on her back. She couldn't remember that ever before, even after her longest and most difficult skating con-
test, had she been so utterly exhausted. Did mothers and
nurses feel like this when children were tucked in for the
night? If they did they should be awarded crowns, nice glittering diamond-tipped crowns.

What was that? She sat up. Listened. Outside the wide-
open window the wind played through the trees with the
sound of fingers brushing low somber notes from a cello.
There it was again! She looked toward the door. Snapped
on the bedside light. Thrust her bare feet into silver sandals.
Flung a matching satin coat over her turquoise blue crêpe
pajamas. Her day wasn't over yet apparently. She tiptoed
across the room. One of the children was crying. She turned
on the light. Sister was sitting up in bed. She blinked and
sobbed:

"I want my Muvver!"

Now what do I do? Gay wondered as she crushed back
an hysterical urge to laugh at this development of her adventure in child care.

She drew forward a chair. Tenderly smoothed back Sister's fluff of golden hair.

"Come on, angel, let's you and I rock and tell stories,"
she suggested.

"Don't want to wock wif you. Want my Muvver!"

Her wail wakened Billy. He raised heavy lids.

Is he going to join the chorus? Now what? Gay asked herself.

"What's the matter, Sister?" he mumbled sleepily, yawned
and sat up.

"I want my Muvver!"

The boy's eyes big and blue and troubled sought Gay's.
She answered the question in them.

"You know that Mother is ill. She can't come here. Tell
Sister to be a good girl and go to sleep, Billy."

"Don't want to go to sleep. Want my Muvver," sobbed
the child.

On his knees the boy leaned over and patted her shoulder.

"Don't cry." His blue eyes, now wide and brilliant, flashed

with inspiration. "How'd you like to have Brian rock you? Gay will bring him, won't you, Gay?"

Now that's an idea, Gay scoffed to herself and braced for battle.

Sister's wail broke in two.

"Want Bwian to wock me an' tell me Muvver de-ar, Muvver de-ar," she intoned with a sobbing breath.

"Well, you can't have Brian rock you." Gay's exasperation was not lessened by a mental close-up of herself knocking at her almost ex-husband's door at midnight.

Sister snuffled, sobbed, renewed her chant.

"Want Bwian to wock me."

Billy patted her shoulder and transfixed Gay with wide incredulous blue eyes.

"You must get Brian, Gay. Sam always tells me that girls should have everything they want and Sister's a girl, isn't she?"

"Even if she is, she can't have Brian tonight, so that's that."

Gay was aware that she was talking through clenched teeth and tried to relax. She smiled and cajoled:

"You and I'll rock in this comfy chair, angel, and I'll tell you a lot of lovely stories."

The little girl flung herself flat on the bed.

"Don't want lovely stowies. Want Bwian to wock me an' tell me Muvver de-ar, Muvver de-ar!"

"Very well, if you prefer to stay there and cry, you may. Lie down, Billy. I'm putting out the light."

Gay left the connecting door open and returned to her room. She could hear the child's sobs and Billy's comforting:

"Gay's an ol' meanie, Sister. Don't you mind."

Was she an "ol' meanie" not to call Brian? Gay asked herself passionately as at the window she looked out upon a star-spangled sky and waited for the children to quiet down. She could see the windows of his room in the tower. No splinters of light tonight. What would he think if she were to appear at his door? Silly! Why worry about that. She wasn't going. Wild horses couldn't drag her there.

A tug at her sleeve derailed a train of undesirable memories.

"Billy, what are you doing out of bed?" she demanded.

His eyes were big with concern. He rumpled his short curls.

"I'm 'fraid, Gay, that if Brian doesn't come quick, Sister'll be sick." He swallowed hard. "It—it hurts me to hear her cry. We—we just got to do somethin'. Won't you please do somethin', Gay?"

Gay dropped to her knees and put her arm about him. She thought, You're all Romney, you adorable thing, tender of your womenfolk. You've licked me. Aloud she said:

"Oh, all right! I'll get him. Go back to bed, Billy, and tell Sister to stop crying."

"What'll we do next if he isn't home?"

Gay's spirit ballooned. Joyous thought! Perhaps Brian wasn't at home.

"We'll plan that 'next' when we find that he isn't. Trot back to bed, sweetness."

She waited outside the door of the children's room until she heard him tell Sister not to cry, that Brian would come. Then, electric torch in hand, she stole to the head of the stairs and looked down at the tower door. It seemed miles below. Step by lagging step she descended. Was something moving in that shadowy corner? Her heart zoomed to her throat and beat its wings.

Why be silly? Hadn't she boasted yesterday that she had no nerves? Yesterday! She shivered. Why should the blinking eyes of that evil thing she had seen on the road flash through her mind when she needed to be cool and debonaire to carry off the present situation? Blinking eyes! She stopped on a stair and gripped the balustrade. She had seen lights that looked like eyes at the old mill! Had the creature who had tried to stop her come from there? She had had so much to think of since she hadn't connected the two. Now they had rushed together like trains in a head-on collision. She must tell Brian. Not now. That could wait until the present situation was disposed of.

Her heels clicked across the flagged floor of the hall. She opened the tower door and peered in. Hesitated. Perhaps Sister was asleep and had forgotten that she wanted Brian. She'd steal back and see. No. She'd better go on. The angelic Sister might stage another riot and rouse the household. Major Bill must not be disturbed—though the cuts made by flying glass had healed he hadn't entirely recovered from the effects of the nervous shock.

She stole along the narrow corridor and stopped before the door of Brian's bedroom. She raised her hand. Dropped it. Believe it or not, the next time she offered to take care of two spoiled children she'd be centuries older than she was now.

She set her teeth and knocked. Waited. No answer. Brian had not come home. What a break! She would tell—

"Who is it?"

He was tying the cord of his crimson lounge coat over his pajamas when he flung open the door.

"What's hap—Gay! *Gay!*"

His eyes changed from amazement to sudden flaming intensity. They sent the stinging blood surging upward from her heart to her face. Did he, could he think she would come to his door after Bee Ware's "Don't kiss me again, darling, until you are free"? She'd smash that idea and smash it hard.

"Nothing has happened, *nothing*," she declared furiously. "It's that abominable child! Sister's homesick. She's cry—crying. She won't go to sleep until you rock her and tell her 'Muvver de-ar, Muvver de-ar!' She's maddening! Mad—dening!"

Why had her voice broken like that? If only he wouldn't look at her as if she were a specimen under a microscope. Would he never speak?

"So that's what brought you here?" he said finally. "For an instant I thought—we won't go into my thoughts. They wouldn't interest you. Come on." He closed the door.

"Almost crying yourself, aren't you?" he asked as side by side they crossed the hall. "Where are the kids sleeping?"

"Sleeping! If by any stretch of imagination you can call what they are doing 'sleeping,' they're in the guestroom next to mine."

As they reached the head of the stairs, Billy dashed forward and seized Brian's hand.

"Billy, I told you to stay in bed," Gay reminded sternly.

"I know you did, Gay, but I couldn't. You were so cross I wasn't sure you'd bring Brian an' I came to look for him myself. I had to tease an' tease before you'd go for him. I'm 'fraid Sister'll cry herself sick if you don't rock her, Brian."

"Lead me to her, Billy. What price popularity! If you were 'cross' you must be completely tuckered out, Gay. Go to bed. I'll look after the children." Color swept into his face. His eyes, clear, clean, amused, met hers. "That sounds domestic, doesn't it?"

He bent his head and kissed her lips, tenderly, quickly.

"Good night, Muvver de-ar! Muvver de-ar!" He cut into her angry protest. "You asked for it. You told me I might kiss any woman I wanted to, remember?"

He swung the boy to his shoulders.

"Come on, Bill, you and I are off to comfort a lady in distress."

XVI

OUTSIDE the Administration Building of the Plant sun and storm were battling for right of way. Enormous white flakes drifted lazily but persistently down. They turned to glistening marble the tall iron fence which enclosed the buildings where the work of the Romney Manufacturing Company was begun, carried to completion, and from which the finished product was shipped. They partially veiled the Orb of Day which hung in the sky like a round copper tray that badly needed polishing. The factory chimneys loomed like lean, shadowy giants. The roofs of the white cottages of the employees on the streets which radiated from the enclosure glistened. The pond gleamed like a huge platinum platter which had been carelessly dropped at the base of the hills which were vague, gun-metal blurs.

Vanquished, the sun disappeared. A light wind slanted the snow till it resembled white sheets blowing; murmured at the windows like hushed voices whispering secrets; coated with downy fluff the trucks laboring like dinosaurs in and out of the frozen roads.

"Looks as if we were in for an old-time winter with snow starting early in November," observed Brian Romney as he turned from a window in his office and faced his uncle and two cousins. The Major was thoughtfully tapping an arm of his chair. Mac, in checked brown tweeds, was tamping tobacco into his pipe. Sam, pale from the effects of his late attack of influenza, was penciling fantastic curlicues on a pad. He looked up.

"Well, Brian, here's your advisory board all present and accounted for. Sorry I had to hold the conference up for a week while that confounded flu laid me low. What's on your mind?"

Was it only a week since the night Gay had knocked on

his door, Brian asked himself. He hadn't had a moment alone with her since to go back to the subject of Bee Ware and her emerald. She had shown genius in avoiding him. Why not? She hated him, didn't she, and loved Jim Seaverns? He tore his thoughts from her and forced them to the matter at hand. He answered:

"Eddie Dobson. He knows that I suspect he damaged that machine two years ago after I put our maid, Lena, wise to his philandering. Apparently he is getting back at me by making my job here as difficult as possible. He is trying to undermine the workers' confidence in their new boss."

"Eddie, the Great Lover, again!" Mac groaned. "What does he want this time, Brian?"

"To be taken back as superintendent instead of foreman."

"And you refuse to play Yes-Man?"

"I do, Sam. It's time we had a showdown in this land of the free and home of the brave. Our employees admit they are satisfied with wages, working hours and conditions and always have been, but 'We want Eddie!' is their battle cry. I don't want Eddie and what's more I won't have Eddie. He's a firebrand. He's ganged up with the worst elements in our employ. Men who have no interest in the business, only in the day's pay. I have discovered that they've formed a secret society which has been meeting in the old mill. Someone must have tipped them off. When Mac and I investigated the place it was clean as a whistle. It was so clean that it was proof that it had been occupied recently."

Sam grinned.

"May be just a kid trick. Remember 'The Sign of the Bloody Thumb' society we boys cooked up and the bottles of red ink we used attaching our print to threats of vengeance?"

"Them were the days!" Mac chuckled.

Brian laughed before he said seriously:

"This is no kid trick. The men wear brown regalia with an owl mask and flapping wings. It was—"

"An owl mask? Did you say *owl?*" Sam was on his feet. He was no longer laughing.

"Yes. We figure that it was one of them who tried to stop Gay. We'll come back to that after we finish with Eddie Dobson's demand. He's a menace to the girl workers—"

"And how they fall for him," Mac interjected.

"To such an extent that if he isn't reinstated with full power to do all future bargaining with us—they—and their male relatives—will walk out, and that means fifty per cent., perhaps more of our workers. He's due here in a few minutes to deliver that ultimatum. He is no longer an employee and has no right to bargain but I decided that if we didn't listen to him he would make another grievance of our refusal. He's looking for trouble. I suspect that he has come to hate me beyond caution, beyond fear, almost beyond sanity. That's why I rounded up my advisory board."

"What do you want your advisory board to advise?" Sam inquired.

"Question. Will we allow one disgruntled man who is no longer in our employ to hold up our business at his pleasure, cause us to lose a small fortune, bring tragedy and want on the families of our workers, just to have his own way? I've had our legal adviser give us an opinion on our rights in the matter." He picked up a paper. "Here it is!"

"Can you give it to us without a lot of confusing herebys, hereafters, demurrers, pursuants, and their horde of first cousins? Legal terms leave me haywire."

"I'll reduce it to words of one syllable, as nearly as I can, Mac. Our lawyer quotes a decision which, reduced to the simplest terms, says that a strike brought on because a fellow workman is discharged is unlawful. That while a body of men may lawfully strike to better their condition, the mere refusal to continue the employment of one of their number is not such a condition as to justify them in combining to enforce a strike. Is that plain enough?"

"It is! I vote we stand our ground and take whatever comes. What's your verdict, Major Bill?"

"I agree with you, Mac, but I can't believe that our workers will persist in demanding Eddie Dobson. They always have been so loyal."

"The strike bug is in the air. They've picked it up just as they would the flu bug. Eddie is all set, first, to embarrass me and second to stage a walkout if he doesn't get what he wants. Louis Dubois emphasized that fact when he came here to try to negotiate the purchase of the Plant."

"Louis Dubois can go to thunder!" Mac Romney exploded. "Decided what answer you'll make to Dobson, Brian?"

"First, put the true condition up to our workers, make them understand that if the majority of them strike there is so little in the business for capital and enterprise that we might as well quit, close down. If we do, it will be for an indefinite period. It will mean canceling orders, suffering and loss to many families—but—it is up to them, isn't it, to stop Eddie and his gang? It will mean also a money loss to us all. Luckily the Plant is owned entirely by the family. We won't have to cut the dividends of stockholders. It's a major operation but I believe it's the only way to save the patient. Realizing what it means to us, now what do you say, Mac?"

"A cut in dividends will be a tough break. I've started a new stable, but I can take it." He chuckled. "Janey got her New York whirl just in time and boy, oh, boy, was it a whirl?"

"And you, Sam?"

Sam Romney shook off the abstraction which had been wrinkling his brow.

"I'm with Mac, Brian. If the workers had a real grievance I'd say, 'Go slow!' but if, with the law on our side, Dobson succeeds in holding us up this time he'll get the habit and we'll never feel secure. Walkouts seem to be a part of modern industrial life. I'm all for seeing this through."

The office door was flung open. Sue Dubois stood on the threshold. Her shrill green suit and beret grated along Brian's nerve centers. The color intensified the red lights in her hair, the masculine boldness of her features, the coarseness of her skin and the hard, emerald brilliance of her eyes. She defiantly regarded the four men who stood looking back at her.

"Stop staring at me, Brian, as if I were something the cat had brought in."

"Was I staring? I was wondering what sent you here with the manner of a bill collector threatening to shut off the telephone. You mistake my reaction to your entrance, Sue. Did you cast a Sleeping Beauty spell over the office force that you got in without being announced?"

"Hmp! I suppose you're proud of that wisecrack about my beauty. That blonde menace you call a secretary told me you were in conference. Did she think she could keep me out of any office in my family business? I showed her."

"For the love of Mike, Sue! Pipe down!"

"Too bad about your sensitive ears, Mac. You'll be lucky if you don't hear things harder to listen to than my voice. If a fogy old bach will marry a girl years younger—" hunched shoulders supplied the conclusion.

Mac's already ruddy color deepened. Brian drew an infuriated breath. Before he could speak Sam laughed and admitted:

"Susie, my girl, I regard you with admiration, tinged with

despair. You're an expert in the art of conveying shades of innuendo without committing yourself to a statement. What's the trick? Enlighten a struggling author. If I could do your talent justice in a story my reputation would be made."

Sue Dubois' face flushed a deep and unbecoming purplish red.

"Oh, you Romneys!" she sneered. "Lucie was right—if she is too ignorant to know the origin of the phrase—when she said, 'One for All and All for One!' Right or wrong you four men stand together."

"You're a Romney, too," the Major reminded gravely.

"If I am, am I ever consulted about family affairs? I have Grandfather Romney's genius for business. I could run this enterprise with one hand. Why isn't my husband present at this conference to represent my interest in the Plant?"

"You have no interest in it, Sue. You abrogated that when you sold your share to me," William Romney reminded sternly.

"So that's why you bought my stock, Major Bill? You pushed me out so that neither Louis nor I could have anything to say about the business? You took advantage of an inexperienced woman!"

"Skip it! Where do you get that 'inexperienced' stuff? You were born with the stock market tape in your hand!" Mac swallowed a gusty laugh as he met his uncle's warning eyes.

"Sue, you'll be ashamed of that accusation when you get home and think it over and remember that you asked me to buy you out only a year ago. Why did you come here this morning? Did Louis send you?"

William Romney's stern question noticeably reduced Sue Dubois' temperature. There was a hint of fright in her eyes—her uncle was not only a power in the business world, he had a large private fortune which sometime would be distributed. She replied meekly—for her:

"Louis doesn't know I am here. I went to your office, Major Bill, to ask if you would turn the ice carnival next week into a charity benefit for the hospital. They told me you were with Brian so I came here. I'm planning to ask Gabrielle and Jim Seaverns to put on their pair-skating act—I'm sure they'll do it, practice will give them a chance to be together without starting talk, and—"

"Sue!"

A buzz in the interoffice loudspeaker interrupted Brian's furious outburst. He answered:

"All right! Keep him there till I ring." He opened the office door:

"Sorry to hurry you, Sue, but a man is here by appointment to confer with us. He must not be kept waiting."

Mrs. Dubois' laugh held no hint of mirth.

"All fairly standing on tiptoe to speed the parting guest, aren't you? *Toujours la politesse.* I'll go, but, understand this, I haven't given up my intention of seeing my husband president of the Romney Manufacturing Company. I have money enough to buy it, lock, stock and barrel. Good morning!"

"I don't know how our sweet-natured cousin affected the rest of you but I feel as if my heart and mind had been scraped to the quick with a nutmeg grater," Sam said as the door closed behind her.

"Lovely creature! She took a crack at each of our wives, didn't she? How does a woman get that way?" Mac demanded.

"Let's drop the subject of Sue, boys," William Romney suggested. "Eddie Dobson is waiting, isn't he? Have him sent in."

Brian was behind the desk, Major Romney, Mac and Sam completed a semicircle when Dobson swaggered into the office. He had done himself well in the matter of apparel. He looked like a smartly dressed young business man in a mail-order catalogue. Near the door he stopped. His bold, rowdy eyes narrowed.

"I told you I would confer with you, Mr. Brian, and no one else." There was a hint of strain in the bluster. He looked uneasily at William Romney.

"Any decision of mine has to be backed up by the directors of the Plant." Brian made an inclusive gesture. "Meet the advisory board. Gentlemen, this is Eddie Dobson, whose proposition I have asked you to hear. Go ahead, Eddie."

Dobson stretched his neck out of the collar of his blue shirt and straightened his shoulders. He cleared his voice.

"All right, here goes, I want to be taken back as a superintendent and my pay jumped twenty dollars a week." He cast a suspicious look at Sam who was making a note on a pad.

"*Only* twenty dollars! Sstt, sstt, sstt," Mac chuckled between his teeth. He subsided with a chuckle as William Romney looked at him sternly.

"Go on, Eddie, or perhaps that's all?" Brian suggested.

"You bet it isn't all. I want a raise of two per week for

every woman in the factory and your John Hancock on the agreement that all hiring and firing will be done through me."

The room was so still that the sound of a sheet of paper being torn sharply from the pad split the air like a whistling lash.

"And if we do not agree?" Brian inquired smoothly, too smoothly.

Dobson swelled with the pride of a job accomplished.

"If you don't accept our terms we walk out."

"Does that mean every worker in the Plant?"

"Two thirds of them and they'll keep the others away from the yard."

"I suppose you know that it is unlawful for a body of men to strike because their employer refuses to reemploy one of their members?"

Dobson snapped contemptuous fingers. "That for the law!"

"Eddie, you're magnificent."

Brian's amused tone brought the hot blood surging under Dobson's fair skin. He clenched his hand.

"Kidding me, are you?"

"Not at all. Not at all. Just a moment while I consult my advisory board."

Brian rose and talked with his uncle and cousins. When he faced Dobson again he said:

"We refuse to 'arbitrate' with you, Eddie. You are no longer an employee of the Plant. We'll listen to a group of our workers, not to you. Go back to your followers and tell them that. Tell them also that the day they walk out this Plant closes its doors for an indefinite term."

"That's a bluff. You'll never close the Plant."

"Won't we? There's only one way to find out." He crossed the room and opened the door.

"With that we'll call the 'arbitration' conference closed."

"It's all right with me. Walkout it is," Dobson blustered.

As Brian shut the door he leaned against it and said to the three men looking back at him:—

"We've burned our bridges. So what? Sam, your mind hasn't been on Eddie Dobson. Have you been concocting one of your mystery yarns while we've been fighting him? Snap out of it! We need your advice and attention."

Sam flung the pad to the desk.

"You're going to get it—plus. Remember that a stone was flung through a window not so long ago? I see that you do. When I went into the bookroom perhaps an hour later it lay where it had fallen. No one had touched it. I picked it up in my handkerchief. Later took it to a finger-print expert. I suspected that whoever had hurled it had intended to hit Brian, not Major Bill."

"I know it was intended for me," Brian asserted. "Go on, Sam."

"Since then I've been sleuthing for finger prints."

"Are there finger prints on that stone?" Mac's face was red with excitement.

"There are. Two sets."

"Whose?" three men chorused.

"Louis Dubois' for one. I haven't matched up the others."

"But Louis Dubois was in New York that night. As Mac and the girls and I hurried out of the café he passed us with—"

Brian caught back the name. He hadn't mentioned it at the time, why tell now that he had been amazed to see Bee Ware hanging on Dubois' arm. He tried to make his voice convincing as he assured:

"So of course Louis couldn't have thrown that stone."

"That lets him out as far as throwing it goes. Must have been the unknown owner of the other prints who did the job but Louis had something to do with it. You accused me of thinking up a mystery yarn a few minutes ago, Brian. No need to think up one. One has been handed to me ready-made. Because, the stone that hit Major Bill wasn't a stone. It was a hunk of iron covered with clay. And on the clay besides finger prints was—"

"What?" the men demanded in unison.

"An owl's head etched in brown. A horned owl!"

XVII

IN THE storage-room above the garage Gay closed a trunk which reeked with moth balls. With an ermine turban in her hand she perched on top and looked from one object to another which once had adorned the home she and Brian shared. Shrouded in slip covers, or unshrouded, the pieces of furniture were like so many ghosts flitting and drifting from out the past. Memories tightened her throat and flushed her eyes with hot tears. What would be done with all this stuff when she and Brian finally separated? Would he take it to a new home? Not if it made him as sick to look at it as it made her. But it wouldn't. Little he cared that their marriage had gone smash. If he did, could he have kissed her as lightly as he had that night when she had called him to comfort Sister? Could he have laughed and reminded:

"You asked for it. You told me I might kiss any woman I wanted to, didn't you?" She impatiently brushed her hand across her lips. The kiss still burned.

What a waste of time to think of the past. Hadn't Major Bill told Brian and herself to forget yesterday? Hadn't he said, "Today is yours"? She should have had more sense than to come to this room and throw open the door of her mind to all those yesterdays which had been battering for entrance since the night she had locked Brian out of her life. She could have worn something besides the ermine at the Carnival.

Could she? She pressed the white fur against her cheek. So many happy triumphs and gorgeous star-spangled nights were linked with it. Would Jim send her violets as he had done each time he and she had entered a pair-skating competition?

Jim! He had phoned to ask in a stiff, frozen voice if he should say "Yes" to Mrs. Louis' request that he skate with Gay at the Charity Carnival. It was the first time she had heard from him since the evening when, white and furious, he had left her apartment.

"Of course, say 'Yes,' Jim," she had answered eagerly. "That is, if you can spare the time. The Carnival is only a week off. We'll have to put in a lot of practice to bring our act up to concert pitch."

"I'll find the time, all right!" His voice had thawed. "Mrs. Louis has asked me to stay with them until after the Carnival so we can get a lot of practice on the pond. Something tells me we'll top all other performances. I'll be seeing you."

For the moment enthusiasm at the prospect of skating with him again had wiped possible objections to the plan from her mind. During the week since they had been appearing and burning in letters of fire. She said to herself now:

You shouldn't have told him to come. Perhaps Sue invited him to stay with her for the sole purpose of showing up the true relations between Brian and you. It hasn't helped you to carry on at Rosewynne to meet Jim at the pond every morning at dawn for two hours' practice before he went to the city, and an hour in the late afternoon. It hasn't helped him, either. Major Bill oozes disapproval and as for Brian—he's getting grimmer and grimmer. That isn't my fault is it? I didn't want to return to Rosewynne, did I? The pesky old Plant is responsible for that, isn't it? Thank heaven the Carnival comes off tonight. After that Jim will return to town and I'll see that he stays there until—until my job at Rosewynne is finished.

She crossed to the window, that sunny window from which she could see the cloud-patched sky, the brick walls of the terraced orchard and vegetable gardens, the tops of green pines and balsams and oaks, the glint of glass in the grape house, which Major Bill had had built very near the main house that his wife might reach it easily in her wheel chair. Raising Hamburgs and nectarines had been her hobby.

The snow of a week before had disappeared except where white patches lay in shadowy hollows in the hills, but the cold had strengthened. Far to the right, dots which were men were testing the ice. Last night the pond had been flooded by hose from the boathouse that it might be smooth as a glass floor. Men were placing ice blocks which would encircle the space reserved for figure skating. Two were strengthening the wire fence between the shore and a low ridge which would be open to spectators. Electricians were putting up flood lights at opposite sides of the pond in front of the boathouse and the bleachers, seats on which had been sold at fabulous prices for charity.

Here's hoping that Jim and I give a performance worth the money, Gay thought, as she went slowly down the stairs.

Tim O'Brien was puttering near the door as she stepped out into the clear bracing air. The sun turned his red hair to a burning bush. He had driven her to the pond morning and afternoon. He was taciturn. Sometimes, sitting beside him, she had sensed his seething inner protest. Against what? She looked up at the turquoise sky.

"On top of keeping the thermometer below freezing for a week it looks as if Mr. Weather Man were planning to hand out a grand night for the Carnival, Tim."

"Yes, Madam. They tell me there's ten inches of ice on the pond. The moon will be full. If the wind doesn't rise it will be perfect." A faint smile twisted his already crooked mouth. "Are you nervous?"

I've never seen him show a trace of interest before. He must be getting human, Gay thought. I'll make the most of the thaw. Something tells me he wants to talk. I'll give him a chance.

"I'm not nervous, Tim—but I'll be glad when I've finished my part of the program. Mr. Seaverns and I haven't skated together since last winter and we've had to put in hours and hours of practice—as you know—to get our swoops and spirals and jumps perfectly timed."

"Mr. Seaverns is good but so is Mr. Brian. He has speed. What gets my goat is the way you work over a sport."

"Why not, Tim? I love to do anything I try to do as well as possible. It puts adventure into life. Think how humdrum it would be if every day were just like every other day with no hills to climb—that's what achievement is—if it were always on a dead level."

"That's all right for you—you know you can get off the level—somewhere—you're not strapped down—"

"Are you strapped down, Tim?"

"With all the kids to support? You're asking me!"

"Lena helps with the family, doesn't she?"

"Sure she helps. You know the pay she gets but I'll bet you don't know what it takes to feed and clothe six kids and an old soak who won't work. It takes all our wages and now we're scraping the bottom of our savings. Suppose it was you? Suppose you saw a chance to get a fat bunch of money? Would you take it or would you leave it lay?"

The flaming questions coming from him were as startling as the sudden outburst of a volcano for years considered extinct. What was behind the change? Was he asking her to help him decide which turn to make at a crossroads?

"It would depend on what was tied up with the bunch of money, Tim. There are some things like dishonor or—or treachery which no amount of money could make worth while."

"I'm not so sure. Shall I drive you to the pond this evening, Madam?" In the drawing of a breath he had rebuilt his defenses.

"Yes, and after I'm through to Rosewynne. I shall change from my skating costume before I go to Mrs. Dubois' for supper. After you leave me at the lake, call for some girl you would like to take to the Carnival, you can go back for her after you drive me home. There will be general skating between the program features."

"Me take a girl! Me with a family of seven on my hands? What dame would look at me? It's smooth guys like Eddie Dobson who can spend their money on themselves they fall for, he with a grandmother and mother both drawing pensions from the Plant. He should worry about his family."

He departed on the last bitter word. Gay's eyes followed him. What had the boy on his mind—besides "six kids and an old soak"? Was he in love with a girl who preferred Eddie? Was he fighting the temptation to accept money for something dishonorable, something that would hurt the Plant and its owners?

Should she tell Brian that she suspected Tim was being bribed with "a fat bunch of money"?

She shrank from the suggestion. Having spent an enormous amount of gray matter and all her ingenuity keeping out of his way the past week, she wouldn't seek him now. Whom could she tell? Not the Major; why worry him? Mac? Mac was practical, he always had his feet on the ground. He would be at Sue's for supper after the Carnival. She would get him in a corner by himself and tell him then.

Hours later seated under a canopy in the lee of the boathouse she looked down at the mass of deep purple flowers at her shoulder. Exquisite things. Jim hadn't forgotten. She had had violets sent her many times but these seemed to exhale a special fragrance, to have a special significance. Did her reaction to them prove that she really loved Jim Seaverns? She'd better sign off on that line of thought.

Perfect night. Across the pond, lights like a string of major planets plucked from the heavens outlined the highway. The stars paled by comparison. The moon hung in the sky like a huge gold face dragging the starry milky way behind it like a sequined veil. Clear. Cold. Not a breath of wind. The lighted bleachers were packed to the top tier of seats. Back of the wire fence a crowd covered the ridge. Around and around the outside of the spot-lighted exhibition enclosure glided skaters, singly and in couples, to the spirit-stirring music of a band.

Gay smiled as Cassie Wainwright, straight as a ramrod, hands tucked into a muff of silver-gray caracul which matched her coat, skated majestically past like a smoky shadow. Bee Ware in a scarlet costume was standing on the shore of the pond talking to a group of men. The light caught the blades of the skates on the red boots hanging from her arm and set them a-glitter. As she turned Gay saw the spray of white orchids on her Persian lamb muff. From Brian, doubtless. Where was Brian? She had not seen him for twenty-four hours. She had had a tray in her room at dinnertime. Probably the four Romney men were near the entrance greeting the arrivals. In a way it was their party. Even so, he might have looked her up to wish her luck.

"Ready, Gay?" Jim Seaverns balanced on skates in front of her. She was impressed as always by his lean, dark good looks. A bugle sounded. "There's our fanfare! You're looking out of sight."

"Thanks, Jim. Handsome is as handsome does." In spite of the note of laughter Gay's voice was shaky. "Ready! Let's snap into it."

Perfectly matched in height, the man in a red satin jacket, his legs slim and lithe in black tights, the girl all in white, except for the violets, glided to the center of the spot-lighted enclosure and bowed to the bleachers and to the crowd behind the wire fence. Beams of colored light from opposite sides of the pond drenched them, rippled from rose to violet, to green, to amber. For an instant the thunder of applause drowned the music, then as hand in hand the pair swung off in a swooping spiral, the onlookers silenced their hands.

They danced, they glided on one skate to the music of Paradise in Waltz Time. Back and forth they wove. Marvelous in their timing. Four shadows on the blue ice kept pace with them and sometimes the shadows' shadows. There was perfection of motion in their lightning turns, magic in their leaps to emphasize the beat and rhythm of the music which blended with the hiss of blades. They smiled as their lithe bodies moved in perfect time and co-ordination. With a dance step they came to a sudden stop. Finished in a low fade-away.

The audience broke into a frenzy of applause. Stamped and clapped until the pair-skaters took a bow. Then a second band blared into a Rhumba and spectators crowded the ice outside the enclosure.

As Gay and Seaverns reached the canopied bench where Lena was waiting with her leopard coat, he raised her white-gloved hand and fervently pressed his lips to it.

"Better than ever, my dear," he said huskily.

Gay hastily withdrew her hand.

"I know that used to be part of our act, Jim, but we'll cut it out now. Please—"

"Jim, you were sensational!"

Gay recognized the voice. Behind her Bee Ware the Widow was the center of a group entirely composed of the Romney family. The Major was there, Mac and Jane, Sam and Lucie, Sue and Louis Dubois and—Brian, lean and tall in the white coat, red belt and dark green tights of his Skating Club.

"If you ask me, Gay was the sensation," Louis Dubois corrected suavely. "I've never seen such perfect figure-skating. You mustn't stand without your coat. Allow me." He took the coat from Lena and laid it over Gay's shoulders.

Every nerve in her body cringed away from him. Did he think she had forgotten his rough threat that he would have her eating from his hand? How could Brian stand there laughing with Lucie and allow Louis to touch her coat? He knew how she loathed the man. She waved a dismissing hand.

"Go away, all of you. I want to be alone until after my single."

As the Romneys skated away, Sue Dubois called, "Don't forget, you're all coming to supper with me. Come on, Louis. I want to speak to one of the ticket takers."

He loosened the hand she had caught in hers.

"Can't, Sue. There's a New York man in the clubhouse I must talk with."

His wife looked after him as he broke away. With anger in her eyes and an ugly twist to her lips she glided off.

Lena slipped a stout cushion between Gay's white-booted feet and the ice.

"You were wonderful, Madam. The crowd went wild over you," she babbled excitedly.

Gay nodded and snuggled into the cozy warmth of the fur. She closed her eyes. Every nerve was taut. She must relax or her muscles wouldn't co-ordinate and her single would be a flop.

"Anything I can do?"

Startled, she looked up. Brian might have been a stranger speaking to her, though a stranger's voice wouldn't necessarily be so chill, so rigidly polite. His eyes were brilliantly blue, astonishingly like the Major's when he was angry. He was pale and the lines between his nose and stern lips looked as if they had been chiseled.

For some curious and inexplicable reason she had to steady her lips before she could answer in a voice as chill as his.

"Nothing, thanks. I want to be alone until it is time for my single."

"I get you. Good luck. Thanks for wearing my violets," he said stiffly and glided away.

XVIII

BRIAN'S violets! She had thought Jim sent them! Gay looked at the fragrant purple blossoms against her shoulder. He had remembered that she wore them when she skated. He had remembered also that she loved red roses. Why had he sent them? As a graceful gesture to fool the family? It seemed incredible that the man turning his back so coldly had been her husband for almost two years. What had happened to their love?

That's what happened to it, she answered her own question as she saw Bee Ware beckon to him, saw him drop to one knee before her as she held out her red boots with their glistening skates. She bent forward and playfully adjusted his green turban with its red cockade. He jerked his head back.

Silly thing, Gay thought, with all her experience with men doesn't she know that would make Brian furious? Didn't know she skated, that she cared for outdoor sports, for anything but a stag line, dancing and cards. I hope her skates trip her, that she falls and breaks her "sensational" neck, she concluded vindictively and felt her temperature go down.

The bugle! Her signal. She threw off her coat. She was aware of the nearness of the Romneys as she entered the roped-off aisle. As from a great distance she heard Mac's low "Knock 'em in a heap, gal!" and the Major's tender "Good luck, my girl."

She ran to the center of the enclosure. Shouts of acclaim and applause ceased as she poised on her toes and waited for the music. The lights bathed her in the shimmering colors of the rainbow. The world about her was so still it seemed to be holding its breath.

The silence was broken by the opening strains of the Beautiful Blue Danube. Faintly smiling, dreamily, with effortless grace she waltzed to its music. The rhythm swelled. Her shining skates spun. Stopped. Danced on. With her body in a straight line she leaned to the curve of the circle, turned quickly. Glided. With dash and sparkle spun fast. Spun slow. With ballet pirouettes rolled along to the tempo of the music. Round and round she went followed by the lights and her shadows until with a deep obeisance she backed from the enclosure on one skate.

The spectators on the bleachers went wild. They stamped. They clapped. They shouted "Encore! Encore!" The crowd on the ridge roared acclaim. Gay returned and took her bow. Laughed, shook her head and retreated in a fade-away.

Jim Seaverns' ice-scrolling was an outstanding exhibition. Gay and he put on their most intricate and difficult pair-skating act which flowed in unbroken rhythm and their part of the program was finished. Their charm and personality brought a thunder of acclaim which echoed and re-echoed among the hills. As they reached the canopied seat he said:

"They're still shouting and clapping. Shall we go back?"

"No. Better to leave them wanting more. I'll take a turn around the pond by my lonesome just to stop the tingle along my nerves. Tim will drive me back to Rosewynne so I can change from this costume before we go to Sue's supper."

"Who sent you the violets?"

"I thought you sent them," she answered his brusque question.

"I didn't. I'll confess that I've been so rushed with business and practice that sending you the usual flowers slipped my mind. I didn't think of them till I saw those you're wearing. Who did remember that you always wore violets when you skated?"

The memory of Brian's voice, "Thanks for wearing my violets," tightened her throat.

"If you didn't, I shall have to turn G-Woman and find out. No card came with them. Do your Boy Scout good deed for the day, Jim. Ask Aunt Cass to take a turn, will you? She'll love to skate with one of the evening's headliners."

"Sure you'll be all right alone? I'll keep an eye on you."

"Don't be foolish, run along."

Feeling that she hadn't a care in the world, now that her part in the Carnival was over, Gay darted through the crowd which was skating to the music of "The Merry-Go-Round Broke Down," their gay costumes contributing to the pageant. What a night! Windless. Clear. Stinging cold. She looked up. The moon, guarded by Venus and Jupiter at their most brilliant, was grinning at her. In the east the two brightest stars in the belt of Orion shone like huge incandescents. A meteor burst with a loud report and scraps of flaming cosmic dust hurtled off into space. Where would those bits of stone and metal land, she wondered, and looked down quickly as if she expected to see them strike the pond like hail.

How smooth the ice was. Why didn't the skaters get away from the crowd and enjoy this? One couple had done so. Looked as if the man were teaching the girl. She was so new at it that he couldn't even hold her up. She was down with a crash.

Poor thing, perhaps I can help, Gay thought, and swept forward in long swinging glides. Not until she was almost upon them did she discover that the man was Brian, that Bee Ware was clinging to his arm and swaying as her skates slid from under her.

Didn't the woman know how to stand up or was she pretending she didn't that she might have an excuse for clinging? Gay noted the dark impatience of Brian's face. Heard his annoyed:

"For Pete's sake, take a long, slow stride, Bee. You can't get anywhere jerking along."

A wicked imp of retaliation seized Gay. She approached, laughed, counseled gaily:

"Don't be cross with the child, *darling*, because she hasn't skate sense."

She spun on one runner, then whirled away in waltz pirouettes.

What evil spirit possessed you to be so hateful? she demanded of herself, as she struck out swiftly toward the upper end of the pond which was heavily shadowed by trees. You have plenty of faults, her accusing conscience persisted, but you've never been catty, and was that return of Bee's fling at your card playing catty? It had claws, sharp, pointed, digging claws.

The claws had dug into Brian too. He had been furious. Lucky his eyes hadn't been knives, they would have slashed her to ribbons. Why care if his feelings had been hurt? If a man who could skate as he could—in some ways he was better than Jim—would stand for the clinging of that poisonous Bee Ware, he deserved to be made furious. Just the same, she wished she hadn't said it, wished she hadn't flaunted in their faces her skill on skates. Show-off, aren't you? she accused, and for the first time in her life felt cheap.

At the end of the pond into which the mill stream emptied she stood motionless looking at the frozen ribbon which wound back into the woods. Moonlight had turned it to silver and the towering tree tops to silver-gilt. In the opposite direction she could see the pink haze above the Plant factories. Curious, it didn't seem so bright as usual.

She drew a deep breath. The air was fragrant with the scent of pine and balsam. How still the world was here. So still that a snap of frost in a branch overhead echoed like a pistol shot. From a distance came the murmurous drone of voices and the beat and rhythm of music.

Something else was coming from that center of life and gaiety. A man at a terrific pace. His skates whined on the ice. Gay's heart did a cartwheel or two. Could it be the monster who had tried to stop her in the road? A chill shivered along her nerves. She had heard the phrase "rooted to the spot," had jeered at its improbability. She knew now that it was possible. Her feet wouldn't move.

She watched the skater in trancelike fascination. There was furious determination in the way he came on. Who was he and why was he rushing toward her? He shot through a patch of moonlight which transmuted his white coat to silver. It was Brian! Brian, coming to have it out with her for her hateful fling at Bee Ware!

Well, he shouldn't have that satisfaction. Fear had rooted her feet to the ice. Not fear, but a wild surge of emotion she couldn't understand freed them. She flew back toward the boathouse. Nearer and nearer sounded the sibilant hiss of blades. Cold air whistled by her ears. Her throat dried. A sense of frenzied futility seized her. It was like a nightmare. Like a page from "Alice" with the Red Queen crying, "Faster! Faster!"

She couldn't go faster. She—

A hand caught her shoulder and whirled her round with a force that almost upset her balance.

"Thought you could get away from me, didn't you?" demanded Brian Romney.

Gay glanced from his white face to the crowd gliding round the spot-lighted enclosure. The music was louder here. Her eyes came back to him. She shrugged:

"You certainly have speed but I'm not too bad myself. I suppose you came to eat me alive for what I said about Bee Ware. I'm sorry. I'll admit that I'm terribly ashamed of myself, if that will make you feel better."

His grip tightened. His eyes scorched down into her heart.

"Didn't know you said anything about Bee. You called me 'darling,' didn't you? Well, I'm here to tell you once and for all that I won't be called darling by you in that mocking tone."

His icy voice roused the little demon which had taken possession of her when she had seen Bee Ware clinging to him. Her laugh was a derisive tinkle.

"No? What are you going to do about it?"

His eyes were points of light in his stony face. He caught her in his arms and kissed her till she struggled for breath.

"That's what I'm going to do about it!" he said in a controlled voice more deadly than one which slashed.

His answer loosed a primitive self, a person she never before had met face to face. She felt like tearing, hurting, crushing.

"Is that the way you keep a promise?" she flamed. "Is that the way you kiss the irresistible Bee? That settles it."

"Settles what? I knew 'it' was settled when I saw Jim Seaverns kiss your hand. You'd better be getting back. Have you forgotten you are due at Sue's supper?"

"I've forgotten nothing! *Nothing*. Have you forgotten that you sent Bee Ware to me with that note to ask for your freedom? Coward! Didn't dare ask for it yourself."

"What do you mean? What note?"

He caught her shoulder in a grip which should have crushed the bone. His face was white as he repeated:

"What do you mean? What didn't I dare?"

"Pretending to forget, aren't you? Let me go!" She wrenched free. Waved to the man speeding toward her.

"Here I am, Jim!"

"What's the trouble? Was that Romney holding you?" Brian heard a voice demand before he turned and sped away.

Back and forth, back and forth he skated. Scrolling over and over the most difficult figures he knew, trying to rid his mind of the picture of Gay, trying to deafen his ears to her voice as she had called him "Coward!"

She had accused him of sending Bee Ware to her with a note? What note? He never had written a word to the woman that couldn't have been read from the housetops. Had Bee's treachery been behind Gay's "I'm through, Brian"? He'd have the truth about that before another twenty-four hours had passed.

Perhaps though, it had been merely Gay's excuse for securing her own freedom. The afternoon she had returned to Rosewynne she had said she loved Jim Seaverns and intended to marry him.

His heart felt as if it had been shredded to tatters, aching, burning tatters. In the distance the crowd was gliding to the music of "How Dry I am," under a multitude of heavenly stars which the glare of earthly flood lights faded to white gold.

Lights in the boathouse twinkled an invitation. The members and their guests who were not going on to Sue Dubois' would be warming up there with something to drink and eat. He would remain at the dark end of the pond until there was no chance of meeting Bee Ware. The next time he saw her he would have a question to ask that he would make her answer; it couldn't be done in a crowd. Until tonight he had not seen her since in the library at Rosewynne he had roughly ordered her to "Get out!" when Gay had crumpled on the threshold. He had been furious at her intimation that he had been kissing her, he who wanted to kiss only one woman in the world—one woman who loved Jim Seaverns and "intended" to marry him.

Well, he had kissed her. He had broken his promise. He had boasted to Major Bill that he had learned to curb his quick temper, but the sight of Seaverns kissing her hand, his own infuriated impatience at Bee Ware's clinging, Gay's mocking *darling*, the exquisite grace of her as she had whirled away, had been sparks to the dynamite which had blown the lid off his control. The events of the last hour on top of the strain of expecting that at any moment the roar and clang of the Plant machinery would be silenced had culminated in his outburst tonight which was calculated to end all outbursts between his wife and himself.

The skaters on the roughened ice had thinned. The bleachers and the ridge behind the wire fence were clear of spectators. The band was dragging out "Good Night, Ladies." He wouldn't return to the boathouse for his car until the floods had been turned off the pond. The moon was all the light he needed.

He turned his back on the music. The blades of his skates sang as he struck off toward the upper end of the pond. He was expected at Sue's for supper, but he was not going. Gay's accusation had left his heart and mind in a tumult. Besides, Dubois was a traitor and a cad. Louis would have to explain his finger prints on that hunk of clay-covered iron before he would accept his hospitality. Who had thrown it through the tower window? Sam had not yet matched up the second set of finger prints. Until he had, Louis was not to suspect that he was known to be linked up with it.

His thoughts snapped back to Gay like steel to magnet. He would skate until he was so tired he would drop to sleep as soon as he tumbled into bed. He wouldn't take the chance of lying awake tonight, not with his blood still racing from the feel of her mouth under his, the fury of her voice still echoing in his mind. Would he be aware of that all the rest of his life?

The rest of his life! That might mean years and years without her. No wonder she had stopped loving him. No wonder she had believed any lie that had been told her. What had he brought to their marriage? Love? Passion? Companionship? Money? Yes. Understanding of the seriousness of the contract into which he and she had entered "in the sight of God"? Common sense? Selflessness? Tact? Sacrifice? No.

He dropped to the bank to tighten a boot lace. A touch on his shoulder brought him to his feet. His heart tore up its roots and mounted to his throat. Two hideous creatures stood behind him. Great round yellow eyes blinked on and off. Owls! Horned owls!

XIX

GAY COULDN'T quite remember the sequence of events after she sped away from Brian. Jim had been with her. He had roughly accused her of loving her husband. Pity he hadn't heard her call Brian "coward." She hadn't meant to do that, had not intended ever to let him know about the note Bee Ware had shown her, but when he had kissed her, not as if he loved her, but as if he wanted to hurt her cruelly, she had been mad with the pain of it. How he must detest her to have done that.

Sitting beside taciturn Tim on the way home, while she changed her frock at Rosewynne, her mind swirled in reckless disorder. Major Bill, grave and preoccupied, was waiting in the hall when she came down the stairs in a lustrous satin gown, which shaded from cool silver at the deep and lovely neckline to glowing blue at the hem of the sweeping skirt.

"I waited to take you to Sue's when I found that Brian had not returned from the Carnival," he explained as he held her gleaming lamé coat. "Ready, my dear? Let's go."

Seated beside her in the limousine as it sped along a smooth road under a purple dome pricked with a million stars, he roused himself from deep abstraction to say:

"You're playing with dynamite to encourage Jim Seaverns, my girl. Marching straight toward inevitable tragedy."

Surprise flushed Gay's face with hot color. Major Bill never before had spoken to her like that. Not a word of praise for her skating. Was he too beginning to dislike her? She had to swallow hard before she could release her voice.

"I can't see where tragedy comes in, if I love Jim enough to marry him when I am free. Haven't I a right to be happy?"

"Don't fool yourself. After a while will you be any happier with Seaverns than you were with Brian? Do you think marriage is all happiness? That it doesn't take effort and tolerance and eternal vigilance to make it a going concern? It has hours of sure-fire ecstasy, the next day it may seem unbearable. It doesn't remain tuned in on the honeymoon wave-length. It's a rich, exciting drama but—it's also a contract between faulty, passionate human beings, who clash and love, defy and surrender, suffer, forget and forgive. There are plenty of misfits and failures, but I was sure that you with your sensitivity and breeding would bring to marriage a rare intelligence and a love that would live and glow, would survive misfortune, illness, even death."

Gay clenched her hands hard and choked back a sob. Fierce, burning pride kept her from dropping her head to his shoulder and crying her heart out. She managed to say contemptuously:

"How about the sensitivity, breeding and rare intelligence your white-haired boy, Brian, might have brought to that same marriage?"

"Oh, Brian!" His voice was harsh with exasperation. "If Brian were only young enough I'd take him over my knee and thrash some sense into him. I had such hopes that you and he would make of marriage a high, beautiful relationship. Instead, you are just another couple who has failed. With which admission we'll bring my broadcast to a close. Don't answer, my dear. You may say something you'll be sorry for later. Here we are at Sue's."

If only he had not shut off her self-justification, had let her confess that, in the depths of her smarting, stinging consciousness, she knew he was right, Gay thought bitterly. Wasn't it her fault that Brian had stopped loving her? So many times she might have laughed off a hurt instead of turning frosty. "Just another couple who has failed." The words burned in her mind as if etched with a red-hot poker.

The Dubois guests were laughing, talking and sipping sherry as she paused on the threshold of the drawing-room. A mirrored wall reflected the fireplace tiled in green, the shiny chromium fender and andirons and the white fur rug; gave back the mirrored screen with ferns and pots of yellow chrysanthemums between its folds and a patch of starry sky beyond the long windows. The flames of candles in old silver sticks were repeated a hundred times in the mirrored furniture, accessories and trimmings.

"Here she is!" someone shouted.

Mac tucked Gay's hand under his arm and drew her forward. "Ladies and gentlemen I have the honor to present—"

They interrupted his pompous announcement by crowding round her, women in colorful evening frocks, men in dinner clothes to which they had changed from skating regalia at their homes before coming on to supper. Their enthusiasm eased the ache of Gay's heart.

"Thanks a million but save some of this heady praise for Jim Seaverns," she protested smiling. "He was the headliner of the evening. Where is he?"

"Upstairs changing. He came in looking white as a death's head," Sue Dubois shrilled. "I wonder what ghost of his past stalked him tonight. Where's Bee Ware? The answer to that is, where's Brian?" she concluded with hateful meaning.

Mac's look should have shriveled her.

"I'll bet Bee Ware had to change that fire-engine-red costume of hers," he grinned. "Tonight she must have realized the truth of the old saw, 'the hardest thing about learning to skate is the ice.' Every time I looked at her she was clinging to the bosom of the pond."

Louis Dubois, slightly unsteady, appeared in the doorway. His wife exclaimed shrilly:

"Louis! Where have you been? Did that New York man keep you all this time?"

"He and others." He offered his arm to Gay:

"May I have the honor of taking in the star—"

"St—ar of the e—e—evening
Beautiful, beauti—ful star."

Sam Romney paraphrased the lines from "Alice" in a melting baritone.

His host regarded him with a bleak and ugly glare before he led Gay to the sun porch which opened from the dining-room. Three sides of it were walled with thick bubbled-glass bricks and the fourth with windows which extended from ceiling to floor.

Perhaps she had been unwise to persuade Mac and Sam against their heated protests to come here tonight, she reflected in a determined effort to push Brian out of her mind and keep him out. But, knowing how Major Bill deplored strife among the cousins, she had backed up Jane and Lucie when they had argued to their husbands that the family must appear at Sue's party. It was a Romney custom for the grown-ups to dine at Rosewynne on Thanksgiving eve. With that festivity but ten days ahead, Sue would make the occasion a nightmare if they didn't attend her after-Carnival supper. They had come. So what?

"What are you doing all by your lonesome?" Mac demanded as he loomed over her.

"Louis is getting me something to eat. I didn't want to

come here with him, he has had too much to drink, but Sue had her baleful eye on us and I didn't dare refuse for fear she would make an issue of it. Thus a sharp-tongued woman does make cowards of us all. That gem of thought is adapted from one William Shakespeare, not from your idol, Mr. Dickens, in case you care, Mac."

"Glad you told me. I was getting ready to memorize it. You're a push-over on the light touch, aren't you, gal? Sam's got it, too."

"Why not? It has been known to turn gloom to sunshine just as a touch of comedy often has saved a perilous situation from near-tragedy." If only she had put into practice what she was preaching, she thought bitterly.

"You've said it. Laugh it off. You were a knockout tonight, Gay. You'll have a swell press in the morning. I haven't been in this house since Sue had it done over. Swank and ultra-modern as it is, I prefer the atmosphere of tradition at Rose-wynne and Dingley Dell."

"So do I. Come nearer, Mac. I want to tell you something. Quick! Before Louis comes back!"

He slid from the arm of the U-shaped couch to a seat beside her. With her eyes on the dining-room door she told him briefly of Tim's troubled question at the garage. She concluded:

"I know he has been appointed a sort of bodyguard for me, though I'm not supposed to suspect it. Sounds as if he were being bribed to do something dishonorable, doesn't it? Don't you think Brian ought to know?"

"Sure he ought to know. It's possible that Eddie Dobson has Tim under pay. The Romney Manufacturing Company is in for a showdown, more likely a shutdown. We're holding our breaths expecting the lightning to strike at any moment. Eddie the Great Lover has gnawed his rope. Gave us his ultimatum the other day. We have it on good authority—Louis himself—that Dubois is in sympathy with him. Sue intends to make her husband president of the Company and indications are that she doesn't care how she brings it off. That's one reason Sam and I fought like steers against coming here tonight but you and the girls insisted and here we are. Where's Brian? Couldn't you make him come after putting the thumbscrews on Sam and me?"

"Let's you and I not pretend, Mac. You know I can't make Brian do anything. He h—hates me and now Major Bill—"

Gay's voice broke. Mac regarded her in shocked surprise.

"Hey! What's all this? Got an acute attack of letdown jitters after your corking performance at the Carnival? You're not going to cry are you—here?"

His horrified voice restored Gay's self-control.

"Of course I'm not going to cry—I'd choose a more responsive shoulder than yours on which to sob out my troubles. Join us, Jane," Gay invited as Mac's wife with a plate in her hand appeared in the doorway. "You're a dream in that frock, a delectable pink and violet dream, isn't she, Mac?"

"She is," Mac responded with convincing heartiness.

"I've caught you twosing, Mackensie Romney, you can't get away with it by flattering me," Jane accused gaily. "That I should live to see it! I'm knocked in a heap."

Mac's color deepened. At the imminent risk of upsetting the plate of salad, he caught her in one arm.

"Jealous, Janey?" he asked wistfully.

"Old mind-reader!" she accused and rubbed her sleek dark head against his sleeve.

The unexpected sweetness of her voice tightened Gay's throat. She thought—I may be a total loss at marriage and I may have made a mistake when I persuaded Mac and Sam to come here tonight, but not when I sidetracked Jane's plan to meet Louis in New York.

Dubois appeared with a waitress carrying a loaded tray. He wavered slightly in his approach.

"Here you are." Unsteadily he drew a small table in front of Gay. "Set it there. Hope I've brought everything you like. You said you were hungry."

"Hungry, but not starving, Louis. There is enough on that tray for a dozen. That lobster salad is the answer to a gourmet's prayer and Sue's Parkerhouse rolls melt in one's mouth. A mushroom and sweetbread *pâté!* Looks luscious. Take away the champagne cup, please, I prefer coffee, hot and fragrant."

"I'll change it," Mac picked up the glass. "Come on, Janey. Feed the brute. You know my disposition cracks when I'm hungry."

Louis Dubois' eyes followed Mac and his wife as they entered the dining-room. Gay watched them go with a sense of panic. Hadn't Mac noticed Louis' unsteadiness?

"Putting on a devotion act, aren't they?"

"Don't sneer at devotion, Louis. Especially when it's the real thing. Jane and Mac are terribly in love."

"Oh yeah! Is that why she made a date with me in New

York and never showed up while I hung round waiting for her? Luckily I had another string to my bow. You're telling me she's in love with that guy!"

He seated himself close beside her.

"Why am I wasting a minute on the Mac Romneys when for the first time since your return to Rosewynne I'm alone with you? Don't move away! I'm crazy about you, Gay. Have been from the moment I met you. You didn't mean it, did you, when you said that night at the Dobsons' that you detested me? I don't believe it. Tonight your beauty tore me to pieces. You don't care for Brian. You can't fool me with your devoted wife act. I wasn't born yesterday. I hate Sue. We'll junk them and then—"

Emotion and alcohol choked his voice. Horrified by the white distortion of his face Gay shivered. Fierce passion had torn away the superficial polish his wife's money had laid over an ordinary, vicious and insufferable person. What should she do? If she left him abruptly he was tight enough to risk making a scene, he wouldn't do it if he were sober— there was too much to lose if his wife heard him. Why didn't someone come? In the dining-room she could see the flickering scarlet and blue flames of crêpes Suzettes. From the distant radio drifted the rhythmic music from some supper club and a woman's husky voice singing of love and a broken heart.

"Well?" demanded Dubois.

"You've had too much champagne cup, Louis. You'll regret this when you're sober. Don't try to be melodramatic because you're just screamingly fun—ny." Gay's ripple of amusement was calculated to throw cold water on his ardor. It did.

"Laughing at me, aren't you?" he sulked. "Never have thought me fit even to tie the shoes of the great Romneys, have you? Where's your model Brian tonight? He's probably—" he caught back the next word and substituted a tipsy chuckle. Went on:

"Thinks my house isn't good enough for him, I suppose? I'll show him. Before long I'll be president of the Romney Manufacturing Company and then—"

He rose unsteadily as William Romney approached with Mac.

"My dear, we must go at once." The Major's face was white. He spoke to Gay without looking at Dubois.

"What's happened, Major Bill—? Brian? Is Brian—?" Gay's voice caught in a choked whisper. Something crashed inside her. She looked appealingly from him to Mac, to Dubois. Louis' expression steadied her. His eyes were aflame with malicious eagerness, his skin was the ghastly color of the face of a girl she had once seen under a green umbrella.

"What has happened, Major Bill?" he asked with exaggerated concern.

White to the lips William Romney looked back at him. "You're asking me? As if you didn't know! Come, Gay."

XX

BRIAN ROMNEY glanced from one blinking-eyed horror to the other standing rigid with menace, with deadly purpose, each side of him. He thought of the clay-covered hunk of iron marked with the head of a horned owl. Had the man behind one of those masks hurled it? Unsuccessful in that attempt to injure him, was kidnaping the next move? No wonder Gay had been terrified when a creature like one of these had tried to hold her up.

A pair of shoes dropped from a huge brown wing.

"Put 'em on!" The falsetto voice squeaked from the taller of the two. "You're goin' places. We can get you 'long faster without skates."

Brian measured the distance to the beam-lighted enclosure where skaters still glided. Should he trip these creatures and dash for the boathouse? No. If he succeeded in breaking away he might never know who was behind the scheme to kidnap Gay and himself. Shrouded as the shorter "owl" was in hideous regalia there had been something vaguely familiar in the way he had stepped forward. Could it be Eddie Dobson? The situation smacked of his theatric mumbo jumbo. He had threatened that night in the library. "If you don't give me back my job you'll be sorry." He wouldn't break away. He would see this thing through and Eddie would be the "sorry" one.

"Goin' to take off them skates or will I do it for yer?"

"Thanks so much, but I'll do it myself," Brian replied to the squeaked threat.

He dropped to the bank where the mill stream entered

the pond, choked back a startled exclamation as he picked up a shoe. It was one of a pair he had given Tim O'Brien to put in his locker at the boathouse when he had changed to skating boots! How had these men—

Suspicion seared his mind. Tim! Tim a traitor! Tim in whose care he had placed Gay! Was he planning to give her up as he had the shoes? No matter if he never found out who these creatures were, he wouldn't go with them.

He must find Gay. Perhaps already she was— He forced his imagination to heel. Not a second to think of what might happen to her. Every thread of his mind must be on making his getaway. He fumbled with the lacing of his boot.

"Hang this thing, it knots!" he gritted between clenched teeth.

"I'll cut it!" the big owl squeaked and produced a wicked-looking knife.

"That's an idea," Brian agreed and struggled to keep his voice cool and detached. "But take a pointer from me—while you're cutting the laces, your pal had better watch the boathouse. I'm expected there for supper. If I don't come soon my friends and the five plain-clothes men hired to check up on the crowd will be looking for me. If they should even see you holding me up here—well, it's the chair or life for kidnaping, you know." Brian was proud of the lightness of the last suggestion.

The big owl grunted and looked uneasily toward the lights.

"Shut your mouth. Who's kidnapin'?" He poked his companion. "Keep watch of that boathouse while I cut off his boot."

"*Mais oui!*"

The shorter owl set his head nodding like a mandarin and turned his back.

Lavalle speaking! Lavalle whom he had discharged! Who was the other? Brian asked himself and tensed for a spring.

"Stick out that foot, you—"

The foot stuck out with speed and force. The skate blade caught the bending owl full in the blinking eyes. Backward he crashed. Ice crackled. Brian leaped on the shorter creature. He went down with a sickening crunch.

Brian swung clear of the cursing, groaning mass. Struck off in swift curves. He swirled. Sped. Swung. Whine of blades behind him. The owls were on skates! Good God! The pond was big as an ocean! Almost at the enclosure! Two minutes more and he'd be safe! What in thunder—

His left skate turned under him! Fumbling with the boot

lace had loosened it. He stumbled. Looking over his shoulder. Four round yellow lights blinking on and off! Eyes! Coming! Coming fast! He dropped to one knee. His icy hands were numb. He set his teeth. Forced his fingers to steadiness. Tied the lacing. Swept forward. Shouted.

"Hold the light! I'm coming," and in an instant more was at the boathouse. He looked back. As far as he could see the pond was clear. No sign of the creatures. They must have switched off the light behind those huge eyes.

Pity he hadn't grabbed his shoes, he thought, as avoiding the path which led from the pond to the boathouse he stumbled, scraped, smashed through shrubs to the place where he had parked his convertible. Perhaps he wouldn't find that. Perhaps—

There it was. Someone in it! Smoking. A pal of the two he had left behind him? He approached cautiously. The man at the wheel leaned out.

"Well, for the love of Mike! Brian! Where do you think you are? On a skating rink?"

"Mac! How did you know where I was?"

"Hop in! Quick!" As Brian sank to the seat beside him and the car shot ahead Mac explained in a voice rough with excitement:

"Couldn't locate you. Had a flash of intelligence. Phoned the boathouse from Sue's. Asked if your convertible was still here. It was. Sam drove me over. Got bad news for you."

"Gay? Gay? Did they get her?"

"Hey! What's the matter? Sit still! Got the jitters? Gay's with Major Bill. The fires are out at the Plant! That's my bedtime story."

"My God! Is that all?"

The blood flowed through Brian's veins again. Gay was safe. Nothing else mattered.

"All! All! What do you want? Isn't that the opening gun of the walkout? Isn't that enough to stop production?"

"Yes. Yes. But, you see, Mac—"

He told of the hold-up on the pond by the hideous creatures, of the surprising appearance of the shoes he had left in Tim O'Brien's care, of his conviction that Tim had proved traitor, of his agony of fear for Gay's safety.

"I'll bet that explains his uneasy conscience."

Mac repeated what Gay had told him of Tim's questions. He awkwardly patted Brian's knee.

"Snap out of it, stout fella. We'll find out what it's all about. Gay's okay. The only danger she was up against was having her host tumble into her lap at supper. Louis came in late with a fine edge on. It isn't like him, he's too cautious. Must have had something on his mind."

"Then you went to Sue's for supper?"

"Sure. Sam and I walked up to the firing line like perfect little gentlemen. The girls made us."

"How did you hear about the Plant?"

"Someone phoned Major Bill. I went to the sunroom with him to find Gay. If you'd seen her face when she whispered 'Brian? Is Brian hurt?' you'd be beating a tom-tom for joy. Must be great to have your wife so crazy about you."

"Gay! Crazy about me! You're spoofing. You know better than that, Mac. Where's Sam?"

"After he left me here he made a beeline for Rosewynne. He's sure the Brown Owls are mixed up in the Plant walkout. He's matched the second set of finger prints on that hunk of clay-covered iron."

"Whose are they?"

"Lavalle's, and Dubois' were the others."

"What a team! The Frenchman was one of the two who held me up at the pond."

"It's darned lucky you broke away. Now when Sam finds out who frightened Gay—he's working on it—he'll be all set to spring his trap. Look! As long as I can remember I've seen a pink haze above the furnaces of the Plant; now there's hardly a glow. That's calculated to make Great-Grandfather Romney shiver in his grave. Darn it all it—it hurts."

"It does, infernally, but it has come. I've been cock-eyed waiting for the shell to burst. Now we're up against a situation we can get our teeth into. Don't let a word of what happened on the pond leak out, Mac."

At Rosewynne Sampson flung open the door. His eyes were enormous, his face was the curious pasty color of Negroid skin from which the blood has been drained.

"You know what done happen, young gent'men?" he whispered hoarsely.

"Yes. Fires out at the Plant. Where's Major Bill?" Brian clanked across the flagged floor on skate blades to the tower steps and began to unlace his boots.

"He's gone to de Plant. Let me do that, Mr. Brian."

"No, Sampson. Pick up some flashlights while I'm putting on my shoes. Does Jane know where you are, Mac?"

"Yes. I told her that Sam and I had business with the Major—suggested that she and Lucie fade away together from

Sue's party without letting anyone know their husbands had gone ahead. Get a move on, stout fella."

"Where's Mrs. Brian, Sampson?"

The butler stopped fumbling in the drawer of the carved Italian commode.

"She an' Madam Wainwright an' Mr. Sam, dey gone along with Major Willum."

"To the Plant! Mac, did you hear that? Major Bill's crazy to take those women there tonight."

"Perhaps he couldn't help himself. Gay has a way with her and it would take a harder-boiled lad than our Major to wear down Cassie the Battle-Ax when she gets her mind set. Perhaps she came along a remedy to quiet the strikers' nerves. Get going! Don't you want to see what's happened to the business your great-grandfather founded?"

Brian thought of Mac's question as they stopped the convertible in the shadow of a skeleton tree opposite the Administration Building. Was the grand old business of the Romney Manufacturing Company already on the toboggan?

Mac grabbed his arm.

"Look! On the East Gate! Can you read it? Don't flash a light! Pickets may be watching for us!"

Brian thrust the electric torch back into his pocket. The moon had dropped behind the tree tops but there was still light enough for him to read the great black letters on the two white placards on the double gate.

THIS PLANT UNFAIR
TO
EMPLOYEES

"Unfair! With our bonuses, hospital, nurses, gymnasium, playgrounds, pensions and now the training school! Drive round the outside of the yard, Mac. Go slow," Brian ordered gruffly.

As the car circled the iron railing the two men looked down the radiating streets. Not a light visible in the white cottages. Not a gleam in the factory buildings. Stillness brooded over the place like a spell. On the North and South gates white placards announced:

THERE IS
A
STRIKE ON

The West Gate repeated the message of the East Gate:

THIS PLANT UNFAIR
TO
EMPLOYEES

Mac relieved his pent-up excitement in a long, low whistle.

"Kind of gets you, doesn't it? Spooky. What? Not a sign of life. No pickets—visible. What do you make of it, Brian?"

"Perhaps they're hidden behind trees. Waiting to pop out if we make a move. We'll disappoint them. We'll make no move tonight. Even now I can't believe it."

"Where do we go from here? Had we better snoop around the town?"

Brian looked toward the twinkling lights of the small thriving city, whose business activities and prosperity were founded on and to a large degree supported by the activities and prosperity of the Plant.

"No. I wonder what the city fathers will think of this. It will put a crimp in their upward and onward march. Major Bill— Where is Major Bill, Mac? Where are Gay, Aunt Cass, Sam? You don't suppose they've been—"

"Hey, don't go haywire! They've probably taken a look-see and gone home."

"Step on the gas. If they are not at Rosewynne—" Brian left the sentence unfinished to plunge at once into plans of what was to be done if they were not there.

William Romney was in his accustomed chair by the fire, Sam was perched on an arm of the broad couch when Mac and Brian burst into the library at Rosewynne.

"I told you they were safe," gasped Mac breathless from his run up the steps.

"Where's Gay?" Brian demanded. Imagination had stalked him with every turn of the car's wheels.

"In her room. You're white as a sheet, where'd you think she was, boy?"

Brian drew a hand across his eyes.

"Guess I haven't been thinking, Major Bill. Sampson told me that she and Aunt Cass went to the Plant with you and when we didn't see you there— Why live that over again? You're all safe." He flung himself into a chair. "Now what do we do?"

TODAY IS YOURS   143

They discussed and argued, planned and replanned. The clock in the hall put on its musical Westminster-chime act and sonorously struck two. Brian stopped his restless pacing and, back to the mantel, regarded his uncle and cousins. Was his face as lined and white as their faces? The Major's tired eyes roused him to fury. He had been unfailingly fair and considerate of his workers and how were they repaying him? That line of thought wouldn't get him anywhere. Straight, clear, constructive thinking was what was needed. He said slowly, as if each one of them had not already said it in different words:—

"We've got to pull off a peaceable settlement of this thing —no violence—without knuckling to Eddie Dobson. If we don't, outside labor organizations will butt in or we'll have the Conciliators of the State Labor Department on our backs. We don't want either. It's a family fight and we'll keep it so. We've always been friends with our workers. They're seeing crooked. They'll snap out of it. We won't admit to anyone that it is serious. We'll—"

"Laugh it off? Oh yeah! Well, Gay's method won't work here, worse luck," Mac predicted gruffly.

Sam, who sprawled wearily in his chair, sat up.

"What do you mean, 'Gay's method'?" he demanded.

"She was sort of low tonight and then shot out of it with a sparkle, you know the way she has, and when I kidded her and said she was a push-over on the light touch, she came back with:

"'Why not? It has been known to turn gloom to sunshine just as a touch of comedy often has saved a perilous situation from near-tragedy.'"

"A touch of comedy," Brian repeated thoughtfully, then let out a whoop, tempered to the hour and a supposedly sleeping household.

"I've got it! I've got it!"

"Well, if you ask me, you've got the heebie-jeebies, grinning like a Cheshire cat when we're in such a mess."

"Don't mind Mac's crabbing, Brian, he's always grumpy if his sleep is cut. Spill your plan, and spill it quick," Sam urged.

"If you see any possibility of a way out of this mix-up, boy, tell us," William Romney prodded eagerly.

Brian's nerves tingled, his heart pounded. Had he found a way out? His low voice vibrated as he outlined his plan.

"What do you think of it?" he asked.

Mac's excitement exploded in a guffaw. "It's a knock-out."

"If it works," William Romney approved dubiously. "It will take time to prepare for it."

"All the more dramatic when we pull it off. I'm all for it," chuckled Sam.

"It will take only time enough to let the strikers think we're licked, Major Bill," Brian reassured. "Sit down, all of you, while we make a list of the men we'll ask to help. Gosh, I've got another hunch. Wonderful how an idea grows. Know any newspaper editors, Sam?"

"What do you mean, know 'em? If you mean well enough for them to buy one of my mystery masterpieces, I don't. If on the other hand you mean well enough for them to call me 'Old Sam,' I do. What's on your mind?"

"Front-page publicity for our side."

Brian elaborated his idea. Even William Romney, realizing, as his nephews could not, what this strike might mean to the business to which he had devoted years and energy and money, joined in the laugh which followed.

Gay heard it. She had been tense since her hurried departure from Sue's. She couldn't forget the feel of Brian's mouth on hers, nor his eyes when he had blazed, "What didn't I dare?" After Major Bill's stern announcement in Sue's sun porch, "My dear, we must go at once!" she had had an instant of terror. If anything had happened to Brian— She tried to rebuild her defenses against him with the memory of his note to Bee. She couldn't. It did a complete fade-out. She had the feeling that she was back from a far country, a far, lonely country.

In a wave-green lounge coat she snapped on the light in her boudoir and cautiously set the hall door ajar. Voices in the hall. Chuckles. What did it mean? Weren't the Romneys anxious about the strike? Didn't they *care?*

She rested her head against the crack. Listened. Muffled good-nights. The front door closing. Mac and Sam leaving? The diminishing purr of a motor. Major Bill's voice in the hall. She would ask him if—

"Good night, Major Bill. Don't worry. We've got 'em licked."

"Good night, boy. I hope we have."

Brian was at home. Safe. The Major never called his other nephews "boy."

Gay stole to the gallery and looked down. Brian was crossing the hall to the tower door. Dreamily, softly, he was whistling the Beautiful Blue Danube.

Back in her boudoir she frowned incredulously at the look-ing-glass girl.

"A strike on and he's whistling. *Whistling!* Just what do you make of that?" she demanded.

XXI

FOR TWO DAYS pickets from twenty-five to fifty in num-ber had patrolled the road which encircled the Plant yard and the broader highway which led to the city. Hoisted placards proclaimed that a strike was on. Others demanded in even larger letters:

JOIN US
AND
HELP WIN

and a few informed:

WE ARE STRIKING
FOR
EDDIE DOBSON

During that time the Romneys had made no attempt to enter the yard by the placarded gates. Brian or Mac or Sam occasionally had walked through the streets. Their appear-ance had excited no demonstration except when a nonstriker would approach to assure them of his loyalty. Then he would be seized by pickets and dragged off. Not too rough-ly handled while he remained in sight.

The city fathers had called in a body at Rosewynne to offer police protection. With his uncle and cousins standing behind him in the library, Brian replied:

"We don't want your help at the Plant. We can handle this ourselves, but what we do want, is to have every road which leads to it policed and if a member of an outside organization of any kind appears, he is to be turned back. We won't permit parasites. The property is ours. We have every legal right to say who shall step on it. This is purely a family fight and we won't stand for outside interference. Do you get that?"

They did. They departed with the assurance that no stranger, no matter how innocent his errand, would be permitted to approach the Plant. The leader, who had the body of a jockey and the head of a Napoleon of finance, had paused at the door to suggest:

"Don't try to paddle your own canoe too long, Mr. Romney. The strikers and nonstrikers are good-natured enough now, but they're likely to get ugly if their food lines are cut, if that's the remedy you have up your sleeve."

The warning recurred to Brian as at a few moments before nine o'clock, on the third morning of the strike, he approached the gate in front of the Administration Building. Cutting food lines was not the owners' plan. He was sure they had a better one for breaking this strike. He glanced at his wrist watch. In five minutes the test would come.

An Indian-summer day left dozing behind in the procession of November days had suddenly waked up and made itself felt. Men were topcoatless; heads were hatless; bees were tumbling out of hives. Brian glanced at the cloudless sky. High against the clear blue three large hawks circled slowly southward. On the tiptop of a tall oak a lone crow perched like a shiny black enamel sentinel. The warm sun was baking the scent of balsam from dark green trees and only a week ago there had been thick ice for the Carnival.

The Carnival! Memory surged through him like unbearable physical pain. No matter what you did, somehow, sometime, you paid for it. Gay had barely spoken to him since he had caught her in his arms and roughly kissed her. For a few hours after Mac had told him of her concern for his safety his spirit had spread wings of hope; that night, even with the strike presenting its pressing problems, he had gone to his room whistling. Those wings had folded tight again during the last two days. She had said that Bee Ware had shown her a note in which he asked for his freedom. How could she believe it? How— He'd better ring off on that line of thought. He must keep his mind clear for what was ahead. After this mess was behind him he could tackle his personal problems, not before.

A hand gripped his arm. "Watch your step, sir!"

A striker had flung himself at Brian's feet. Between him and the gate others dropped like a row of cardboard soldiers in a breeze. Beyond them inside the yard girls and women, arms locked in arms, made a living barricade against the iron railing.

"Thanks, Ferguson," Brian answered the gaunt foreman's

muffled warning. "Had I stepped on him it would have started a riot, I presume. Beat it! I know you're loyal to us. Here comes the Dictator. Better not let him see you talking to me."

The foreman melted into the crowd which gathered as Eddie Dobson mounted a chair. His skin was chalky in contrast to his heavy red sweater. His rowdy eyes roamed over the faces confronting him. Someone set up an amplifier. In a high, shrill voice he began to harangue his audience.

Hat pulled low over his eyes Brian listened, listened not only to the voice, but for the sound which would announce the opening of the employers' campaign to end the strike. He glanced at his watch again. One minute more. He forced his attention to the man on the chair. He'd have to hand it to Eddie for his flow of language. He couldn't believe this wild stuff he was saying, but where would his argument be without its red-hot charges, its bluster, its venom? Nowhere. It was apparent that Dobson was desperate.

Who the dickens was shouldering through the crowd? It was not—it couldn't be! It was Aunt Cass!

For an incredulous instant Brian stared at the stiff, straight, gray-clad woman striding across the narrow space which separated the speaker from his listeners. He saw Dobson's jaw drop and waggle in surprise; saw Cassie Wainwright grab his red sweater and yank him from the chair; as in a nightmare saw her mount in his place. Heard her voice, amplified a hundred per cent., accuse:

"Fools! Fools! Don't you know when you're well off? Don't you know—"

Hoots of derision from pickets and strikers, catcalls from the women behind the iron fence roused Brian from his coma of amazement. He dashed forward. Pulled her down.

With his arm about her he faced the menacing rumble of the glowering crowd and reflected that it wasn't a pretty situation for a woman. There was a glint of glass in upraised fists—that would be bottles suddenly produced from pockets —bricks and sticks and stones in infinite variety. Then he looked straight into Eddie Dobson's anger-glazed eyes and reflected that it wasn't an especially pretty situation for himself. Where were Mac and Sam and the others? Time for them. Why didn't they come? Could he hold back this threatening crowd until they appeared?

"Break it up, boys! Break it up!" he shouted. "You haven't gone so cock-eyed that you'd fight an old woman, have you?"

"Brian Romney! Don't you dare call me an old—"

A bugle interrupted Cassie Wainwright's furious protest. High and clear it sounded assembly in an ineffable blend of music and command. Zero hour.

"Troops? Troops?" The word soughed through the air as the crowd pushed, stumbled and surged toward the highway. Only Eddie Dobson stood his ground. Gaunt, haggard, threatening, he faced Brian who still gripped Cassie Wainwright in one arm.

"So you had to call in the troops! 'Fraid of us, aren't you?" he sneered.

Even in this moment, which he knew to be a crisis in his life and the life of the business his great-grandfather had conceived and cherished, anticipation of what was ahead stirred a spring of laughter deep in Brian's spirit and twitched at his lips.

"Not afraid of you, Eddie. A little sorry for you, that's all."

With a muttered threat Dobson turned away. Brian said sternly:

"Look here, Aunt Cass. You must get out of this. I'm not looking for trouble, but you never can tell which way a crowd will jump. We're banking on its jumping our way but if it doesn't—it may mean a mix-up. I ought to join Mac and Sam but I can't leave you alone after your attack on Dobson."

"Go right along. Don't worry about me, Brian. I walked here. I'll walk back."

"Does Gay know you came?"

"She does not. You left orders that the Romney women were to stay at home, didn't you? I'm not a Romney and here I am and I'm staying too."

"Aunt Cass!" Brian made a futile grab for her but she disappeared in the milling crowd. He took a roundabout course to the highway.

Here they came! Marching men in a column of fours. Brian's throat tightened. He hadn't realized that the Romneys had so many friends in the community. Of the hundred marching, only the department heads were employees of the Plant. They were dressed as alike as a battalion of soldiers except that their uniform was a gray serge sack suit, blue shirt and gray Fedora slanted over one eye at a snappy angle. There was a curious bulge in the left-hand pocket of each sack coat.

"A touch of comedy often has saved a perilous situation from near-tragedy," Gay had said. If only it would work this time. It was a gamble to try it, of course, but it must work. It must, Brian told himself passionately. Even if it didn't it was worth trying, anything was worth trying which would avert a prolonged war with their workers.

Sam Romney came first swinging a drum major's baton. He was followed by three men supporting a huge placard with the inscription:

THIS STRIKE IS
UNFAIR
TO EMPLOYERS

Then came a band of twenty blowing lustily on wind instruments the quick-stepping notes of Yankee Doodle. Many feet in the crowd of onlookers, standing with backs turned to the Plant, kept time to the rhythm. After the musicians marched four men carrying banners which advised:

JOIN US
AND
HOLD YOUR JOB

Then came Mac, red-faced and short-breathed, whirling his drum major's baton as the band behind him played "Pack Up Your Troubles in Your Old Kit Bag and Smile! Smile! Smile!"

On and on they came. Rhythm of feet on the sun-patched road, blare of brass, beat of drums, the rippling splendor of the Stars and Stripes.

One banner proclaimed to the world:

WE DON'T WANT
EDDIE

The next asserted:

WE WON'T HAVE
EDDIE

Brian joined the last line. Behind it lumbered a sound wagon. Following that were automobiles packed with laughing, grinning photographers and newspaper men. They bulged over the doors. They balanced on the running boards. They perched on the hoods.

At first the strikers hooted. Then someone laughed and

shouted "Attaboy!" as Sam Romney gave his baton a dancing-dervish whirl. Brian watched the faces they passed. Some were ugly; the majority saw the humor of the situation. A man left the strikers and fell into step behind the last four. Another and then another. Each deserter was greeted with hoots and catcalls from the crowd he had left, but no missiles flew.

No violence to be feared as long as the majority smiled. Brian glanced at the bulge in the pocket of the gray coat beside him. Out of abundance of precaution each marcher had been provided with a tear-gas bomb for self-defense. He hoped they would not be needed.

Past one radiating street and then another marched the gray procession with bands playing, banners waving, the rumbling sound wagon, photographer- and reporter-laden cars trailing them. Older women peered from the windows of the spotless white cottages or stood on the steps and waved.

Back in the broad highway Sam Romney halted the column. The line broke into groups. He said in a low voice to Brian:

"The tail of this kite is lengthening."

"Yes. Two hundred men must have joined our procession. They jauntily thumbed their noses when the strikers hooted. If only we can keep this a comedy, put it across without a riot. If someone of our crowd doesn't get excited and let go a load of tear gas, I'm sure we'll get by."

From the watching crowd rose the strident cries of the pickets:

"There is a strike on!" "This Plant unfair to employees!" "Join us and help win!" And a shrill feminine chorus: "We want Eddie!"

Where was Eddie? How was he taking the desertion of his followers? Brian wondered. Then he saw him. Gaunt. Haggard. Eyes no longer rowdy. Haunted. He had stopped beside a photographer who was training a camera on a group of gray-clad men who were lighting cigarettes. Dobson caught the man's shoulder.

"What you doin' here? Those aren't the fellas you want! The strikers are behind you at the yard."

The man shook back a mop of hair, tawny and thick as the mane of the M. G. M. lion, grinned and waved an impatient hand.

"Oh yeah! Out of the way, bully boy, out of the way! My paper's not interested in strikers. Fed up on 'em!

What they're doing is old stuff but this, boy, oh boy, this is news! Red-hot news!"

Sam caught Brian's arm. "Look!"

Brian's eyes followed his to where three men had surrounded and were jostling one who had left their group and taken his place under a placard:

BE FAIR TO
EMPLOYERS

"Get going, Sam! Quick! Trouble's loose!"

"You're telling me!" Sam blew a long sharp blast on a whistle.

"Close up! Close up!" someone shouted.

Instantly the gray-coated men fell into the column of fours. Both bands burst into:

"Pack Up Your Troubles in Your Old Kit Bag and Smile! Smile! Smile!"

On they marched, gathering followers as they circled the yard. As Brian looked back he was reminded of the Pied Piper of Hamelin Town enchanting the children with his music as he led them to his cave.

The strikers watching them were no longer amused, they looked defeated, ugly. There had been more than one clenched fist as the column passed. The joke was wearing thin. Why didn't Sam start for home? Brian's nerves tightened. It had gone well so far. No use crowding their luck. Why didn't he go?

"Too late!" he muttered, as a bottle flew high and crashed to the road. Other missiles followed. Crackle. Click. Clatter. Clang. Crunch. Had Sam seen them? He couldn't hear with that band bleating directly behind him. He must get word to him. As he stepped out of line he saw Mac loping forward.

The bands stopped playing. The world was still as if holding its breath, as if every living thing in it were tense, ready to spring. Good Lord, why had Sam stopped? Brian saw the hand of the man next to him reach for his pocket. He gripped his arm.

"Hold everything. If you let that fly we'll have a riot on our hands!"

The column was moving! Not forward! Was Sam crazy? He was entering the road around the yard again. He was singing! Alone!

Brian swallowed hard as he marched forward to the Welsh tune Ton-Y-Botel and the words in Sam's rich baritone:

> "Once to every man and nation
> Comes the moment to decide,
> In the strife of Truth with Falsehood,
> For the good or evil side;
> Some great cause, God's new Messiah
> Offering each the bloom or blight,
> And the choice goes by forever
> 'Twixt that darkness and the light."

On marched the column. Men were deserting the troublemakers in bunches now as the leaders passed into the highway headed for Rosewynne. Hundreds of voices swelled in song:

> "And the choice goes by forever
> 'Twixt that darkness and the light."

Brian stepped aside to watch the men pass. He looked back. The girls and women inside the yard leaned against the iron railing. Their arms no longer interlocked.

Eddie Dobson stood in front of the East Gate surrounded by his pickets. He saw Brian and charged forward. He stopped within two feet of him. His face was ashy-pale. His eyes burned. His mouth worked.

"Think you've got me licked, don't you?" he sneered. "Well, it's between you and me now. I still have a card or two up my sleeve."

XXII

"GOING ABROAD, Major Bill!" Gay exclaimed incredulously. "What shall I do? I can't stay here at Rosewynne without you."

"You mean, you won't."

She had been snipping faded blossoms from the plants in the court when William Romney entered and made his announcement. She glanced over the feathery chrysanthemums, patches of marguerites, clumps of callas, and towering acacias, their varying shades of yellow turned to gold by the Midas touch of the morning sun streaming through the glass roof.

Her eyes came back and met the blue eyes regarding her with troubled intentness. With a surge of contrition she flung down the clipping shears and pulled off her gardening gloves. She slipped her hand under William Romney's arm and pressed her cheek against his tweed sleeve.

"I'm a selfish wretch to think first of myself. Of course you should get away. You rate a vacation if anyone in the world does. Let's sit on this marble bench while you tell me your plans. I love the warm, earthy smell, the sound of dripping water and the darting splashes of scarlet and gold in the pool."

"Stop and get your breath, my girl. I'm not leaving today."

"That's a relief, Major Willum. Your *au revoir*-but-not-good-by tone suggested that your departing plane already was whirling its propeller in the drive. Do Mac and Sam and —and Brian know your plans?"

"Not yet. I wanted to talk with you first. I have a guilty feeling that if I go I shall be letting you down. You agreed to stay at Rosewynne with Brian *and* me."

"The agreement was that I was to stay until Brian was 'well established,' until he could 'swing the job.' He has 'swung' it. The Plant won out on the strike, didn't it?"

"I don't like that word 'strike' applied to us. In our case it was not a conflict between labor and capital, it was a struggle between the common sense and loyalty of our workers and evil influences, Dobson and Dubois. We met it with your recipe for saving a perilous situation from near-tragedy by a touch of comedy. It worked. It brought the men to their senses and it resulted in the determination of the majority to possess their own souls. They sent a spokesman to us to say they were ashamed and sorry. Except for a few who stand by Dobson they'll be on their jobs next Monday. We're giving them time off with full pay till then."

"Do you anticipate trouble with Eddie?"

"He's quiet. Too quiet. I don't like it. He has a persecution complex. It's got him under control and it's a hard thing to beat."

"When you leave, Major Bill, I'll go traveling too. I'll trek to Reno and get a divorce."

"On what ground?"

"Does one have to have a 'ground' in Reno? Well, then, incompatibility. That will give Brian his freedom."

"Sure Brian wants his freedom?"

"I know he wants it. Apparently you didn't observe his devotion to Bee Ware the night of the Carnival or you wouldn't ask that question. When an expert skater like Brian will allow a woman to cling to him while she flounders round on the ice, that's love. I'm so sure he wants his freedom that he's going to get it. Then everybody will be happy. Bee Ware the Widow and—"

"Jim Seaverns? He is the real reason for your divorce, isn't he?"

"You're unfair, Major Bill. I haven't seen Jim since the Carnival and sometimes I think I don't want to see him again—ever. You may be sure of one thing—I won't, while I am legally Brian's wife."

"Sure of that? Don't make rash promises, my girl. Lucie wants to bring the twins to our Thanksgiving-eve dinner tonight."

His change of subject was so quick that it took Gay an instant to orient herself. Then she exclaimed:

"Those children! It's absurd."

"I tried to convey that idea tactfully but Lucie insisted that as they were the only Romney heirs of their generation, they should begin to observe family traditions. She reminded me that young Princess Elizabeth of England has been trained since infancy for future responsibilities."

"Prerogatives of royalty. It's ridiculous. I adore those twins, but from my previous experience I wouldn't put it past them to do something which will wreck your party. Does Sam approve?"

"Sam's a yes-man where Lucie is concerned. It was he who suggested that the family spend the night and that the children be put to bed here. I said a hearty 'yes' to that. It will mean that our contract game won't be broken up early. Sue Dubois' reaction to the plan will not be sunny. We'll be treated to a crackling display of verbal fireworks. However, we'll let the children come. Having broken the news of my contemplated outing to you, I'll get Brian's reaction. He's working in his bookroom. He had the Plant mail delivered here."

Gay went slowly up the stairs trying to get the confusion of her thoughts, her emotion which seemed to have constricted in one aching lump in her throat, under control, to stop the ceaseless repetition in her mind of Major Bill's contemptuous, "You are just another couple who has failed." Ten minutes ago she had seen nothing ahead but an endless procession of days tinged with heartache and self-accusation. In the drawing of a breath the pattern had been juggled into another and more complicated design. She had spoken of going to Reno as she might have said lightly, "I'm off to New York." It wouldn't be so easy as that.

As she entered her boudoir the poodle who had been absorbed in watching Madam Wainwright poke the logs in the fireplace dashed forward and thrust her long black nose into Gay's hand.

"Can't get this room warm," Cassie Wainwright complained. "A week ago the weather was so mild that the bees were flying from the hives. Today the thermometer registers ten degrees above." Her eyes sharpened. "What's the matter? You look as if you'd lost your last friend."

Gay regarded the mirror-girl in her navy wool frock with its white collar and belt who looked back at her from across the room.

"The corners of my mouth are turning down, aren't they? It's most unbecoming. I've had a shock. Major Bill is going abroad."

Still gripping the poker Cassie Wainwright seated herself stiffly on a chair beside the fireplace.

"Good idea. I'm going home day after tomorrow. You and Brian will have the house to yourselves. I've never approved of a young couple living with their elders. They should be able to agree and disagree and work out adjustments without an audience. The presence of a third person often magnifies into tragic dimensions little rifts which would have been laughed or kissed away if husband and wife had been alone. That's neither here nor there. Why shouldn't Major Romney take a vacation? Dobson the trouble-maker has quieted down, hasn't he?"

"At present, but something tells me he isn't beaten. Eddie has hated Brian since he warned Lena against him. Brian will fight him to a finish, his finish, I'm afraid. I'm sick about it."

She crossed to the window to avoid her aunt's boring eyes. Purple shadows were patching the hills and moving on as snowy fluffs of cloud were blown like feathers in a breeze between the wooded slope and the sun. Her throat felt as if clamped by a steel band as she watched an upside-down white-breasted nuthatch busily pecking at the bole of a silver birch. The poodle, perched on a chair, whined with desire to be out and at the bird.

"So, that's what's making the young man look as if he were headed straight for an old-fashioned decline." Cassie Wainwright's voice temporarily derailed Gay's train of thought.

"What young man?" she demanded.

"Brian, of course. He's lost pounds these last few weeks and most of his bronze. He's as pale and peaked as Tim O'Brien, but not from the same cause. Something is gnawing at Tim's conscience. Ever thought what a curious thing conscience is? It is one more proof of the Divinity in us, else why do hardened criminals confess their sins? That's neither here nor there. When I came into this room a few minutes ago Tim was filling the wood box and Lena was whispering to him. They were both white as ghosts."

Startled, Gay remembered her conclusion that Tim would bear watching. Was he drawing Lena into a net of trouble?

"It's six brothers and sisters and a worthless father gnawing at their wages, not conscience that makes them look white," she asserted.

"Hmp! To return to Brian's health. You must insist that he take something to build him up, Gay. He's worrying. It's worry not work that kills people. Neither Mac or Sam have lost flesh over labor conditions. Those twin brothers grow to look more alike every day now that Mac is happier. I guess his wife realized where an affair with the Dubois man would land her and dropped him. I didn't credit her with so much sense. Now that affair has blown over I wish that Jezebel of a widow, Bee Ware, would stop trailing your husband. She's shameless. I've seen her when I've been walking, hanging round the Plant in that cream-color roadster waiting to pick him up."

"He could stop it if he didn't like it. Have you ever seen a man who didn't know how to get away from a woman if he wanted to? The know-how is born in them."

"Don't shrug your shoulders, Gay. Hope you haven't picked up the habit from Sue Dubois. Her hunch at about every

fifth word would drive me out of my mind if I had to live
with her. Perhaps Brian does like to be trailed by that
widow. Most men would rather be with a woman who invites by the warmth of her eyes, the lure of her smile, than
with one as chilly as an ice-machine."

"Just what are you implying, Aunt Cass?"

"I'm not implying, I'm saying it. If I were your husband
I'd as soon have a shining white enameled Frigidaire for a
companion as you. At least the amount of frost in that can
be regulated. I'm disappointed in you, Gay. I'd heard rumors
that you and Brian were going your separate ways, but I
wanted to see for myself. That's what brought me to Rosewynne, not my doctor's advice. You're not doing your share
to keep your marriage from failure. Don't let that cheap
woman beat you."

"Just another couple who has failed." The words echoed
through the corridors of memory before Gay asked:

"And just what would you do to prevent it, Aunt Cass?
Your point of view on matrimony is interesting if strictly
mid-nineteenth century."

"Don't be sarcastic, Gay, it isn't your type. Show your husband that you love him. You do. You can't fool me. A wife
holds the winning cards in a three-cornered game if she has
the brains to play them. I didn't intend to tell you this until
I left for home but— What do you want, Lena? You're pale
as a ghost. Are you sick? If you are I'll mix you—"

"I'm not sick, Madam. I—I—please may I speak to you
alone, Mrs. Brian?"

Gay was startled by the tenseness of the girl's voice and
the hunted look in her eyes.

"Certainly, Lena. We'll talk in the other room."

As the maid closed the bedroom door behind them Gay
encouraged:

"What is it? Don't be afraid to tell me. Is Jim in trouble?"

"It's trouble but it ain't for him. It's for Mr. Brian."

"For Mr. Brian! What do you mean?"

"You needn't grip my arm so hard, Mrs. Brian. I'll tell you
if you promise first that you'll never let on how you heard."

Gay hesitated for a split second.

"Unless you swear you won't bring me into it—it isn't myself I'm thinking of it's Tim—I won't talk."

"I promise. Go on."

Standing in the middle of the room Lena whispered:

"It's Eddie and his gang. They're out to get Mr. Brian!"

"Lena!" Gay put her hand to her throat to relieve the fierce pressure that was choking off her voice. "What—what will they do to him?"

"They'll keep him till he takes back Eddie Dobson and makes him superintendent."

"He won't do it! He'll never do it, Lena."

"That's what I told Tim. You should have seen his eyes when he said 'Won't he?' he says, 'Wait till the Owls get hold of him. They'll make him change his mind.' "

XXIII

GAY HAD an impression of peacocks trailing iridescent plumage on the panels of the tall screen but she wasn't seeing them. Instead she was seeing a huge creature with fiery eyes. Hopping. Flapping. Beckoning with a hideous wing. She was hearing the poodle's blood-curdling howl, a yell. "Look out! You crazy—"

She shuddered. Flexed stiff lips.

"Owls? Owls?" she repeated woodenly. "What are 'the Owls,' Lena?"

"They're something fierce. One of them secret societies, you read about, Eddie Dobson's gang. They met in the old mill till after that Sunday afternoon you and Mr. Seaverns went down there. Lucky for you that Tim was the lookout that day. He found your watch and brought it to me to put in your room after he'd pinned a warning to it for you to keep out of the ravine. He made me swear I wouldn't tell how it came on your desk. He said terrible things would happen to him if Eddie found out he'd done that. He'd go to town for you, Mrs. Brian. I had to tell you now, though. You did so much for our mother."

"How did Tim get drawn into a club that does 'terrible' things to its members?"

"He used to be crazy about Eddie and when Eddie told him he'd got a big idea for a club which would give the boys in the Plant a great time and help 'em fight for their rights, that a big swell who'd run one like it—"

"Who was the big swell, Lena?"

"I don't know, Mrs. Brian. Honest to God, I don't. Tim thought the club was grand at first but then they got to doing wild things, like smashing that machine at the Plant and setting fire to a man's house if he doublecrossed them. They'd draw lots to see who'd do it. He wanted to get out but they threatened him an' said what they'd do to him and me if he did. After that he knew he was watched. Two days ago he overheard two Grand Horned Owls—grand means they're the leaders, no one knows who they are, because they're always masked when they meet—planning to snatch Mr. Brian out of his room in the tower tonight."

"Tonight! Coming for him—tonight!"

"Sh-sh! Please, Mrs. Brian, not so loud. I've taken Tim's life and mine in my hands to tell you this. If one of the gang found out—" The sentence ended in a shiver.

"It won't be found out, Lena." Gay's husky voice was steady. "I promise. Whatever I do your name and Tim's will be kept out of it. What time will they come?"

"They know the Romneys always have a Thanksgiving-eve party here. They'll come after the guests have gone. They reckoned you'd all be dead with sleep by midnight. Who's knocking? I mustn't be seen—"

"The dressing-room! Quick!"

Gay waited to hear the cautious closing of the door. She called:

"Who is it?"

"You're wanted on the telephone, Gay," Madam Wainwright replied.

She answered the unimportant call. Then sat like a stone girl with hands clenched in her lap. What next? Of course Brian must be told. Could she make him realize the seriousness of the situation without telling him whence the information had come? She must. She glanced at her watch. Major Bill had said that he was working at home.

She ran down the stairs and across the hall. Almost before she heard the response to her knock she was in the bookwalled room, with its deep crimson leather chairs, its cabinets of athletic trophies, shelves of balls Brian had pitched in winning games, and a fire of blazing logs. She was aware of William Romney's surprised exclamation, of Brian's searching eyes as he stood up behind his paper-strewn desk. He seemed abnormally tall. And grim. And cold.

"Gay!" he said. "Gay!" Then he laughed. Not a pleasant

laugh. "You must be in a rush to tell me that you'll leave when Major Bill leaves—to come here."

Without answering, she quickly turned the key, quickly crossed to the desk. Even as she looked up at him she thought that Aunt Cass wouldn't think Brian peaked if she saw him now. There was deep color in his face, strength and determination in every muscle of his taut body. Stern lines about his eyes and mouth made him look old. Old! Brian old! The word stabbed at her heart. She said quickly:

"I haven't come about that, Brian! It's about you. Come closer, Major Bill. Listen. And think! Think! What is to be done."

She told them. All that Lena had told her.

Brian pushed a chair behind her.

"Sit down and stop shaking. This sounds more like Grade A movie material than truth. Sure you haven't been dreaming, Gay?"

"Don't laugh, Brian! Major Bill, make him believe me!"

"Who told you, Gay?"

"I can't tell. I promised on my word of honor. It might mean tragedy if it were found out. You've got to believe me without knowing, Brian. You've got to."

"I believe you. You said they were to drag me out of the tower after the guests go?"

"Yes. Oh, I wish your rooms weren't on the first floor! I've been thinking, Brian, you could come to my room. They wouldn't find you there."

"Thanks. I don't care to come that way."

"You know I only meant to—to—"

"To help," he finished the furious assertion for her. "I understand."

"But what will you do?" she persisted, anxiety routing anger. "Tell me! I might crash through with an idea."

"He doesn't know yet, Gay. Give us time to think it over," William Romney suggested. "It still sounds too much like old-time mellerdrammer to be true. Our men wouldn't do anything like that."

"That's the trouble with you Romneys. You don't believe anyone can be really bad," Gay declared passionately.

"Oh, yes we do," Brian contradicted. "As I said once before I suspect that Eddie Dobson's hatred for me has gone almost beyond sanity and there is one other—"

"Louis Dubois?" Gay whispered. "But he's dining with us tonight. How could he be in on this?"

"Want to help?"

"Of course. I'll do anything! Anything, Brian."

"All right, then. I'll ask the hardest thing I can ask. Carry on as if you'd never heard of the party the Owls have planned to pull off tonight. Fill your day full. Keep going. Don't give yourself time to worry. You were tops in the dramatic club here. You have the chance to stage the finest acting of your life. Can you do it?"

"I can." Her lips trembled into a smile. "I don't like to talk about myself but—I'll knock 'em in heaps. I'll begin practicing on Aunt Cass at once."

She was aware that Brian stood on the threshold looking after her. From the room behind him came the Major's voice:

"Great Scott, lucky we didn't return those tear-gas bombs. Where are they, boy?"

"In that chest—" The door closed on the sentence.

What would Brian think of this way of filling her day, Gay wondered, as in midafternoon she drove toward the Dobson cottage. If only she could do something. She had thought of a dozen plans to avert the attack only to be brought up short by the stone wall of her promise to Lena that she would not even hint at the source of her information. Headlines of midnight attacks by hooded men she had read and thought forgotten blazed in her memory like electric-light signs through city smoke.

She forcibly thrust a horde of hectic images from her mind as she entered the Dobson living-room with the black poodle at her heels. Her heart did a cart wheel and came right side up with a bang as she saw Eddie lounging in the kitchen doorway. She had boasted that she could act. This was her chance to prove it.

She nodded to the man regarding her from under lowered lids and smiled at his flustered mother.

"Good afternoon, Mrs. Dobson. Is that delectable smell of sage and onions a Thanksgiving turkey roasting? You are forehanded. I've been so busy preparing for our family party tonight, that this is the first minute I've had to bring Mrs. Bascom her pep'mints."

She untied a white package and laid the opened box on the shawled lap of the old woman huddled in the wheel chair.

"A double quantity for the holiday," she said and smiled at the man in the doorway. "Something tells me your grandsons like them too."

Mrs. Dobson made a sound that was a blend of sob and

exasperation. Her eyes flooded, her large mouth quivered as she frowned at her son.

"What you waitin' for, Eddie? I'd think you'd be ashamed to stay in the same room with pretty Mrs. Brian who's so kind to yer grandmum an' me after all the trouble you've made fer her folks. Go along now an' you jest listen to me. Don't you let Joey trail 'round with that gang of yours no more. He says you've let him join that club; hev ye?"

"Keep your shirt on, Mum. Joey's old enough to do what he wants to," Mrs. Dobson's elder son reminded roughly.

"He ain't old enough to go with your crowd. You see that he's in the house early tonight. If he isn't—you needn't never come back yourself—understand?"

She was white as she met the eyes that looked back at her with rowdy impertinence. Eddie Dobson shrugged:

"He'll be in the house all right, tonight, an' I'll be here Thanksgiving to carve the turkey. So long, till tomorrow."

He disappeared into the kitchen and slammed the door behind him. His mother drew her breath in a harsh sob. The old woman in the wheel chair peered at her with sharp beadlike eyes.

"What you cryin' fer, Liza?" she demanded in a cracked quaver. "You ought to be glad that fer once ye had the spunk to stand up to Eddie. He's done nawthin' but make trouble ever since he was growed. Give me one of the pep'mints. Give that funny fella one too," she cackled, as the black poodle laid a reminding paw on her knee.

"You're awful good, ma'am, to bring these to Ma," Mrs. Dobson said in a choked voice.

"Why shouldn't she?" croaked the old woman as she sucked on a mint. "I ain't done nawthin', hev I? Jest because Eddie's made a fool of himself—"

"That's all right, Ma," her daughter interrupted nervously. "No one's blaming you fer anything."

"I guess they'd better not. Your folks havin' a party tonight, M's. Brian? I remember one Thanksgivin' eve I went up to help. It was a grand sight with the table all shinin' with glass an silver an' the old man—he would be your husband's grandfather—at the head of it an' his four sons an' their wives an' their children—my—my so many of them gone now an' I'm still here. What's that gold stuff glitt'ring on your dress?"

Gay slipped off the leopard coat.

"Sequins. There are cuffs as well as a belt. See. The shimmering gold is rather nice with the cinnamon brown wool. Like it?"

"Yes. You have such pretty clothes and I like pretty things. I like—"

The quavering voice died away in a whisper, the lids drooped over the old eyes. Gay put on her coat and stole to the hall.

"You've been so kind, ma'am," Mrs. Dobson said as she opened the front door. "An' I'm so ashamed of the trouble Eddie's made."

"Don't worry about it. The Plant will be running again Monday and most of the men will be at work. The others will realize how wrong they've been and come back, I'm sure."

"You're awful kind. I—"

"Liza! Close that door! You're coolin' this room!" a cracked voice reminded.

"Good night, ma'am. A happy Thanksgiving to you," Mrs. Dobson said hurriedly.

"The same to you and many of them," Gay answered.

Minute by minute Time checked off the hours as the day marched on to keep its rendezvous with the Past. Hours when Gay had felt the silent currents of preparation surging through the house. No reference to what was coming. No confusion. But tense lines in the Major's face and Brian's even while their voices were light and they smiled.

Was it only this morning that Lena had whispered of the kidnap plan? It seemed an aeon away. Only this afternoon that Ma Bascom had described a party like this of years and years ago? Gay looked down the long table in the dining-room at Rosewynne, over the massive silver nautilus shell filled with yellow chrysanthemums, which flanked on each side by smaller shells heaped with the purple bloom of Hamburg grapes, past the tall branching candelabra with their lighted tapers to William Romney at the other end.

How could he smile? How could he appear so at ease as he talked to Aunt Cass at his right, knowing, as he did, what might happen later? Perhaps he didn't believe what he had called "old-time mellerdrammer." Maybe he was right. It might be that her consciousness had lapsed for an instant and she had had a flash of nightmare.

The hope was as iridescent as a soap bubble and as short-lived. Of course she hadn't dreamed it. She glanced at Lena who was assisting Sampson and the waitress. Even the expertly applied rouge couldn't disguise the stark pallor of her face. Would it be noticed? She looked at Brian. He was thoughtfully regarding Lena. He turned to answer Sister who sat beside him. She and Billy had waged a battle royal as to which one of them should have the seat. It had jeopardized their pale blue costumes and sadly disarranged their golden hair. Jane was on his other side.

As if he felt Gay's glance he looked up. His eyes flashed a warning. He did believe her incredible story. That helped.

"Gay's sighing like a porpoise," Mac at her right announced jocularly. "What's on the little mind, gal?"

"I object to having my mind classified as 'little,'" Gay retorted gaily. "If you must know why I drew that long ragged breath of relief, it was because Sister shook her head when Sampson asked her if she would have plum pudding."

"It's a wonder she did," Sue Dubois shrilled. "Those kids have eaten everything in sight. Someone's going to have a merry time with them later. I can see little black nightmare imps peeking out of Sister's eyes now."

The child put her finger between lips that trembled.

"I don't want little black imps peekin' out my eyes, Bwian."

"There aren't any, dear," he comforted. "Aunt Sue was joking. Why don't you and Billy go upstairs and play with Mrs. Fezziwig while we finish dinner?"

With shrieks of approval the children dashed for the door. "It's absurd having kids that age at dinner. The nursery—"

"But I like having them here, Sue," William Romney interrupted his niece's shrill protest. "I like having my entire family here. Who knows, I may not have returned from my round-the-world trip by next Thanksgiving and the circle may not be complete."

"You won't be the only person missing if rumor is to be believed." Mrs. Dubois looked at Gay. "Other forces than travel break family circles."

"How about adjourning to the living-room for coffee, Major Bill?" Brian asked quickly. William Romney rose.

"The motion to adjourn is made and seconded. All those in favor—"

Laughing, the women drifted to the hall in a wave of color. Pale rose accented the dark brilliance of Jane Romney's eyes. Golden-haired Lucie appeared to float in frothy, azure tulle. Sue glittered in harsh sequined green.

Gay wore layer over layer of nasturtium shades of chiffon that swirled out at the hem. Cassie Wainwright's silvery gray was like a rift of moonlight on a sea of gorgeous color. The high collar of diamonds which hugged her long thin neck, much as protective wire fencing encloses a tree trunk, sparkled with every movement of her angular body.

As they crossed the hall trills of childish laughter, pierced by the shrill obligato of the poodle's bark, drifted down from the floor above. Gay smiled in sympathy. Then memory stiffened her lips. Would the twins be safe in this house to-night?

She glanced at the four Romneys and Louis Dubois as they entered the softly lighted, rose-scented library. Brian and Major Bill would not have permitted the children to remain at Rosewynne had they a doubt of their safety. Surely she could trust those two men.

Lucie flitted from the room to put the twins to bed. Sampson set out the card tables. On the pretext of helping Lucie, Gay excused herself. She felt driven, desperate with anxiety. It was like groping in the haunted dark not knowing what horror lay in wait in the hours ahead. How would Brian meet it?

She stood at the window of her boudoir fighting a mounting sense of panic. As if her eyes were drawn by a magnet she looked up. How clear the sky was. How bright the stars. So calm. So steadfast. A golden mesh of glory above the beat and throb of the earth and the restless surge of the millions on it. Some of their peace stole into her troubled mind.

She joined Lucie on the balcony above the pool in the fragrant court. Candles burned in each of the eight Gothic windows. The effect was one of breath-taking enchantment.

"Perfect, isn't it?" Lucie whispered as if fearing to disturb the scented stillness if she spoke aloud.

As they went down the stairs giggles and low voices drifted from the twins' room.

"Those children are wide awake," their mother deplored. "They are so excited they'll never go to sleep. They begged so for 'Fezz' that I left the poodle with them and their door open."

"That's asking for trouble."

"But what else could I do, Gay? They would have raised a riot if I hadn't."

"I am quite sure you could do nothing else, Lucie."

To herself Gay said, You're exquisite, you bear beautiful children and you keep your husband deeply in love with you. Perhaps that is enough to expect of one woman.

The card players were intent on their game in the library. Lucie perched on the arm of her husband's chair and rested her head against his. He kissed her.

"Kids all right, honey?" he asked tenderly.

"For pity's sake, Lucie, keep away from Sam," Sue Dubois protested and snapped down a card. "He may succeed at the writing game—I hear he's sold another mystery story—but he's not so good at this game that he can afford to have his attention diverted."

"Just for that dirty dig I'll take the last three tricks from you and Major Bill, Susie, my girl." Sam grinned at Jane across the table as he laid down his cards. "Who says we're not good, partner?"

Gay watched the game at the adjoining table where Cassie Wainwright and Brian were playing against Mac and Louis. The rubber finished, Dubois rose.

"String along for me, will you, Gay? I've got to talk with a man. I'll use the hall phone."

Gay's heart lost a beat and quick-stepped on. Had Louis' call anything to do with the midnight kidnaping? That was a thought. Was Brian wondering too? His eyes were on the man hurriedly leaving the room.

Through the wide-open door she saw Louis stop. Came a burst of childish laughter. Ear-splitting yelps. Billy's high voice:

"Grab it, Fezz! Shake it! Shake it at Louis!"

"Now what," Gay thought. She reached the door as the twins in gay striped bathrobes rushed down the stairs like an avalanche in top flight. Each one hugged a small red can under an arm. Mrs. Fezziwig, who made the descent first, worried and shook another held between her teeth by a metal ring. In a split second the poodle was playfully tossing and dexterously catching it, in front of Louis Dubois.

"Shake it! Fezz! Shake it!" the twins chorused.

The poodle steadied the red can on the floor with one wool-braceleted leg and tugged at the metal ring with sharp teeth.

"What you got there?" Dubois bent over the dog. He jumped two feet. Shouted:

"Look out! You crazy—"

Gay's blood froze. That voice! Those words! The hideous thing in the road! Louis Dubois!

XXIV

"DROP IT! Fezziwig! Drop it!"

As through a fog Gay heard Brian's shout. Saw him snatch up the red can and hold it high out of reach of the yelping, leaping poodle and the shrilly protesting twins.

"Mac! Take those things away from the kids! Quick!"

"What is it, Brian? What have the children done *now?*" Lucie demanded from among the group of startled women and men at the library door.

"Give me those!" Mac carefully removed the cans from the grip of the scowling, grabbing twins. "For the love of Mike, where did you kids dig up these tear-gas bombs?"

"Sam!" snapped Brian. "Put the children to bed and make them stay there. It isn't their fault we're not all crying our eyes out and sneezing our heads off."

Sister caught him round the knees and with golden head tipped back pleaded tearfully:

"Wock me an' tell me Muvver de-ar, Muvver de-ar, Bwian?"

He looked down sternly at the angelic upturned face.

"I will not. I don't like a naughty little girl who takes things from my room."

"Not naughty little girl!" pouted Sister.

Billy put his hand on her shoulder and regarded Brian with reproachful blue eyes.

"We only went there to get one of your baseballs to throw for Fezz, Brian. An' when we couldn't find that—"

"You bet you couldn't find it," Brian interrupted. "I'd heard you kids were coming to dinner."

Sam grabbed a shoulder of each offspring and personally conducted them to the stairs.

"Up you go! Scram!"

Halfway up, Sister, finger in mouth, looked back.

"Don't want to go, Sam. Want Bwian to wock me an' tell Muvver de-ar, Muvver de-ar!"

Her father scooped her up on his arms and took the steps two at a time with Billy trailing him.

"What shall I do with these confounded things, Brian?" Mac demanded as he held the red cans gingerly by the tips of his fingers.

"Put them on the tower steps. I'll take care of them."

"Just why are you storing tear-gas bombs at Rosewynne, Brian? Preparing for a siege?" There was a strident note in Louis Dubois' amused question.

"Nothing so exciting. Out of abundance of precaution we carried them in the historic Employers' Parade. I've had so much else on my mind I didn't return them to Police Headquarters. You may bet your last dollar they will be out of the house tomorrow. Lucie, play a hand or two with Aunt Cass until I come back, will you? Gay, bring Mrs. Fezziwig upstairs. We'll lock her in your boudoir."

Mac linked his arm in Dubois'.

"Come on, Louis. Let the telephoning go till Brian comes down. He and Aunt Cass were wiping us off the earth. With Lucie—" his voice drifted to a murmur as the two men entered the library.

At the head of the stairs Gay whispered:

"Does Mac know, Brian?"

He nodded.

"He's staying. They're all staying. Get the guestroom on the front of the house ready for Sue and Louis. We'll put him where he can be watched. That's part of our plan, Gay."

"Louis was—was the Owl who tried to stop me, Brian. I recognized his voice tonight when he said—" her breath caught.

"Steady. I know he was. I've found out a lot. I've been waiting for a few more facts before dropping a bomb—not tear-gas—which will blow him out of the Plant forever. We've got Lavalle's confession of his part in the 'stone' throwing. Draw the hangings across the windows before you light up. We'll put Jane and Mac in the tower. Shut the poodle in your boudoir. Be quick. Come back to the library. You'll hear the rest of my plan."

Would she ever feel warm again, Gay wondered, as ten minutes later she sat on on edge of the library couch with her icy fingers linked round one knee.

"Rubber!"

Laughter and voices raised in gay post-mortem discussion were interrupted by the sharp sound of cards dropped to the table as Brian Romney rose. Mac strolled to the door and stopped on the threshold to light his pipe. Sam pushed Lucie into Major Bill's chair and stood in front of her.

Gay's throat tightened. It's coming! She told herself and rigidly controlled a shiver of nerves.

Louis Dubois lighted a cigarette.

"If the 'show's' over, Sue, let's—"

"But the show isn't over, Louis," Brian interrupted genially. "There is a second act. To be staged at midnight. Soft music. Red light. All the trimmings. Major Bill wants you all to remain for the night to see it through."

From bored indifference Louis Dubois' expression sharpened to alert attention.

"Spend the night here!" his wife shrilled. "Don't be ridiculous Brian! We can't. We are off tomorrow for the holiday in New York. Besides we are not prepared. You should have let us know yesterday if you expected us to stay here until morning, Major Bill."

"You're right Sue. But, I didn't know until a few hours ago that I would need you. Tell them, Brian."

Brian told them. Of the plan for the midnight attack. Of the secret society.

"Secret society! Who cooked up that crazy yarn?"

Gay held her breath as she waited to Brian's answer to Louis' contemptuous question. He did not know the source of her information but he might suspect. If he did would he tell?

"Perhaps you would call it a 'club,' Louis. Police headquarters evidently didn't think it a crazy yarn when I was warned what to expect," Brian retorted calmly and Gay unclenched her tense fingers.

Dubois flexed thin lips. His left lid twitched. His eyes burned like coals in his colorless face.

"Headquarters!" he sneered. "If the police knew what was to happen why not let them handle it instead of dragging the family into the mess?"

"We didn't ask the police to handle it, Louis, because as it is a family affair—we still consider the workers as part of our business family and presume that some of them are mixed up in this—we assumed that the Romney men would prefer to take care of this latest unpleasantness themselves."

"Of course, of course it's up to us men." Dubois hastened to repair a tactical error. "But, why involve our wives? I'm surprised, Major Bill, that you would consent to endanger the lives of women, of delicate, helpless women," he concluded with a burst of bombastic oratory.

"Hmp! Speak for your own woman, Louis Dubois, and not

for the rest of us," bridled Cassie Wainwright. "Don't call me delicate and helpless! Nothing I like better than to sniff the smoke of danger."

"There will be no danger, Madam Cassie," William Romney reassured. "Can't you understand, Louis, that if any of you left this house tonight our knowledge of the threatened attack would get on the air? It would be bound to leak out. The marauders—whoever they are—would be warned that they were expected and would postpone their plan and attack when we were not prepared. We'll get it behind us once and for all tonight. With four Romneys in the house and Police at Headquarters geared up to answer our call, I repeat that *you* and Sue are in no danger."

Gay's eyes were on Louis Dubois. She thought of his betraying shout in the hall and she thought of the monster who had signaled to her in the road. What had he wanted? How had he dared try to stop her? Did he know she had recognized his voice tonight? He was white and his left lid twitched incessantly. His eyes flashed to the large window that opened on the terrace. Had he seen something outside? Was someone waiting for a signal from him? She had been so intent on her own thoughts she hadn't heard his response to Major Bill's announcement. What was he saying now?

"Well, Sue, if we can't go, we can't." He shrugged resignation. "You've forgotten one thing, Brian, our cars are here. They will give away the fact that your guests are remaining."

"We thought of that, Louis. The cars have been driven away. Your household has been informed that you and Sue decided to stay here for the night and return home in the early morning. Now, please go to your rooms. At once. Everybody. Don't stop to talk with one another. Put out the lights as soon as possible. And not one of you women is to poke her head outside her door, understand?" Brian's voice which had been cool, tensed. "One false move and our plan of defense will go blooey. Go! Hurry!"

Without speaking the women ran up the stairs. At the door of the boudoir Gay stopped and looked down at the four Romneys and Dubois who stood in the hall. She heard Brian say:

"We've decided not to drag you into this, Louis. After all, you're a Romney by marriage only. Stay in your room no matter what you hear and keep Sue there. That will be your contribution to the midnight entertainment."

"If you've decided I can help more by keeping out of the

scrap, I can't do anything but agree, can I?" Dubois' question was tinged with amused indulgence. "You couldn't have asked anything harder than for me to avoid a fight. I eat 'em up. Don't worry about Sue. I'll keep her quiet. Good night."

Gay slipped into her room as he started up the stairs. When he reached the head she heard him say:

"I still think someone has pulled a practical joke on you. I'm willing to bet a cool thousand there will be no midnight attack. No takers? Good night again."

Gay softly closed her door and leaned against it. Why was Louis so sure there would be no midnight attack? Was he planning to warn the Owls? Why not? He was one of them. He would try to get out of the house. She was sure of it. There had been something in his eyes when he looked at the window in the library! Would he attempt to escape that way? He shouldn't succeed. She would be there first. But she couldn't pull off a G-Woman stunt in this frock.

Pulses beating a tattoo of excitement, she stepped out of clouds of nasturtium chiffon. Slipped on a house coat of jade-green brocade. With hands unsteady from haste, knotted the long, fringed sash about her waist. Tense with impatience, waited.

Fifteen minutes later Brian Romney slipped into the dusky library and flattened himself against the wall in a dark space near the light switch. It seemed as if he waited hours before the hall clock slowly sounded each melodic note of the Westminster chimes. Then deliberately, distinctly, intoned the hour. The last sonorous stroke of twelve echoed through the still house.

He held his breath. Listened. A sound! Only red coals settling in the fireplace. His nerves must be strained to the snapping point to twang at that. The hangings at the long windows which opened on the front terrace were not quite drawn. One brilliant star glowed steadily in the streak of indigo sky visible between them.

The stage was set to trap whoever might try to warn the Owls that their plan for a midnight attack was known. He was sure an attempt would be made. He was equally sure that Louis Dubois would be the person, that he would try to escape from the front of the house. He had seen his furtive glance toward the terrace windows.

Louis was the Owl who had tried to kidnap Gay. How had he dared? What had been his object? At the office conference he had bragged that he had a fact up his sleeve which would

prick the pride of the Romneys like a pin in a balloon. That
had been the day he had had a date with Jane. When Jane
failed him had he planned to kidnap Gay?

Brian unclenched his hands. This was no time to see red
with fury. He would settle with Louis later. The present and
immediate future required every atom of his attention. How
quiet the room was. Scuttlings in the wainscoting. A mouse?
In the stillness it sounded like a moose crashing through
underbrush.

A sound! Not the fire! He leaned forward. A creak! Someone on the stairs! Quick breathing at the threshold. A shadow! Stealing toward the windows! The hangings moved! Shut
out star and sky. They were held together. Why? To let
someone in? To help someone out?

He gripped the automatic in his pocket. Started forward.
Shrank against the wall. The glass door to the court moved!
Swung open! Slowly. Cautiously. Another shadow! Slinking
toward the long windows! A rendezvous? Were two sneaking
out to warn the Owls?

XXV

"STOP! Don't move," Brian called. He snapped on the lights.
Dubois, chalky with fury, backed against one of the hangings
at the long windows. He glared like an animal at bay. Thrust
his hand into his pocket. Then laughed.

"It's you, Brian! You gave me the heebie-jeebies appearing out of the dark. You see, I decided I must get home to
attend to an important matter. Thought it a pity to disturb
you, so decided to slip out this way." His low voice mocked.
A cornered brute peered from his eyes.

"Go back to your room, Louis."

"What sort of a run-around are you giving me? You may
boss the Plant, Brian, but you don't boss me."

He whipped a revolver from his pocket. A hand flung up
his arm. A bullet struck the ceiling. Brian seized his elbows.

"Hold them! Tight! I'll strap them down," whispered an

unsteady voice. A green sash was flung around Dubois' waist. "Don't stop to stare at me, Brian! Quick!"

"So you've added spying to your other charms, Gay?" Dubois sneered.

"Shut up, Louis! Grab his gun, Gay! Here's Mac! Quick, Mac! Take this end of the sash. Yank it! Hard! Swell job! That pinions his arms. One yelp from you, Louis, and it will be your last for a time," Brian warned.

Dubois' response was a cross between a curse and a snarl. He kicked at Mac who promptly produced two handkerchiefs.

"Hand over yours, Brian," he whispered. "This buckaroo needs hobbling." He pulled and knotted. "There! That will hold!"

"I'll drag you Romneys through the criminal court for this," Dubois gritted.

"That's enough from you, Louis! Grab him, Mac. Smack him if he makes a sound. We'll hustle him out. Give me his gun, Gay. Switch out the light. Wait here."

Brian and Mac pushed and dragged Dubois into the court. His rasping laugh filtered back through the dusk before the glass doors closed softly.

Seated on the edge of a chair Gay clenched her hands, held her breath lest she miss a sound. Silence. Spooky silence. Had the three been spirited away? The room was ghostly. No light but the dull red glow from the dying fire. She couldn't bear it to wait like this.

She sprang to her feet and caromed into Brian, as, breathing hard, he entered the room. He caught her arm.

"Where were you going?"

"I had to know what was happening to you."

Even in the dim light she could see his burning eyes. If only she could know the thoughts behind them.

"Nothing happened to me. It all happened to Louis. If he doesn't like vegetable cellars with strong locks, he's out of luck. Why didn't you stay in your room?"

"Don't growl at me! They'd be personally conducting you off in an ambulance this minute if I hadn't left my room."

"You came nearer that joy ride than I. When you slipped between those hangings, I drew my gun, ready to spring at whoever was behind them. The glass door opened and—when I think—what might have happened—" He drew his hand across his eyes.

"I'm sorry, Brian. I—"

"They're coming!"

The warning was a mere shiver of sound from the hall. Brian gripped Gay's arm and drew her toward the stairs.

"Help me, Gay. Stay in your room? Promise?"

"I promise."

In her bedroom she crouched by the open window. The world outside was filled with midnight mystery and quiet, and the scent of frosty evergreens. The rush of the wind through icy branches set them tinkling like fairy chimes broadcasting to the twinkling stars. Two white fluffs convoyed a snowy squadron of cumulus clouds sailing majestically toward the misty hills. The waning moon, thin as the paring of a silver coin, hung above them like a ship's pennant. She could see the window of Brian's bedroom, on the first floor, the faint tracery of the iron balcony on which it opened. Not a splinter of light. Was he waiting in the dark? Waiting for what? She shivered.

She rested her chin on hands clasped on the sill. Her physical eyes were on the window but her spiritual eyes were turned inward. And all this time I thought I was out of love with him, she admitted to herself, that the night he said "There are other women" my heart froze for keeps. How do I know that the note Bee Ware showed me had anything to do with marriage? If it hadn't, will he ever forgive me? Aunt Cass was right. I have not done my share to keep my marriage from failure. I was so hurt I was an easy mark. I have gone on from day to day, getting a certain amount of pleasure and inspiration from mere living, but always aware of that frozen lump which once had been my heart. And now a threat of danger to Brian has shown me that during this last year my love for him has been deepening, strengthening as if growing under icy ground.

Is that what true marriage is? her turbulent thoughts surged on. Something between a man and a woman which isn't of the body, but which lives and glows in the soul and survives all storm, all influence, all fate? And just where will that conclusion get you? Suppose that note meant what Bee Ware implied and your husband does want to marry a gay widow?

She swallowed the sob the question rocketed to her throat. According to Aunt Cass, Bee Ware had warmth, her smile allure, while Brian's wife had all the fire of an ice-machine and about as much human appeal.

"Even so, she shan't have you! You're mine! I'll keep you!" she flung at the dark blotch which was the tower window and knew in that instant that the feeling she had had for

Brian when she married was nothing to compare with the present passionate outpouring of her love. She had changed. She no longer felt bewildered. She felt grown-up, competent to meet life as it came with head erect and a sense of marching forward to the rhythm and beat of far-off music.

She looked at her clenched fists. Her reaction was as swift as that of a chameleon to its color medium. Her laugh was tinged with scorn.

"Them be brave words, my proud beauty. Just how will you keep him?" she asked herself aloud.

Cassie Wainwright's caustic advice bubbled to the surface of her mind.

"Show your husband that you love him."

Could she do that? Not knowing if Brian loved her even a little. Not knowing that he was not satisfied with his life as it was. Suppose she went to him and told him she was sorry—she knew now that she alone was responsible for their separation—and he looked at her with cool amused eyes and said—

"Gay! Gay!" Jane stole up behind her. "Did I frighten you? You jumped a foot. I couldn't stay alone another minute. I would have screamed from nervousness. Listen! Something's moving in the garden!"

Her fingers bit into Gay's arm.

"Look! That shadow! It slinks! Hear my t—teeth ch—chatter! N—Now what?"

At that instant, Brian watching from the dark bedroom asked himself the same question. His nerves and muscles relaxed their frightful tension. At last there was something definite to meet.

"They've come," he whispered into the dusk behind him.

"How many?"

"Can't tell. One shape moved. Sam, go the rounds. Make sure that Sampson, the chauffeur and gardener are at their posts. Come back. Remember, don't chuck a gas bomb unless I give the word. Flood light ready, Mac? When I step to the balcony turn it on."

"Brian! You're not going out?"

"Sure, I am, Major Bill. The light will be in their eyes. How many pairs? I'd give a grand to know. Ready, Mac? I'm stepping out. Let go!"

A beam of blinding light. A sound like the oncoming surge of a tidal wave. Eyes! Enormous eyes! Dozens of them. Brian's breath caught. His heart pounded. Owls! Huge. Hideous. Scores of brown Owls!

"What do you want?" His clipped question slashed the cold air like a whistling sabre.

Three huge creatures stepped forward. A rough voice croaked:

"We want Dobson back on the job! Come down! We've got things to say to you. If you don't we'll come and get you!"

Was the scene below him real? It was too fantastic to be anything but a bad dream, Brian assured himself.

"Now that you've pulled off your masquerade party, break it up, boys," he advised. "Get going, Eddie, unless you want to be locked up with the leader of your gang. We've got him."

The three Owls conferred. Then something struck the wall above Brian with the sound of a blow-out and showered him with fine glass. He shook his head. The splinters in his face weren't dream stuff. They were chips from an electric light bulb. Another struck his shoulder without breaking. He caught it. Flung it! Straight at the tallest Owl. Glass splintered against glass.

"Expensive ammunition you're using, boys. Did the Plant supply it?"

There was no response to his contemptuous shout. Silence. Ominous. Vibrating.

"Come in! Brian! Quick! A head! Above the rail!" Mac warned. "Chuck a dose of tear gas, Sam!"

"Not yet! We've got to get Dobson! He'll be the first over and here he is!" Brian exulted.

He tore the concealing hood from a creature with a man's body and the head of a horned owl.

"I was sure it would be you, Eddie. So like you to hide behind a mask. Order your gang off the place unless you want them gassed."

"I'll order nothing you—" Dobson lunged. Brian caught the fist before it touched his face. He shouted:

"Mac! Knock off the Owl coming over the rail. I'm busy."

He caught Dobson's wrists in a crippling grip. Mac struck. Chuckled: "How'm I doin'?"

"Hear that crash, Eddie?" Brian demanded. "Another Owl has bit the dust. Call off your gang, or you'll follow him."

"You ain't got the strength! Hey! Let up on my wrists!"

"Not till you call off the gang! What's that?"

"Smashed glass. Your grape house," Dobson sneered. "An' a good job. We'll finish up with a nice little fire. It's so near this house perhaps 'twill scorch this too. You'll be enjoyin' baked fruit for breakfast."

His grin was sardonic. With superhuman effort he freed his wrists. Grabbed Brian. Lifted him! Mac shot a fist into his face. His hold loosened. Another jab. His wrists were gripped.

"I could smash you over the rail but you'll be better off, Eddie, in jail, than in a hospital with a broken back," Brian panted. "Come along! Mac give me a hand. No you don't break away! You'll walk, not run to the nearest exit. In you go!"

A banshee's screech split the air. Quavered and died. Rose again. It was as if the demons of an inferno had broken loose and were screaming with exultation at their release. Not another sound in the world.

"Cops!" Dobson muttered through stiff lips. "You had to send for them, didn't you?"

Brian's laugh was short.

"Your mistake, Eddie. Your gang sent for them when they smashed the grape house and set off the alarm. What's that flickering light on the wall? Who's yelling? Listen!"

"Let me out! Eddie! Eddie! It's Joey! I'm locked in! It's burning!" The last word ended in a piercing scream.

Eddie Dobson wrenched his hands free. "Joey? *Joey?* I told him to stay home tonight or I'd—"

"Quick! Over the rail! We'll get him out!" Brian pushed the dazed man ahead of him.

"Let me out! Eddie! Eddie! It's burning! Help! Help!" The frenzied shriek rent the still air.

XXVI

IN THE late afternoon Brian Romney lingered on the step of the white cottage. The face of the woman in the doorway was a mask, only her eyes were burningly alive. Her control was more heart-wrenching than a burst of grief.

"I wish I could help more, Mrs. Dobson." The fervent words eased a little his crushing sense of futility.

"You've done everything, Mr. Brian. They told me how you went into that burning hell side by side with Eddie to get Joey—after his gang ran out on him like rats—an' how when the frame fell in an' they were both tangled in the vines you pulled and hauled to free 'em, till they dragged you away before you got buried yerself. What more could ye have done? Look at your bandaged hands."

"That doesn't mean a thing. Just a few burns on the backs of them. The palms are okay. Merely a fussy doctor's precaution." Even as he made light of them Brian winced from the smart of the burns and the memory of that writhing red-hot frame that once had been the grape house.

Mrs. Dobson caught at her throat as if she were choking. "I'm the one should hev done more. When he was nawthin' but a youngster I let Eddie get out of hand 'cause I loved him too much to paddywhack him when he done wrong. An' then he pulled Joey down wid him, my Joey, who wasn't nawthin' but a little boy who wanted his Mum to tuck him into bed at night. Mother of God! I'll never tuck him in again!"

Grief wrenched off the mask and showed her face quivering, distraught. Brian laid his bandaged hand on hers.

"It wasn't Eddie's fault last night, Mrs. Dobson. He had told Joey not to go to club, but the boy slipped in, in his regalia. When lots were drawn to clean out the grapes for the gang before they burned, Joey drew the job. The house already had been drenched with gas outside. When he started to come out the door jammed. Eddie was wild with fear when he heard his yell for help. He kept muttering, 'I told him not to come! I told him not to come!' He worked like a madman to save his brother before he was trapped himself."

Mrs. Dobson shuddered.

"What difference does it make now, Mr. Brian, whose fault it was, wid both me boys in the room back there with only candles burnin' fer light? God rest their souls! The last thing Eddie said to me was, 'I'll be here Thanksgivin' to carve the turkey. So long, till tomorrow!' Well, it's Thanksgivin' an' it's tomorrow an' he'll never come back. I'm an' old woman widout me boys. Alone. Left alone!"

Her breath came in a bursting sob. Two great tears rolled down her cheeks.

"Liza! Come in an' shut the door," a querulous old voice quavered. "You're coolin' off this room!"

Mrs. Dobson drew a print sleeve across her streaming eyes.

"I ain't quite alone. Things happen queer in this world. There's Ma, ninety-six, who don't care 'bout nawthin' but keepin' warm an' munchin' candy, stayin', an' me boys so full of life—" She broke off and steadied her voice.

"Mr. Brian, if they'd been yer own flesh an' blood, you an' yer folks couldn't hev done more. Yer pretty wife was here all mornin' helpin' me, 'twas her that brought them beautiful red roses, in there with—"

"Liza!" the old voice reminded.

"Comin', Ma!" Mrs. Dobson called with an attempt at cheeriness and closed the door.

Bandaged hands in his pockets, hat pulled low over his eyes, Brian Romney strode toward home. He filled his lungs with the cold air. It helped clear away the fog of tragedy and confusion. Would Joey's agonized shrieks echo on forever in his mind?

Memory projected and blacked-out pictures with the speed and fidelity of a newsreel. He saw Mrs. Dobson's terrified eyes when he had brokenly prepared her for what the ambulance was bringing. Followed the scene in the library at Rosewynne, the fire blazing, the white-faced women in bright house coats, the Romney men in dinner clothes, their shirts smooched and blackened, their faces line by grief and fury as they listened to the confession forced from Louis Dubois by William Romney under a threat of a prison sentence if he didn't come clean.

And he saw Louis, as with eyelid twitching, face cadaverous, he admitted with a touch of bravado that he had suggested and financed the secret society of Owls; that he had instructed Lavalle to watch the tower windows and at the first chance fling that clay-covered hunk of iron at Brian. There had been a hint of jauntiness in his voice as he had added that Lavalle had been stupid not to recognize the Major, he had no grudge against the Major. He went on to admit that he had ordered Lavalle and someone whom he might select, to bring Brian before the tribunal of Owls the night of the Carnival. That he had backed up Dobson and encouraged the men to strike.

"Well, I guess that about covers it."

"Why did you do it?" William Romney asked sternly.

"Sue was bound I should have it and I wanted Brian's job."

"You wanted his wife!" Sue Dubois shrilled. It was the first time she had spoken.

"And that brings us to the most important question of all, Louis. Why did you, dressed in Owl regalia, try to hold up Gay in the road?"

"Who told you I did, Major?" There was confession in the harsh question.

"You've told us now."

"I'd been talking with her a short time before. She was so cocky I thought I'd frighten her." He glanced furtively at his ashy-faced wife.

That scene was pushed out of Brian's mind by the vision of himself questioning Tim. The boy had said with convincing earnestness that when Mr. Dubois had told him that Mr. Brian had sent him for his shoes he had handed them over without a suspicion that the man was lying. He had stumblingly confessed that he had taken part in some of the "cussedness" pulled off by the secret society, that he had tried to square it with his conscience by warning of the midnight attack.

Next on the screen of memory flashed the picture of dawn creeping up on the horizon to blend with the purple sky and turn off one by one the twinkling stars. With it came the sound effects of the waking chatter of birds and the acrid smell of smoldering wood. He had stood with Major Bill on the steps and seen Mac and Jane depart for home in their car which had miraculously arrived. The twins, exhausted from the unusually late hours, had slept straight through the night. He thought of Dubois' brutalized, defeated face as he had slunk into his sedan, of Sue's red head held high as she had seized the wheel from her husband. He had said to the Major:

"I'm guessing that in the future Sue drives. I can almost feel sorry for Louis."

"Sorry! He ought to be heading straight for jail. He knew us when he said, 'You Royal Romneys are puffed with pride.' He knew we wouldn't let our name be mixed up in scandal if we could avoid it. He traded on that. My boy, sentiment is the most costly thing in which one can indulge," the Major had growled as he went into the house.

All that had happened in the night and early morning. Every moment since had been filled to the brim. He had not seen Gay.

What was she thinking? Feeling? Now that trouble at

the Plant was over, it would be running fully staffed on
Monday, he would attack his personal problems. But not
tonight. He hadn't slept for forty-eight hours, he was unutterably weary from emotional strain and the smart of his
burned hands. He would mess up things worse than they were
if he tried to talk with Gay now.

He stopped in the drive at Rosewynne and looked off
at the hills in an attempt to clear his mind of tragedy and
perplexity. Glow from the departed sun had transmuted the
pond to an enormous pigeon-blood ruby and fused a dark
blotch of cloud above it with the iridescence of an abalone
shell. Then he saw the broken shrubs, the trampled garden
and the blackened frame of the hothouse that looked like
the skeleton of a prehistoric monster, the burned, twisted
vines which had taken years to grow. Anger made his brain
light.

"Darling!"

The cooing voice and the white hand slipped under his
arm increased his fury. He contemptuously regarded Bee
Ware's seductively smiling eyes and pouting lips. Being
seductive was her best bet, he remembered, and forcibly
freed his arm. She clutched it again.

"Darling! I've been almost out of my mind about you.
I heard in town that you had been frightfully hurt trying
to rescue that poisonous Eddie Dobson and his kid brother."

"Stop and get your breath, Bee. I haven't been frightfully hurt." Her possessive attitude infuriated him. He
might not be in the mood to meet Gay but he was all set
to show Bee once and for all where she stood with him.
He caught his shoulder.

"Now listen to me!"

"Oh, your hands! Bandaged! Why didn't Gay tell me?
I've just come from the house. She was so absorbed giving
Jim Seaverns his tea that she didn't pay much attention to
me. What happened to you, darling?"

Jim Seaverns with Gay! What did it mean? He couldn't
stop to think of that now. He had other business.

"Bee, do you understand English? Just everyday plain
English?"

"What a question, darling! It's so fun—funny."

"It's so funny I'm practically in stitches over it. Now get
this. I love my wife. I never have, I never will love any
other woman. There never will be a 'second Mrs. Brian
Romney.'"

A faint color flushed her face. She gave a furtive glance at her emerald ring before she shrugged and questioned slyly:

"Not even when there is a Mrs. Jim Seaverns?"

"Not even then. Now that that subject is washed up, we'll go on to the next. What note did you show Gay when you told her that I had sent you to ask for my freedom?"

"I—show her a note? Excitement has turned your brain, darling."

"You're lying! Come across with the truth. If you don't— Sue will be told of your meetings with Louis and you'll be dragged through the divorce court. No matter how innocent those meetings were—you see I'm giving you the benefit of the doubt—she won't leave you a rag of reputation. Can you take it?"

It was a wild shot. He had suddenly remembered his quickly dismissed suspicion the night of Mac's supper when Louis and Bee had left together; of its recurrence when he had seen them entering the café. He had nothing to back it up, but he was fighting for his wife. He held his breath as he waited for her answer. Her face was ghastly, her eyes terrified as she forged his suspicion to conviction.

"You wouldn't do that, Brian?" The last word was a shiver.

"I would. What note did you show Gay?"

She told him.

"You mean you tried to wreck my marriage with the note I sent explaining that the Romneys wouldn't sell a block of Plant stock outside the family? Why you—you—"

He caught her arm.

"Come in and tell that to Gay!"

"No! No! Brian! I will not!"

"*You're* telling *me* what you'll do! Come on!"

He half lifted, half dragged her across the terrace, through the hall to the library, his burned hands forgotten.

Jim Seaverns, who was holding Gay's hands as they stood in front of the fire, dropped them and looked toward the door. She took a quick step forward. Brian's tired face with its burning eyes, its strained bitter mouth, hurt her intolerably. Had he and Bee come together to demand his freedom? she wondered. What she said was:

"Just in time for tea. How nice."

"Bee has something to say to you. Go on, Bee! Quick! Don't keep us waiting," Brian commanded.

Brazenly, if haltingly, Bee Ware told of the note Brian had written her in regard to the sale of Plant stock, admitted that he had not known of her appeal to Gay to free him. She concluded with a high tinkling laugh.

"You'll have to admit that it was a good try, darling. If that's all I'll go. Too bad to interrupt the act being put on in this room when we entered. Bye-bye!"

That was done and thoroughly done, Brian throught as he closed the massive entrance door behind her. Bee was hating him with a deep and purple hatred. She'd not get over that in a hurry. Louis was even more of a bounder than he had thought him. Had Gay believed Bee's explanation? Her white face had given no indication of the thoughts behind it?

Would there be a Mrs. Jim Seaverns? Why not? He asked himself the question as he dropped heavily to the couch in his bookroom. The fight had gone out of him. He was as flat as a deflated balloon. Exhausted from emotional strain. Nothing mattered. He hadn't stopped a moment since he had heard yesterday morning of the threatened attack. Major Bill, Mac and Sam had helped all they could but there had been so much that only he could do. He was dead with sleep. He would close his eyes for a moment, only for a moment, he must tell Gay—

A sound brought him back from the unreal world in which he had been drifting. Where was he? In the dark. The sound again. A knock.

He swayed as he sprang to his feet.

"Who is it?" he called, switched on the light and opened the door. "What is it, Sampson?"

The butler's eyes rolled like black marbles in puddles of milk.

"De Lawd be praised. You're here, Mr. Brian. Dey've been waitin' ten minutes for you to come to dinner an' Major Willum an' me got a terrible fright."

"Dinner! Tell them not to wait any longer. I'll join them for coffee. Send a tray here. I'll eat while I change. Come back when you've finished serving and bow my black tie. My hands are stiff. Scram, Sampson."

When, refreshed, rested, inexplicably light-hearted, he entered the living-room Gay was pouring coffee. Her white frock was spattered with bouquets of gay old-fashioned flowers. She looked up. Brian's heart threatened to pound its way out of his body. She was wearing her pearls!

"Brian! Your hands! You've taken off the bandages! He shouldn't have done that, should he, Major Bill?" she asked anxiously.

William Romney rose from his deep chair beside the fire.

"His hands can't be very painful, Gay, or he wouldn't appear as if he were on the tiptop of the world. There's a repressed fire in his eyes that gives me the merry-pranks up and down my spine. I'm cutting out. Now. This minute. I'm off to see Mrs. Dobson. Don't have her on your mind, children, you've done all you can. I'll see you when I get back."

The fire snapped. The scent of flowers drifted from the court to the accompaniment of the soft drip of water. The silence in the great room vibrated with electrical currents. With an effort Gay slashed through it.

"Why do you look at me like that, Brian? What do you want?"

"I want my wife. How long have you been wearing pearls?"

Gay became absorbed in arranging the coffee tray.

"I asked Major Willum to give them back to me—yesterday."

"Come here!" He caught her hand and drew her to her feet. "Yesterday! Before—before you knew what the note was that Bee showed you?"

She nodded.

"You said once that you loved Jim Seaverns and intended to marry him. How about it?" he demanded sternly.

"I was so surprised to see you that day, Brian, that I said the first thing I could think of to make you believe that I wouldn't stand between you and—and Bee Ware. When you came into the library this afternoon Jim was telling me that the night of the Carnival he knew he had no chance. I'm a poor-spirited creature to admit all—"

Her voice was smothered under his lips.

"Gay! Gay!" he said softly after a moment. "You do love me again?"

Head tilted back against his shoulder her tender eyes met his.

"I know now that I never stopped loving you, Brian."

His arm tightened.

"Never since the day I met you, never since we parted have I had even a mild flirtation with a girl or woman. Believe me?"

"Yes."

"Going to hold on tight if I get crabby? Going to know it will blow over? Going to know that I love you, always will love you as long as I live?"

"Yes."

"Seal that promise."

Softly, sweetly, the Westminster chimes drifted into the room.

"I'll never hear that clock again but what I'll see myself as I stole down the stairs last night at the first stroke of twelve. I could hear my heart pound," Gay confided and shivered.

"Forget it, lovely. I've got an idea! Let's get away from it all. The smoke. The tragedy. Let's elope! Now!" Passionate intensity shone through the smile in his eyes.

"Elope? How exciting!"

"The Plant won't open until Monday. Your greatest admirer and friend invites you to honeymoon in the Big Town. How about it? Will you come?"

Her laugh was sweet and gay and daring.

"Of course I will. Thanksgiving is my favorite day for eloping. Wait until I pack a bag and I'll be with you."

Twenty minutes later she returned to the library in a soft brown beret that matched her frock with its belt and cuffs of glistening sequins.

"We mustn't make a social blunder," she whispered. "It's a time-honored custom for elopers to pin a note to something."

Brian bent to read the words on the slip of paper she fastened to William Romney's chair.

Off to New York. Back Sunday.
Heaps of love from
          The Couple Who Will Not Fail.

"What does that sentence mean?" he asked gravely.

"Major Bill will understand. I'll tell you on the way."

"Give me your coat." As she slipped into it he pressed his lips to the back of her neck.

"Changed your hair line this last year, haven't you?" he observed huskily.

Night had set a million stars in the dark purple heavens. They twinkled like a million candle flames in a breeze. Frozen branches clashed an icy symphony as they swayed.

Brian put the bags in the car and looked back at Gay on the terrace.

"What are you waiting for?" he called softly.

"I forgot! We can't go!"

He was beside her in an instant.

"What do you mean? Can't go?" he demanded.

Her eyes were alight but her voice was grave with assumed concern as she said:

"Major Willum! Aunt Cass! We can't leave those gay young people here unchaperoned."

The color swept back to his face.

"Woman! If you scare me like that again—" His buoyant voice broke. "Come *on!*"

Radiant, laughing, they ran across the terrace to the car.